A MURDEROUS TRYST

BEATRICE HYDE-CLARE MYSTERIES SERIES
BOOK XI

LYNN MESSINA

potatoworks press • greenwich village

To Philippe and Emmanuelle,
Thank you for making French Bea so awesome

Chapter One

Although generally happy to receive a visit from her grandmother-in-law, Beatrice, Duchess of Kesgrave, frowned as she watched the septuagenarian enter the drawing room. Her expression was so disconcertingly fierce, the other woman paused on the threshold to apologize for interrupting.

"I hope you know you are not obligated to welcome me every time I call," the dowager said, her gaze landing briefly on the book lying next to Bea on the cushion. "You are allowed to tell Marlow to send me on my way and continue with your reading. This is your home, and I would hate it if you felt as though you must stand on ceremony with me."

"With you, no," Bea said, smiling as she rose to her feet. "I am happy to treat you with all the rampant disrespect the situation requires. But Marlow is another matter, and I will happily inconvenience myself in a dozen ways to avoid ruffling his feathers. Refusing your call so that I may finish the chapter of a dreadful Minerva Press novel would upset him greatly. That said, I *am* pleased to see you because it is, in fact, a dreadful Minerva Press novel, and I must be saved from my own compulsion to finish it. Your timing is impeccable. Please sit down while I ring for a tray. I had just noticed the first rumblings of hunger and was about to summon rout cakes. I hope you will stay and join me."

The dowager flashed a knowing smile as she lowered onto the settee. "I expect you are famished as I was during much of my time. My husband insisted on hiring an accoucheur to attend to me, and he was a beastly combination of medieval superstition and Roman hearsay. The nonsense he spouted! I was allowed only bland foods because he swore too much salt would result in a child without fingernails, which I knew was nonsense because my own mother ate daily rations of salt pork when she was increasing with me. But even if the science held under scrutiny, I thought it was a fair exchange and I had my maid smuggle salt to my room in vials of perfume. And, la, both my sons were born perfect, their defects materializing only years later."

Bea, who had been confounded by the dowager's presence in Berkeley Square when the duke had left not thirty-five minutes before for her home in Clarges Street, realized now Kesgrave had made a grave miscalculation. Having set aside the afternoon to help his grandmother hire a new physician, he should have known to wait until after the appointments to inform her of his wife's condition. No doubt the dowager had seized upon the excuse to dash out of the house and leave her grandson to conduct the interviews on his own.

Although the desertion might seem like an ill-considered abdication of responsibility by the woman who would be subject to the doctor's supervision, Bea knew it would make no difference in the end. The dowager, whose various complaints—her stiff joints, her aching muscles—were the result of the inexorable problem of aging, was determined to be dissatisfied with the medical care she received regardless of its quality.

The fact that the duke had made such an obvious blunder was, Bea thought, a testament to his delight at his impending fatherhood. She opened her mouth to make a teasing comment to that effect because she did not like the way the dowager's bright expression had dimmed at the mention of her own progeny, neither of whom had grown up to be the sort of man of honor for which a fond mother might have wished, but her guest preempted her with an observation about how well she looked.

"Tilly said you were stout and would ride it out well," the dowager continued.

Tugging the bell cord, Bea furrowed her brow, startled by this information. "Tilly?"

"I had a note from her this morning regarding your condition. It was a model of decorum and restraint, saying all the right things about your health and well-being and the promising future of the Matlock line. But I could feel the smugness emanating from the paper and ink," the dowager said with a moue of disapproval. "She knew precisely what she was doing, and that is why I am here: to take my scapegrace grandson to task for daring to tell the heartless Countess of Abercrombie about your condition before his own grandmother. If your wretched aunt also knows, then I shall do something very unpleasant indeed, like caterwaul until Marlow comes in to see how you are abusing me."

Although ordinarily the terrifying prospect of the butler's disapprobation was enough to cause Bea to shudder, she was too unsettled by the information to react.

Kesgrave had lied to her.

Why had he lied to her?

No, she told herself sternly, she did not know that that was what happened. Any number of things could explain the discrepancy, which seemed like a lie only because she did not fully comprehend the situation. Possibly, he had gotten his days or appointments confused, or she might have misunderstood his schedule. She had been distracted during breakfast, had she not, considering how to tell her family about the cherub and contemplating what the tormenting Twaddle would write when he found out.

In all likelihood, she had simply heard him wrong.

And even if Kesgrave *had* misled her, she had no reason to assume his motive was sinister or underhanded. He might have slipped out to the jeweler to have some absurdly lovely and useless bauble made to commemorate the cherub or to the modiste to commission gowns to accommodate her growing belly. Typically, such errands would not require excessive secrecy, but men had funny ideas about expectant mothers—the dowager just said that her own husband's advocate denied her salt—and she was willing to concede that the duke could have his own logic. As close as they were in mind and spirit, he was still his own person, with his own thoughts and beliefs, and she could not know his every rationale.

Sometimes people did things that seemed unfathomable to others.

And that was entirely normal, she assured herself. There was no reason for a cold pit of dread to settle in her stomach.

Everything was fine.

And yet her fist clenched so tightly around the bell cord, her fingernails pressed half-moons into the flesh of her palm and she had to force herself to loosen her grip. Although there was never an appropriate time to indulge in wild fantastical thinking, now was especially inopportune because she had a visitor to entertain—one who was rightly offended by her grandson's slight.

Arranging her features in what she hoped was a reasonable facsimile of amusement, she rushed to assure the dowager that such theatrics were not necessary. "My family do not have the least notion of my condition. The only reason Lady Abercrombie knows is Damien sought her advice regarding physicians to consult."

But that was the wrong thing to say because it immediately brought to mind Kesgrave's falsehood and Bea noted with resentment that it had been very slapdash of the duke to draw his grandmother into his deception without taking the precaution of informing her of her usefulness. It was a courtesy he owed both women, so that at the very least his wife would not be obliged to entertain the dowager while her mind reeled with theories and conspiracies. At the same time, she took solace in the oversight, for it indicated a lack of calculation. Failing to account for every contingency was out of character for the usually pedantic duke, which made her think he had not intended to lie to her.

Somehow it had just happened.

And everyone knew a hastily constructed fiction did not count as much as a well-thought-out one, she thought satirically, annoyed at herself for trying to mitigate the action. It was better to accept the big lie ... the Great Fabrication ... for what it was and not try to contort it into something lesser. The only way to grasp the enormity of a situation was to see it with wide-eyed clarity. It might have been a lone falsehood told extemporaneously to address an unexpected problem, but it could just as easily be one more fib in an elaborate web of half-truths and misdirection.

There was no way to know without more information.

Oh, yes, that is very helpful, your grace, Bea thought, disgusted with herself for turning a single unexplained event into a full-fledged crisis.

Aunt Vera could not have done it better herself.

Recalling her relative, who possessed an unmatched ability to see a gangrenous limb in a minor scratch, Bea was reminded of the scene outside of the orphan asylum in Lambeth. An imposing building, all gloomy stone and Gothic decay, it dredged up childhood fears long buried, and although she could not articulate the terror that had over-taken her as she contemplated the structure, Kesgrave did. He perceived everything.

That had been only three days ago.

Nothing significant could have changed in three days.

Determinedly, she resolved to cease thinking about the matter until she could ask him directly why he had lied, and said, "The countess's recommendation appears to be a sensible man who does not think breeding women must be coddled in cotton. He has proposed that each of my training sessions be cut by fifteen minutes to ensure I have enough time to rest but did not suggest that I stop them altogether, which is what I was anticipating."

Although this defense reasonably explained why Lady Abercrombie had the news, it failed to address why the dowager did not. "Having dashed off an informative note to Tilly, the least he could have done was dash off an informative note to me!"

"I expect he wanted to tell you in person," Bea said.

"Do not make excuses for the scoundrel," her grace said, shaking her head. "And if that is the case, then where is he? I have been here a full five minutes and he has yet to appear to tell me the happy news."

"He is not at home," Bea said, grateful for the evenness of her tone. Holding to her resolution was all but impossible in the face of point-blank questions bringing the Great Fabrica-tion to the fore, and she smothered the impulse to add that she did not know where he was.

"Is that not just like a man," the dowager said with an exasperated sigh. "They are rarely where you want them to be. But no matter! You are here and looking so well. Do tell me how you are feeling. Is the nausea in the morning very terrible?"

"Actually, it is not horrible," Bea said, then paused briefly as Joseph carried in the tray, which he placed on the low table opposite the settee. She waited until he left before resuming because the staff had yet to be told of the cherub. She believed Twaddle would find out about it only seconds after the servants and wanted to forestall that moment as long as possible. "I am queasy upon rising, but a slice of plain toast usually calms it. I have thrown up only a handful of times."

"Excellent!" the dowager said approvingly. "As Tilly noted, you are stout, and I do agree that you shall come through this with flying colors. One worries about the more delicate girls fading at the first hint of a challenge, but I am certain you will triumph whatever the setback."

Although Bea's stomach clenched at the use of these euphemisms to describe the perilous undertaking that was childbirth, she smothered her anxiety and curved her lips in a placid smile. The only way human beings managed to continue to procreate despite its ever-present dangers, she was convinced, was by not mentioning its ever-present dangers. "I appreciate your and Lady Abercrombie's confidence."

"You must let me know if you need anything at all," the dowager insisted. "My great-grandson will not be denied anything—and before you mount your high horse and point out that you could be carrying my great-granddaughter, let me remind you that there has not been a Matlock girl in six generations. Will I be surprised if you break the mold? Not at all, my dear. But one hundred and fifty years speak for themselves."

"Duly noted," Bea replied as she raised the teapot to pour.

"Now I am most curious about this call you and Kesgrave made to Fortescue's Asylum for Pauper Children," the dowager said, accepting the delicate porcelain teacup, with its lovely pink floral motif. "I find it very difficult to believe you had any business there. It is such a dreary place! And it was vexing of Twaddle to mention your visit but provide us with no explanation for it. I do not believe for a moment that he does not know why you were there."

Bea, who expected the complete story of her interest to emerge in the next column if not the one after that, was genuinely amused at the august dowager's inclusion of herself among the scurrilous gossip's readership. "Us?" she murmured inquisitively.

"It is twice as irksome because he usually includes too much detail," the dowager continued as if the other woman had not spoken. "I do not care what the Leaky Fawcett was sipping when she made yet another young miss cry by the refreshment table at Almack's. I only want to know what she said and how many minutes passed before she issued one of her flagrantly insincere apologies."

"Perhaps a letter to Mr. Twaddle-Thum's employer requesting a more rigorous editing process might bring about the desired improvement," Bea suggested.

Ignoring this provoking comment, the dowager confessed she genuinely appreciated Twaddle's dispatches, for they were a reliable source of information—unlike her grandson. "Unless the report of your visit is untrue, and Twaddle has taken to making up stories out of whole cloth. If that is the case, then I shall grow cross, as I have come to enjoy his nonsense."

"It was an investigation," Bea replied.

Although this communication should not have been shocking given her host's proclivities, the dowager pulled back sharply, causing the teacup to rattle in its saucer. "Oh, my, that is dreadful. I do hope the victim was not one of the orphans."

Reassuringly, Bea said that it was not. "It was an elderly man who lived in St. James's Square. He died last week."

"Roger Dugmore," the dowager said with a knowing nod, startling her host with the display of familiarity. "Do not look so surprised, my dear. I read the obituaries religiously to keep abreast of how people my age or older typically die. I am sure it sounds morbid to you, but I find it an instructive guide of things not to do as I settle into my dotage. In that regard, Dugmore's death was deeply distressing because there is no way to avoid climbing out of bed upon waking, and you may be sure I have devoted some energy to figuring out alternatives. But if your involvement means he was murdered, then I will feel much better about the endeavor."

Not sure whether she should be amused or horrified, Bea assured the dowager that rising from one's bed remained a relatively safe activity. "Dugmore's head was bashed against the table so that it appeared as though he had sustained an injury in a fall."

"Aren't you clever, figuring that out," the dowager said admiringly.

But Bea was not clever, not at all, and she launched into an account of the investigation, which was instigated by Dugmore's preening peacock of a grandson in a bid to garner Mr. Twaddle-Thum's attention. Here, she provided a diverting description of the popinjay, with his high shirt points and ladybird races, but the dour cynicism in her tone stripped Viscount Ripley's absurdities of their humor.

In the end, the investigation had been a chastening experience for her as much as for his lordship, and Kesgrave, observing an air of melancholy, announced with portentous grandiosity that it was high time he taught her how to play chess. With her analytical mind, habit of remembering everything she read and ability to identify patterns, she might actually be able to provide him with a challenging game. Then he set up the board in the library, explained the history and capability of each piece in stultifying detail, and lectured on a series of opening moves with increasingly implausible names.

She was reasonably certain that the red-tailed coachman gambit did not exist.

The following morning, they had enjoyed a leisurely meal in bed before Kesgrave bracketed himself in his study with his steward to discuss estate business. He emerged three hours later to greet the physician, who had called to meet Bea and assess her condition. In the afternoon, noting the improvement in the weather, they had taken a drive in Hyde Park before briefly attending a musicale at Mrs. Pateman's home.

That was yesterday.

It had been a pleasant day, noteworthy only in its lack of noteworthiness, and she wondered if Kesgrave had known then that he would lie to her today. Was it knitting away in the back of his mind as he swept toast crumbs from the sheets and questioned Stephens about the roofs and directed the gig around the sharp bend at the corner of Hill Street and Deanery? Had he known all along that he would use his grandmother as his pretext or did that idea occur to him during Angelica Gabrielli's performance of "Al desio di chi t'adore"?

And there she was, Bea thought churlishly, back to useless speculation.

The clock struck two, reminding her that it was still early, and it would most likely be hours yet before Kesgrave returned home from his secret errand.

Disheartened by how long she would have to wait to satisfy her curiosity, she was grateful for the dowager's presence, for it gave her something to do other than brood, and when she finished her account of Dugmore's murder, she asked how the older woman knew of Fortescue's. "An orphan asylum in Lambeth does not strike me as the sort of place that would earn your attention. As far as instructive deaths are concerned, I am confident it does not provide useful guidance."

The dowager waved her hand airily and admitted she could not recall how she knew half the things she knew. "It might have appeared in a newspaper article or someone could have mentioned it at a rout. It is probably the latter. Society matrons who devote themselves to charity are so engrossed in their good works that they sometimes refuse to talk about anything else. They will chatter on even in the most unsuitable setting! On one occasion, Lady Uckfield told me all about the home for wayward women she planned to establish while we were standing in a field in Chalk Farm. It was a dawn appointment. Between Witherall and Ditching, I believe."

Fascinated, Bea leaned forward to pepper her guest with questions: how many duels had she attended during her career, what was the point of contention between the two men, how did one dress for an affair of honor?

On a light laugh, the dowager admitted that it was the only one of its kind to which she had been invited. It was just as well, she added, as the affair had given her a hearty disgust of the enterprise. "Witherall was a jackanape and Ditching was a pompous ass, and if they had succeeded in killing each other, then they would be doing the world a kindness. As it was, they were both terrible shots and missed each other by several feet."

They finished the plate of rout cakes, and Bea, reluctant to be alone with her thoughts, rang for more. The dowager stayed for another hour, happily regaling her with tales of her physicians' incompetencies and relatives' ineptitudes, and by the time she left, it was a little after four. Bea picked up her book to resume reading, but in light of the current circumstance—dreadful novel, lying spouse—she found it impossible to become engrossed. Irritably, she tossed the volume across the room and watched it land with a thump next to a marble pillar. If she wanted to keep her mind off the duke until he returned, she would need a more consuming volume.

It should not be long now, she thought, noting it was almost five. As he had not mentioned having alternate plans for dinner, she reasonably concluded he would be home in time for it.

Unless that was a lie of omission.

Angry at her seemingly endless capacity for suspicion, Bea darted to her feet and stalked across the room. If she was going to brood about it no matter what she did, she might as well call on the lending library to find more interesting reading material. The physician had recommended fresh air and exercise, and a vigorous walk met the description.

Alas, her walk was not vigorous.

Hoping that Kesgrave would be home by the time she got back, she trudged slowly, almost sluggishly, to provide him with an extra half hour.

Despite these machinations, he had not yet returned to Berkeley Square, and although Bea initially told the house-keeper to hold off on serving dinner so that she could eat with the duke, she changed her mind when the clock struck eight. By that point, she was starving, and the thought of asking for a snack now and then eating alone later mortified her. It would reveal too much to the staff and would only be repeated by Twaddle at some later date.

It was, she thought two hours later as she climbed the stairs to her bedchamber with a morose heaviness, a relief to know she had the ability to worry about the banal scribbler when she was so awash in dread all she had managed to do was pick at her food.

She was being foolish, she knew.

It was one little lie.

Just one.

It was not the end of the world or the end of her happiness or even the end of the day. It was barely ten o'clock. There were hours yet for Kesgrave to breeze into their bedchamber, his deep blue eyes alight with mischief, and present her with a horrifyingly extravagant necklace. And then he would tell her about how painstaking it had been to fashion and how he had had to stand over the poor jeweler the entire time directing him as to where to place each diamond, and how he should have sent a note when he realized it had grown so late but he had been so consumed with the idea of surprising her that time had simply flown by and before he knew it. ...

Bea drifted off to sleep while concocting this fantasy.

Hours later, she woke, first slowly as she wondered why she felt so strangely unsettled and then with a start as she recalled the duke's inexplicable absence.

His *continued* absence, she realized, noting the bed was otherwise empty.

Calmly, she rose, lit a candle from the embers in the fireplace and looked at the clock on the wall.

It was three.

Three in the morning and Kesgrave *still* had not returned.

Fear rose in her throat as panic swept through her.

Something was wrong—horribly wrong.

All those hours nursing her hurt feelings when Damien may have been lying under a carriage wheel or in a ditch or beneath a horse's hooves.

She almost screamed.

Inhaling sharply, she opened her mouth to cry for Marlow to wake up the house and send out a search party to find the duke.

That was the panic.

But she did not give into it, not yet.

The thought of the dour butler regarding her with benign contempt, his black brows drawn in derision, stopped her, and she decided to confirm that he was not at home. It was late, yes, but many a town gentleman arrived home at that hour to enjoy a glass of port in his study before retiring to bed. It was not typical behavior for Kesgrave, but then, nor was lying.

It could be a whole day of firsts.

Before tiptoeing down the stairs, she slipped on her dressing grown and passed through the enfilade connecting her bedchamber to the duke's. She expected it to be empty, as he had shared her room every night since their wedding, and yet she knew she could take nothing for granted. Issues long settled suddenly felt up for negotiation, and when she made out a dim shape beneath the covers, she was not even surprised.

Oh, yes, a whole day of firsts.

Although not a shock, it was nevertheless a blow, and she sank to the floor rather than hunt for a chair in the darkness. She sat there silently for a long time, struggling to regain her breath, her head pounding as she thought about what to do.

The one urge she must resist at all costs was waking him up.

Two months married, a few weeks expecting, she would not instigate an argument that would expose her to the charge of female irrationality. Everything she was feeling was logical and based on fact, but she knew how easily a woman's emotions could be turned against her. If roused now to be asked why he had lied, he might accuse her of treating a minor event with inappropriate urgency, shifting the focus of the conversation from his behavior to hers.

Bea had seen her uncle do it to his wife too many times to count, Aunt Vera wringing her hands with anxiety and remorse as she struggled to clarify her position, which had seemed so sensible at the beginning of the discussion. Kesgrave had too much respect for himself, let alone her, to resort to the defensive feint.

Or so she had believed.

But she did not know, not for sure.

In truth, she felt as though she did not know anything.

It is the exhaustion, she assured herself, her mind muddled by fatigue. She had worn herself to a nub with apprehension and now she was awake but just barely.

Rising to her feet, Bea returned to her room and climbed into bed. She did not extinguish the candle. As tired as she was, she did not want to be alone in the dark with her thoughts, and being alone with them in the light was the only alternative. She watched the flame flicker for hours and only closed her eyes when it guttered out, sometime after six. Then she drifted off to sleep.

She woke a few hours later to the gentle clatter of silver against porcelain and opened her eyes to see her maid laying toast and tea for her on the table. Aghast, Lily apologized for both waking her up and allowing her to sleep so long. But his grace insisted she needed all the rest she could get.

Bea cringed slightly at this revealing sentence, for, combined with the plain toast, it all but shouted that the duchess was with cherub, and rose from the bed. She did not have to put on her dressing gown, she realized, because she still wore it from her late-night foray. Taking the seat set for her by the window, she noted her nausea was improved from the morning before, as was the weather, and decided these omens portended good things. Nothing was ever as hopeless as it felt in the early hours, and it was fortunate that she had retained enough of her self-control not to wake the duke to enact a Cheltenham tragedy at three in the morning.

How mortifying that would have been—for both of them!

Poor Kesgrave would not have had the least idea what was happening to him.

Swiftly, she gulped the cup of tea, swallowed a few bites of toast and asked Lily to select a morning dress for her. "And do not fret about which one. Any old thing will do nicely, thank you," she added, familiar with her maid's tendency to thoughtfully deliberate over the day's selection. Often, Lily considered and rejected three or four options for seemingly incomprehensible reasons.

But Bea did not have time for that this morning. She was eager to find Kesgrave and hear his reasonable explanation for everything that had occurred the day before.

It was all a tempest in a teapot, she was sure of it.

Lily complied with a reluctant grumble, pulling from the wardrobe a simple muslin gown with an unadorned hem and only the mildest flounce to the sleeve. It was ideally suited for cozy domestic tasks such as attending to one's correspondence, but far too plain for anything outside the home.

And given that it was already after ten. ...

"That is perfect, thank you," Bea said when she observed the look of hesitancy on Lily's face.

Thirty-nine minutes later—indeed, yes, she *had* been counting the minutes—she was dressed and groomed to her maid's satisfaction and had to forcibly stop herself from racing out of the room. Undue haste was not ducal.

Even so, she was able to restrain herself for only so long, and by the time she reached the bottom of the staircase, she was running lightly. Spotting Joseph, she ascertained Kesgrave's location and promptly changed direction when he said the duke was in the entry hall. Given the hour, she had assumed he would be in his study, either reading the newspaper or meeting with Stephens. But a visitor had just arrived —presumably the dowager making another attempt to take her grandson to task for his shabby treatment—and he had gone to the door to greet them.

Happy to watch him get his due, she strode into the entry hall to see that the caller was not in fact the dowager.

No, it was not.

It was a beautiful raven-haired woman, and she was clasped in the duke's embrace.

Chapter Two

Oh, but *beautiful* did not do her justice.

The woman Kesgrave held in his arms was stunning.

Gorgeous.

Ravishing.

And it was not simply that the lustrous dark hair complemented her creamy complexion and set off the ethereal light blue of her eyes to perfection, although those were the things Beatrice noticed first. Her eyes were so unusual and appealing, the way they tipped up toward the temple, giving them a slightly feline cast. It was also that her features appeared as delicate as glass in her heart-shaped face.

There was an encompassing fragility about her, as though even a high-pitched squeal would cause her to shatter, and although the effect struck Bea as alarming, she assumed most men found it charming.

Did Kesgrave count among their number?

The truth was, Bea did not know.

He had an innate decency that would respond to female helplessness with resolute determination, and men of his rank were raised from infancy to value beauty above all else. Among the *ton,* aesthetic perfection was worshipped, and the two of them made an exquisite pair, his bright blond curls offsetting her sleek black waves in a kind of irresistible equilibrium: the living embodiment of the golden ratio.

Together, they were everything the beau monde wanted for itself—and everything Kesgrave had rejected by legshackling himself to an impertinent spinster with an impish grin.

Bea was not insensible to the gravity of that action.

Whatever insecurities she possessed from her own long career as an awkward wallflower and unpaid servant, she was not so lacking in confidence that seeing the duke in the arms of the magnificent stranger made her doubt the solidity of their union.

No, that distinction belonged to the Great Fabrication.

And the separate bedchambers.

Compared to those unnerving events, the lovely newcomer was barely an afterthought.

Even so, she was an afterthought in a pretty gown of the deepest rose with intricate rosettes lining its lace trim, and as Bea stepped farther into the entry hall, she felt every inch of her plain frock.

Poor Lily!

The girl had always known this moment would come and had done everything within her power to avert it. Alas, it was not at all the thing for a maid to tether her noble employer to a chair and compel her to care about her appearance.

That Bea regretted her haste was undeniable.

All those extravagant gowns filling the wardrobe upstairs and she was turned out like an apple seller in Covent Garden.

It is funny, she told herself, pressing forward despite the sudden unease. Spinning sharply on her heels and scurrying away would make her look more foolish than any plain dress ever could.

The caller noticed her first, for she was looking into the room while Kesgrave was facing out, and she examined Beatrice with frank curiosity as the duke stepped back. Catching sight of her next, he moved away from the woman with unhurried steps, his arms falling to his sides as he smiled at Bea.

And what a smile it was—easy, relaxed, nonchalant, pleased.

It contained not a glimmer of guilt for the lie, not a twinge of remorse or discomfort or even a hint of embarrassed awareness at being caught embracing the most breathtaking creature Bea had ever beheld.

There was nothing but delight at her presence, and she felt her apprehension return tenfold because she could not fathom how he could act as though the Great Fabrication did not matter at all unless the Great Fabrication did *not* matter at all.

It was, in fact, an everyday occurrence: the Great Mundanity.

Husbands lied to their wives all the time. Uncle Horace frequently twisted the truth to evade his wife's censure, and although those instances almost always involved purchases the household coffers could ill afford, Kesgrave might have a similar motivation. Although she could not recall a particular topic of which she had signaled disapproval, Bea allowed that she might have conveyed it unintentionally and immediately resented the implication that it was *her* fault.

As she struggled to maintain her composure despite her racing thoughts, Kesgrave said, "Ah, there you are, Bea. We have a caller. Please allow me to introduce to you Mrs. Penelope Taylor."

It was a gut punch.

Like a blow to the stomach, hard and sure, the name rammed into her, knocking the air out of her lungs, and she felt lightheaded from the lack of oxygen.

Did she waver?

Did she actually wobble from side to side?

From the expression on the duke's face, she decided she did not, for he did not seem troubled by her reaction. He continued to speak, explaining that Penny—and, yes, he addressed her like that, informally, familiarly—had just arrived and desired a word with Bea. The ease of his demeanor, the utter lack of self-consciousness in his manner, made it glaringly obvious he had no idea that she recognized the name of his former mistress.

His first, in fact, for the Duke of Kesgrave had taken five in total.

If prompted, Bea could list the full complement in order of succession.

It was not an accomplishment of which she was particularly proud, nor one she had sought to achieve. It had been imposed on her by spiteful matrons and concerned relatives and cynical countesses who believed there was nothing to be gained by pretending the past did not exist.

In this, Bea had to concede Lady Abercrombie was correct.

As upsetting as it was to stand in her own entry hall and greet the dazzling woman whom her husband had once routinely bedded, she was grateful to have all the information.

And have it all, she did: Mrs. Taylor, who had adopted the honorific at the beginning of her career without going through the trouble of inventing a husband, was older than the duke by four years. She was four and twenty when the affair began and walked away from the alliance with several pieces of noteworthy jewelry, chief among them a necklace featuring a fat diamond surrounded by a dozen smaller ones. Last spotted at a late-night picnic at Vauxhall in April, it remained a treasured possession.

"She wishes to discuss a murder in which she finds herself entangled," Kesgrave continued.

The beauty laughed at this statement, a deep, throaty purr that had its own seductive appeal, and chastised him for understating the case. "I am *entangled* in a dispute with the fishmonger. In regards to Millie, I am enmeshed or even embroiled."

Bea smiled blandly.

It required every ounce of her self-control, but she pasted a look of benign interest on her face as she struggled to contain her emotions. The other woman had such a deft way about her, a blithe insouciance and lighthearted familiarity that spoke to an easy intimacy, and Bea had the unpleasant sensation of being an intruder in her own home.

Snidely, she considered asking the couple if they wanted to be alone.

But that was just her insecurity rearing its ugly head.

Kesgrave had ended his association with Penelope Taylor well over a decade ago, and if he had renewed the acquaintance any time in the intervening years, Lady Abercrombie would have mentioned it. The countess bore a deep resentment of the courtesan, who had once counted Lord Abercrombie among her smitten coterie.

Bea cautioned herself against responding with panic or fear, for she had long recognized the inevitability of this moment. She was always going to come face-to-face with one of her husband's former paramours. Indeed, knowing the behavior of gentlemen of the *ton*, she knew it was reasonable to assume he had had a fleeting union with at least one of the lovely widows with whom they regularly interacted.

It is nothing particularly shocking, she thought, as

another figure stepped forward and she realized they had a second caller: a man in a rich green-colored coat and gray mixture pantaloons. He was about sixty years old, with a high forehead and heavy jowls, and towered over the dainty Mrs. Taylor, although he barely came up to Kesgrave's nose. Apologizing for the intrusion, he identified himself as Sir John Piddlehinton, magistrate and neighbor to Mrs. Taylor. He was, he added, there in an unofficial capacity, for the issue was soon to be turned over to the coroner, who had already been alerted.

"But Penny was adamant that she speak to you, and given the direness of her circumstance, I could not deny her," he explained, crossing the threshold into the house. "I fear the dear girl also has a gift for understatement, for neither *enmeshed* nor *embroiled* correctly describes it either. She is, in the words of my long-departed father, as sunk as a meadow."

To this gloomy sentiment, Mrs. Taylor responded with a serene smile, revealing her first imperfection—a trio of crooked teeth, one so out of line it was almost at a right angle to the others—and chastised her companion for being relentlessly pessimistic. "It is an awful business, yes, but I am certain we can come to an amiable arrangement if we all discuss it. Damien, would you be so kind as to lead us someplace where we may sit down? A drawing room, perhaps?"

If Mrs. Taylor was oblivious to the impropriety of the request, then the magistrate was not and suggested they remain there, in the entry hall, as their visit would not be long enough to warrant comfort.

"Discuss Millie's murder in front of an open door?" Mrs. Taylor asked with vague horror.

Piddlehinton winced slightly and said they could close it before looking to Kesgrave for confirmation, clearly sensible to the presumption of speaking so freely of the ducal door.

Bea, listening to the conversation from what felt like a

great distance even though she was only inches away from the other participants, drew a few conclusions: Someone named Millie was dead, Millie had been murdered, the magistrate considered Mrs. Taylor the prime suspect, and the prime suspect was determined to prove her innocence by seeking the Duchess of Kesgrave's assistance.

She allowed that these assumptions could be wrong, but she rather thought she had the correct understanding despite her shock and befuddlement at meeting mistress number one.

Mistress number one, who had lasted nine months.

The young duke rented a house for her on Browder Street and hired a carriage and a team of horses.

It was, according to the countess, an extravagant arrangement, but Mrs. Taylor had several offers from high-ranking men at the time and had simply followed the money.

Kesgrave, agreeing to Mrs. Taylor's suggestion, indicated with a sweep of his hand that she should proceed down the corridor to the left. Pleased, she held out her arm to him, as if requesting his escort to supper, and the duke refused the honor with an amused glance at Bea. Embarrassed either for all of them or only himself, Piddlehinton tilted his head down and kept his eyes on the finely veined marble as he crossed the floor.

It was the nine months that she found most unsettling, Bea thought as she trailed after the group, her steps measured and slow. It was the same length of time she herself had known the duke, but not really, because there were several months between their original meeting and the start of the season when they did not have any contact.

So, in effect, Mrs. Taylor had known him longer.

Did she know him better?

Bea wanted to believe it was not possible for anyone to know Kesgrave better than she because their bond was so profound. But that was just insipid sentimentality. In reality, even Lady Abercrombie knew him better.

Arriving to the drawing room, she found Mrs. Taylor already settled on the settee, her eyes sweeping upward as she admired the frescoes on the ceiling. Next to her, Piddlehinton squirmed. Kesgrave stood at the entrance, the affable smile on his face an indication that he suspected nothing, and there was no reason why he should. His relationship with the courtesan was a dozen years in the past—ancient history, as they say—and more to the point, it was none of Bea's business. The activities a man chose to pursue outside of the bounds of matrimony had little bearing on the marriage itself.

"How rich Dido's throne is," Mrs. Taylor said with a note of awe in her voice as she observed the influence of Menescardi in the deft hand of the artist.

It was an erudite observation, which was, Bea supposed, precisely what a mistress did: offered insightful commentary on Botticelli's *Birth of Venus* while looking like Botticelli's Venus.

"Yes, it is by one of his apprentices," Kesgrave replied, taking the seat next to Bea.

"It is gorgeous, Damien," Mrs. Taylor said warmly. "So vibrant and lifelike. Your ancestor did very well for himself when he hired the painter."

Watching the exchange, Bea was struck by how composed the courtesan was for a murder suspect and assumed that was also part of her appeal. While a wife might pester her husband with fears, anxieties and expectations, a mistress refrained from indulging in any of the messier emotions. She provided only pleasure in all its forms.

In that respect, it was a logical arrangement.

She did not wonder for a moment why a husband would take a mistress.

Why *her* husband would take a mistress—well, yes, that was an entirely different matter.

It was not something she worried about as a matter of course. Kesgrave had been unstinting and generous in his affection, demonstrating it in hundreds of little ways that transcended words.

In this, at least, she was secure.

And yet it was easy to dismiss the idea of a mistress when she was only a specter wafting gently on the periphery. The proposition became much harder to ignore when it took on full corporeality in the dazzling form of Penelope Taylor. As confident as Bea was that the duke would not make an offer to *this* courtesan, she could not quite convince herself that he would never make an offer to *any* courtesan. It was simply what men of his rank and breeding did, and although it would seem to imply something disheartening about the quality of his regard for his wife, it in fact meant nothing.

Lady Abercrombie swore to it.

And Aunt Vera, who could not acknowledge having flesh, let alone discussing matters that pertained to it, warned her in an inordinately concise speech not to take the duke's inevitable defection to heart.

Knowing they could never understand the nature of her bond with the duke, Bea had brushed aside their concerns, and now suddenly all their dire warnings swept to the fore with a relentless vigor. In the wake of the Great Fabrication and their separate bedchambers, she felt herself succumbing to a sort of cynical futility, as though comprehending the inexorable truth that Kesgrave's actions were dictated by a force greater than himself.

Mrs. Taylor trilled lightly at an observation the duke made, and Piddlehinton, his shoulders tensing as he leaned forward, said, "With all due respect, your grace, this is not a social call. Penny stands charged with a very serious crime, and I would appreciate it if you would address it. Then we may be on our way. I would not like to take up more of your time than necessary."

"Yes, of course," Kesgrave replied affably. "Please do proceed."

Although the magistrate opened his mouth to clarify, Mrs. Taylor spoke first, insisting that she could not allow Piddly to explain because he was a small-minded beast who could see no farther than his own nose. "The only reason he thinks I murdered Millie is killing our rivals is simply what women do. We are all vain, hateful, vicious creatures, always wrangling over men, and we cannot make rational decisions because we are constantly enfeebled by jealousy," she said, turning to look at Bea, her gaze all springtime and splendor, and appealing to her directly. "Please tell him, your grace, how little he understands our sex. You and I, for example, are not at each other's throats. We are models of civility despite our both being intimately acquainted with Damien."

Piddlehinton gasped. "Penny! You must choose your words more thoughtfully!"

Mrs. Taylor curved her lips into a sly smile and insisted she *was* being thoughtful. "It would be cruel for me to sit in her grace's own drawing room and have information she did not—information, by the bye, that everyone else in the room has. You might consider that the height of propriety, Piddly, but I think it is decidedly ramshackle."

Unimpressed, the magistrate scowled and said she always had some high-minded ideal to justify all her low-minded actions. Mrs. Taylor scoffed, citing this statement of further proof of his lack of charity, and Bea kept her eyes trained steadily ahead. The urge to look next to her, at the duke, was almost overwhelming, but she refused to succumb because she did not want to see his face. She did not want to possess the information she would intuit from his expression while she was trapped there, in the elaborate drawing room, with his mistress.

If it could not be resolved immediately, then she did not want to know.

"I appreciate your consideration," Bea said, her tone remarkably flat for the way her heart raced in her chest. The self-possession was the result of her position. Two months of smothering the pinch of inadequacy she felt every time Marlow or Lily addressed her by her title had equipped her well for this moment. "Regarding the murder in question, is your rivalry with the victim the only reason Sir John believes you killed her?"

Mrs. Taylor said, "Yes, precisely, he is that petty."

Piddlehinton, answering at the same time, said, "Her dress was splattered with blood, and she was holding the murder weapon as she stood over Millie, who was in her bed!"

"You see!" Mrs. Taylor exclaimed triumphantly. "His imagination is so limited that he cannot begin to fathom another explanation. Millie's blood was on my dress so I must be her killer."

"And the murder weapon," he added through clenched teeth. "Furthermore, she was as cool and composed as you see her now. If Millie's dead body had actually shocked her, then she would have been incapable of speech. By rights, she should be inconsolable with grief and horror over these events, which happened little more than an hour ago. And yet she is coolly admiring your frescoes. If that does not speak to her guilt, then I do not know what does."

Mrs. Taylor rolled her eyes in Bea's direction, as if bored by the simplicity of the male mind. "Since I did not dissolve into a fit of hysterics, then I must be a killer, for no natural woman could retain her ability to think in the presence of blood. That is what he believes! Whatever grief and horror I felt at the sight of my dear friend's blood-soaked corpse—and it was, I swear, considerable—was immediately subsumed by terror for myself. The moment he called me a murderer I no longer had the luxury of succumbing to my emotions. I had to keep a clear head and fight for my own survival, which I have been doing ever since. I am sorry if my coherence offends you, Piddly darling."

Stiffly, the magistrate swore he was not offended.

"Only suspicious," Mrs. Taylor replied snidely.

"Who summoned Sir John?" Bea asked, intrigued enough by their exchange to find her compulsion to look at the duke begin to lessen. "If you did not, was it one of the servants?"

"Nobody sent for him," Mrs. Taylor said.

"That is correct," Piddlehinton said. "I was there by my own volition. As it was tattle time."

He said it matter-of-factly, as though it was something Bea should know.

Alas, she did not. "Tattle time?"

"It is our ritual," Mrs. Taylor explained with a fond look at the magistrate. "Two or three times a week we have breakfast together, read the dailies and gossip like a pair of old biddies."

"Our houses are down the block from each other, so it is very convenient," Piddlehinton added. "We have been doing it for three or four years now."

"Five years," Mrs. Taylor amended.

The magistrate received this news with wide-eyed wonder. "Yes, that is right. *Five* years. Amazing. I would swear it was only three."

"We share expertise," Mrs. Taylor added. "I help Piddly woo women, for he was painfully awkward before me. It was a miracle he ever managed to find a wife. His romantic success has increased significantly under my tutelage. In turn, he helps me with my finances. It has been quite mutually beneficial."

Piddlehinton ardently agreed. "Penny has expanded my

horizons, and I have grown quite fond of the girl. That is why this whole thing is so upsetting for me."

The courtesan dismissed his morosity with a wave of the hand. "Pooh, darling! Save your pity for poor Millie, for I do not need it. I have done nothing wrong. You may take my word for it."

But clearly he could not, because he shook his head and said that the law did not work on pledges and promises. It was an official legal affair that must be handled by the coroner. It was beyond his meager contrivances now.

It was, Bea decided, a fascinating exchange, for their friendship appeared to be sincere, with the magistrate genuinely regretful at not being able to save her from herself. "So you came to the house for tattle time and were informed Mrs. Taylor was in her bedchamber, which is why you went upstairs?"

"Rather, I was told she was seeing to Millie, who had arrived earlier that morning in a state, and I went upstairs to make sure they were not at each other's throats," he said, darting a bashful look at his friend, as if embarrassed to be giving evidence against her. "They tended to bicker a lot when left to their own devices, and with things being what they were, I knew the argument could turn ugly. And so I went upstairs by myself, although Mrs. Booth, the housekeeper, offered to escort me. The truth is, we run tame in each other's homes, do we not, Penny? I went up by myself and the door was ajar so I entered without knocking and saw Penny standing over Millie with a bloody hatpin in her fist. I drew the only conclusion I could."

"And that is why we are here, your grace, because what Piddly said is true: He *is* capable of drawing only one conclusion due to the deficiencies of his intelligence," Mrs. Taylor said. "I need someone with your ingenuity and shrewdness to find the real killer."

"Good God, *that* is the reason?" Piddlehinton asked in surprise.

Mrs. Taylor regarded him with confusion. "Well, naturally, why else would we call on the Duchess of Kesgrave? I know you have read Mr. Twaddle-Thum's accounts of her mystery-solving prowess because we have read them together over tea and marveled at her acumen. We are both in awe of your accomplishments, your grace," she assured her host. "Piddly even describes you as 'deuced clever for a female,' which is the highest praise he has to offer. Not even I have earned it. I am only 'sly' and 'managing.' And 'managing' is not really a compliment because he is calling me manipulative but trying to make it sound benign."

Red-cheeked, the magistrate swore he had called her manipulative to her face, and if he truly never had, he was happy to do so now. "For this was a most ill-advised visit and I should never have let you manipulate me into it. I allowed my pity for your situation to overcome my good sense," he said, then turned to address the duke to offer an abject apology. "You must forgive me, your grace, for exposing you and your wife to this horrible occurrence. It has nothing to do with either one of you. I am sorry!"

The magistrate rose to his feet with a beseeching look at the courtesan, who refused to abide by his unspoken command. Instead, she leaned back in the settee rather pointedly and replied that the matter did in fact pertain to the duke. "Damien vowed to provide me with assistance should I ever require it. He said all I had to do was ask."

Readily, Kesgrave acknowledged the offer, stating that he had issued it more than twelve years past, when he ended their association, and Bea, unable to resist the compulsion any longer, glanced at him. His features arranged in mild amusement, he revealed nothing, and she wondered what she would have seen if she had given in sooner.

Mrs. Taylor lifted her delicate shoulders in an elegant display of indifference and replied that she did not mark time as long as time did not mark her. "And as you can see by looking at me, our relationship might as well have ended yesterday. Now do be a darling, Damien, and tell Piddly that you are a man who honors your commitments before I am forced to resort to a pout."

But the duke demurred, noting that it was up to the duchess which murders she deigned to investigate, and the odd munificence of the language—as if she were deluged by so many corpses she had the luxury of picking and choosing —struck Bea as funny.

Relieved that she was still capable of humor, even in this unnerving circumstance and after the Great Fabrication, she agreed to hear more. Piddlehinton pressed his lips in irritation but regained his seat without comment as Mrs. Taylor thanked Bea for her generosity. Kesgrave, perhaps realizing the gathering would not end anytime soon, rose to arrange for tea and rout cakes.

Bea's heart warmed at the request, for it meant that he was thinking about her. Despite the reappearance of mistress number one, she remained foremost in his mind, and although she did not require the confirmation, she was nevertheless grateful for it.

And that gratitude irritated her, for why would she expect anything less?

The answer was obvious—the lie, the beds—and she resented how quickly her sense of security had been undermined. The problem was not the ravishing Mrs. Taylor. She knew the woman would not swoop in with her alluring pout and beguiling manner and lure Kesgrave away.

No, that fire had been extinguished a long time ago.

The problem was far more insidious than one appealing courtesan, for it was the thing that Mrs. Taylor embodied:

physical perfection. It was a reminder—or, really, the revelation—that youth and beauty would always be available to the duke. Temptation in all its enchanting forms would beckon endlessly, and she could not help but gaze into the future and feel crushed by the weight of the looming tragedy.

But it was not even a tragedy.

Her worst nightmare was simply the standard arrangement for married members of their class. Husbands took mistresses all the time, and it signified nothing.

Aunt Vera had stated it plainly: It has naught to do with you.

And Bea had agreed, for the infidelities of other men were none of her concern and they certainly had no bearing on her marriage. Even yesterday morning, she would have found the idea that her relative's warning was relevant to her situation risible.

But today, now, in the presence of the radiant beauty with whom Kesgrave had shared a bed for almost a year, it felt as though the slow dissolution of their relationship had already begun.

She knew her response was overwrought.

The duke would have a reassuring explanation for the Great Fabrication. He would allay her fears and return to her bed and everything would be as it was.

Except it would not, not really, for her understanding of the future had been irrevocably altered. Like a sailor spotting a far-off coastline through the lens of a spyglass, she had gotten a glimpse of what lay beyond the horizon and it terrified her. Having never broached the subject of a mistress with the duke, she did not know where he stood, and she could conceive of a world where he loved her with all his heart and still sought satisfaction elsewhere.

Kesgrave returned to his seat as she contemplated this

devastating thought, and although he tried to catch her gaze, she looked doggedly at her guests.

"You are very kind to serve tea, but it is really not necessary," Piddlehinton said politely. "We do not want you to exert yourselves on our behalf."

Mrs. Taylor, however, swore that was precisely what she desired. "I should like the duchess to go to any lengths necessary to prove my innocence. I cannot pretend that I am not here to inconvenience you greatly. I wish it were not necessary, but Piddly refuses to see reason."

Calmly, with only a hint of exasperation, the magistrate said again that she had held the murder weapon in her bloody grip.

"Yes, yes," Mrs. Taylor scoffed impatiently. "But where was Millie found?"

"In your bedchamber," he said with an air of impatience. "As we have already discussed."

"Yes, but *where* in my bedchamber?" she asked.

With an apologetic glance at the duke, he said, "In your bed."

And still Mrs. Taylor pressed him for more detail. "*Where* on my bed?"

Confused by the level of specificity, Piddlehinton hazarded a guess. "On your counterpane?"

"Yes! On my *silk* counterpane with *embroidered* serpents that Capenhurst brought back for me from *India* at considerable expense to himself and significant discomfort to his valet," she added with particular emphasis. "And what does that make it?"

Here, he had no theories and could only stare blankly.

"My favorite possession," she announced.

Not anticipating this answer, Piddlehinton drew his brows together and said with a confounded hesitancy. "I really cannot see what that has to do—"

"It does not matter how irritated I grew with Millie or how annoyed I was with her inept efforts to be more like me or her constant complaining or her facile attempts to steal my beaux, I would never kill her on my favorite possession," Mrs. Taylor explained forthrightly. "I would have pushed her onto the rug, which was a parting gift from Speke. He claimed the vibrant colors and lovely pattern captured my spirit, but he was just being a nipcheese and trying to pretty it up. Everyone knows you cannot wear a rug to the pleasure gardens, and sapphires and diamonds capture my spirit far more accurately. I have wanted to replace it for three years, and I promise you that if I were going to stab Millie with a hatpin because she got on my nerves one too many times, I would have had the presence of mind to shove her onto the floor first. Ordinarily, I am against physical abuse, but if I were going to kill her anyway, I should think bashing her shoulder against the floorboard would not bother me."

"That is your defense?" Piddlehinton asked, appalled. "'I am innocent, Piddly dear, because I would never dare stain my precious counterpane.' That is ridiculous, and I am sure the duchess does not find it persuasive either."

Bea, however, thought the sanctity of a treasured belonging was a reasonable defense. To thrive in Mrs. Taylor's chosen profession required a certain amount of cold-bloodedness, and she could never have succeeded as long as she had if she allowed herself to respond to minor irritants with unrestrained fury.

Constrained fury, without question.

By Mrs. Taylor's own account, she was frequently at odds with the victim, which meant she was accustomed to dealing with her anger and irritation. Presumably, if she had reached the end of a very long tether, then she would plan in advance, taking pains to spare the items most precious to her, such as the counterpane.

Alternatively, Mrs. Taylor might loathe the bedspread and adore the rug.

"That is not my only defense," the courtesan countered with a waspish smile. "I have another piece of evidence, and it is so obvious, so readily apparent to anyone who looks at the crime scene, I am mortified that I have to say it out loud to you, Piddly. And it is this: Millie was not the intended victim. That honor belongs to me. I am the one the killer wanted to stab to death on my gorgeous counterpane from India. I am the true victim."

Chapter Three

"Oh, for God's sake," Piddlehinton muttered.

Mrs. Taylor continued as though the magistrate had not spoken. "I knew it at once. The moment I saw her lying there with all that blood, I knew it should have been me. It was the hair, you see, on the pillow, so dark and similar to mine. It looked like me. That is to say, even *I* would think it was me. It terrified me, and I stood in the doorway for a long while, staggered by the sight. And then suddenly I heard a loud clap, which must have been the front door closing behind Piddly, and it broke the spell and I ran to Millie. I knew it was too late but I still thought maybe I could help her, and I felt for her pulse but it was all blood and then I felt the holes, and I jumped back, which is when I tripped on the hatpin. I had just picked it up and was staring at it in confusion when Piddly entered the room."

The magistrate nodded, confirming that the picture she described was indeed the one that had greeted him. "Mrs. Booth told me what happened, about Millie pounding on the door at the crack of dawn, irate and demanding entry, and Penny sending her to bed to get some sleep because the poor girl was as drunk as a lord. Then she told me Penny had just gone to rouse Millie, as she had been asleep for more than two hours. That is when I said that I would offer my assistance because I have seen how snippy Penny can get when she is irritated and I knew she was already annoyed at Millie for causing a fracas on her doorstep. So I dashed upstairs to intercede in their quarrel and found Penny looming over her friend with the murder weapon in her hand. There could be no misunderstanding what I saw."

Tartly, Mrs. Taylor replied that there could obviously be *some* misunderstanding. "I know you can be clever, Piddly, because I have heard your tales of your exploits during your long tenure as magistrate. There is the time you outwitted a horse thief by pretending to be a farrier with a broken leg and when you ambushed a burglar in an alley after his accomplice stabbed you in the shoulder with his dagger. You are capable of complex reasoning, and I beg you to employ just a little. It was morning and I had yet to change from my dressing gown, let alone put on my bonnet. Why would I be holding a hatpin?"

Piddlehinton glanced at the duke, as if to apologize again, and said patiently, "To stab Millie with."

"You mean, to stab Millie in a fit of pique because we were squabbling over a man, for that is what females do?" she asked with deceptive mildness.

Defensively, the magistrate insisted that he held no general opinion of women that was so unfavorable. "But you and Millie *do* squabble all the time. You will call her a thick-headed maggot and she will call you an avaricious louse and then you start screeching at each other. And you may deny it all you want but it is almost always over a man, and so, yes, I do believe in this instance you stabbed her in a fit of pique while bickering over a man."

"Well, there, you see, your grace!" Mrs. Taylor exclaimed,

looking at Bea meaningfully with her sly cat eyes. "His account makes no sense. Why would I have a hatpin in my hand if I was not in the process of putting on my bonnet? Either I killed her in a fit of pique, in which case I used whatever weapon was on hand, or it was premeditated. If it was premeditated, then why would I announce to my household beforehand that I was going to wake up Millie? I would do it stealthily while my staff was the busiest, most likely while they were making breakfast, for if there is one thing I know how to do it is sneak around a bedchamber."

Bea could not refute the logic, for killing in the heat of passion and cold-bloodedly planning a murder were two vastly different things. In light of that, the location of the hatpins seemed relevant to the conversation, but before she could inquire about them, Piddlehinton rose again to his feet. "It is not my duty to answer these questions. That is a matter for the inquest. The coroner will address these questions with the jury. That is when you may make these arguments. Until then, you will await your trial in Newgate."

As these words were among the most terrifying in the English language, Bea was not surprised to see Mrs. Taylor blanch. The possibility of spending even a few hours in the notoriously desolate prison would chill anyone to the bone, even the most hardened villain, and the courtesan was not accustomed to deprivation and squalor.

Even so, Mrs. Taylor greeted the prospect with equanimity, smiling with what appeared to be relief as she said, "Why, you are right, Piddly. I *will* be safe there."

The magistrate goggled at her. "*Safe!* In Newgate! Have you lost all your senses, woman?"

"I must take some measure to ensure my well-being, for I am hunted prey," she asserted with fervent certitude. "Whoever killed Millie will soon discover their mistake and seek to rectify it as soon as possible. But they will not be able to harm me if I am beyond their reach in Newgate. It is an excellent suggestion. Thank you, Piddly, for making it."

Piddlehinton was at once horrified and irritated by her response, for he seemed to consider it a personal affront, the notion that anyone would take shelter in the hell pit known as Newgate. He had mentioned it in an effort to chasten Mrs. Taylor, but all it had done was encourage her. "It is not a suggestion," he snapped. "But the law!"

"Of course it is, dear," she said soothingly as she narrowed her eyes pensively. "It would have to be the state side. According to all the guides for tourists, that is where the best rooms are and the most palatable food. I know it is rather expensive to stay there, but I can afford it. I have been saving up to buy my townhouse rather than hand over all that lovely money to my beastly landlord, and this could set me back a few years. You will arrange it for me, won't you, Piddly? You already have access to my funds as you are in charge of my investments."

But Piddlehinton could not fathom what she was saying. "You are mad. Utterly mad. I should have you confined to the insanity ward at Bethlem."

Mrs. Taylor, blinking her impossibly long lashes at him, asked if he thought she would be safer there. "I am happy to go wherever you advise, darling. You have never led me astray."

The magistrate turned purple with frustration, emitted an incoherent grunt and dropped back onto the settee with a thunk.

Joseph, arriving with the tray, entered the drawing room as Kesgrave asked his former mistress why she remained in London.

Mrs. Taylor raised her chin haughtily and said with arch curiosity, "You mean if I truly fear for my life and this is not merely for show to drive poor Piddly daft, why did I not dash off to some obscure village where nobody knows me? Consider what you are proposing, Damien. I would have to give up my life in London, which suits me very well, and establish a new one in a rustic little corner of the country. I spent enough time milking cows as a young girl to know I would rather be dead than ever touch an udder again."

As Piddlehinton muttered about cholera and consumption, Bea decided Mrs. Taylor's sanguine attitude toward imprisonment could be attributed only to a conviction that she would not be in Newgate for long. She was so confident her innocence could be proved that she was willing to subject herself to the horrors on a short-term basis.

It was a persuasive argument, and Bea found the courtesan's assertion that she was the true victim worthy of further consideration. It would explain why someone as clearly calculating as Mrs. Taylor allowed herself to be embroiled in something as messy as a stabbing death in her own bedchamber.

Consequently, she asked about Miss Lloyd's appearance. "You mentioned that she also had black hair. Did she resemble you in other ways?"

"In every way!" Mrs. Taylor replied with a hint of exasperation. "We were very alike in coloring, as we both have black hair and light blue eyes. And our frames are so slight—narrow bones. That said, she did lack my best asset: my breasts. They are pendulous and pert."

A teacup clattered as Joseph, in the act of placing the tray on the table before Bea, turned to assess Mrs. Taylor's bosom for himself. He mumbled an apology as his face turned bright red and he pulled his eyes from the munificence on display. Then he returned the fallen cup to its saucer, straightened the teapot and scurried from the room.

Taking no notice of the footman's response, Mrs. Taylor added that Millie had not been likewise endowed. "She was in no way deficient. It was simply that she could not hold a

LYNN MESSINA

candle to me. Sadly, that was true in many respects, and it did wear on the poor girl! But she had only herself to blame. Nobody compelled her to live in my shadow. That was the choice she made."

"You see?" Piddlehinton asked as if proving a point. "As vicious as cats."

But Mrs. Taylor shook her head as if her own point had been proved. "We had a relationship that suited us both in different ways, which Piddly cannot understand because he has such a terrible opinion of women. Millie realized that if she enhanced her similarity to me, such as wearing her hair like mine, in cascading waves, and adopting my signature color of dusky rose, she could attract a better quality of man. Most of those men were suitors I had rebuffed who were delighted to settle for a close approximation, and that was helpful to me because it took the sting out of my rejection. As I said, they were happy to accept Millie as second best. It is an arrangement we have had in place for almost four years. Piddly introduced us. He found her in a brothel and was struck by the similarities in our appearance. He thought we must be sisters separated at birth."

Piddlehinton, coloring slightly at the revelation that he frequented such low establishments, said the resemblance was astonishing at first glance. "When you put them side by side you could see the differences, but if you looked at them fleetingly or out of the corner of your eye, you would swear they were twins. And although it is true that they both bene-fitted from the relationship, it was never a comfortable arrangement. Millie resented Penny for always having the better thing—house, protector, wardrobe, jewelry—and Penny grew tired of Millie constantly aping her ways. She would buy a new blue bonnet on Tuesday, and Millie would appear with the same blue bonnet on Wednesday."

"That is true," Mrs. Taylor acknowledged solemnly. "I did

42

find it exhausting to have everything I did imitated. Every so often I would buy some hideous garment just to trick Millie into wearing it. Do you recall that black-and-gold fichu or those spotted slippers? The poor girl lacked discernment and simply dashed out to purchase whatever I was wearing."

Again, the magistrate looked at the duke meaningfully. "As you can imagine, Millie was not happy when she discovered she had been duped into spending more than she could afford on a useless scarf. Those sorts of incidents happened all the time, which is why they were constantly bickering."

"I would not say we were *constantly* bickering, but I will allow our relationship was contentious," Mrs. Taylor said evenhandedly. "It came to a head, however, with Waltham. She was upset about him in a way I had never seen before. It is why she was pounding on the door before six in the morning and shouting loud enough to wake every house on the block."

Much of the story had been told out of order, and Bea had only a vague understanding of the details. Miss Lloyd, irate over something, called on her friend early in the morning to air her dissatisfaction, then retired to Mrs. Taylor's bedroom to recover from her outburst.

Regarding the source of the friction, she said, "Waltham?"

"The Marquess of Waltham," Mrs. Taylor replied succinctly.

Kesgrave, finding the answer insufficient, elaborated in some detail, explaining that the gentleman had recently come into the title after a distant relative died without an heir. "It was unexpected and only happened because the line of succession was drastically altered by the war. Presumably, Penny refused his original offer, passing him onto Miss Lloyd, as was her custom, and then changed her mind when his circumstances improved."

Although this understanding of her motivations was

hardly flattering, Mrs. Taylor fluttered her lashes as though deeply gratified by it. "Why, Damien, you do know me so well. We have long been of one mind. You always know what I am thinking, and I you. Right now, for example, you are annoyed at my claiming to know your thoughts."

Blandly, Kesgrave assured her he was not. "I am reviewing my acquaintance to see to whom I may apply for an introduction to Waltham."

Undaunted, Mrs. Taylor smiled broadly and congratulated him on neatly returning her to her place. "And I must thank you for it, as I am most dependent on the duchess's favor. It would never do to alienate her by appearing overly familiar with her husband."

Bea, holding out a cup of tea to her, promised not to allow her personal feelings about the matter to interfere with her investigation. "I am solely interested in the truth. By your response, I can only assume Waltham welcomed your renewed interest, leaving Miss Lloyd out in the cold."

"Well, yes, but her outrage was a little disingenuous, for she must have realized it would happen because she knew I would never allow a marquess to slip through my fingers," Mrs. Taylor said ardently, pausing to inhale the brew and proclaim it glorious. Then she took a delicate sip and nodded with approval. "If I had had an inkling of what was in store for plain old Mr. Pitt, I would never have hinted him toward Millie. But when I met him, around Christmas—I believe it was Boxing Day, in Hyde Park during an invigorating walk with Debenham, who has known him since childhood—he was unimpressively common. Handsome as the devil, reasonably well situated and eager. So very eager! He sent me a lovely bouquet the next day. But he was so very common and Debenham is a baron. Waltham was disappointed of course but decided Millie was sufficient to his needs. That was in January. Then in early May, just as I returned to London from a visit to the country, I learned of his unexpected good fortune and sent a card expressing my condolences on the death of his cousin. He replied when he returned to London, which was about three weeks ago, at which time he resumed his relationship with Millie. But he also continued the correspondence with me and called last week to see if I would be interested in adding a new dimension to our relationship. We arrived at an agreement earlier in the week, and he said he would tell Millie about his decision last night. Apparently, he did not. It is impossible to say what really happened because Millie was foxed by the time she arrived at my home, but it seems as though she woke to find Waltham creeping out of her bedchamber at daybreak and when she asked why, he told her that he was ending the relationship."

Although she knew little about the courting habits of the demimonde, Bea recognized a rotten turn when she heard it and wondered if Waltham's disrespectful treatment of her friend gave Mrs. Taylor pause. "How did Miss Lloyd respond to this information?" she asked, selecting a rout cake from the plate as she awaited the answer.

"As well as could be expected. It was poorly done of Waltham to not have a lovely gift with him to assuage her anger. Now that his coffers are overflowing, he has been quite generous. I heard he paid Bedford's valet twice his annual salary to lure him away, and I am sure he meant to send over a stunning pair of earrings or a necklace. But not having it on his person was a mistake. As I said, she was drunk and incoherent—her breath reeked of brandy and licorice from those odious candies she loved—so I did not understand everything she said or even most of it. I think she called him names, vulgar ones that would put Mrs. Marshall next door to blush, because she kept insisting she was not afraid to say it to his face—'his face,' presumably meaning Waltham's," Mrs. Taylor explained, taking another sip of tea and gently laying the cup on the table before asking if she may partake of the pastries as well. "I know how dearly you enjoy them, so I do not wish to presume."

Naturally, she did, yes, Bea thought cynically, extending the plate of rout cakes first to Mrs. Taylor and then Piddlehinton. Any reader of Twaddle who knew enough to plead for Her Outrageousness's help in finding a murderer was highly familiar with her preference for treats. That her reasonable fondness had been portrayed as excessive love was merely another injustice by the notorious prattler, and she found Mrs. Taylor's hesitation as humiliating as it was humorous.

After taking a dainty bite, Mrs. Taylor continued, noting that Miss Lloyd had wailed and cried and made outlandish threats for the better part of an hour. "It was mostly babble and none of it followed any logical sense. That said, I believe she threatened to tell Mr. Twaddle-Thum that Waltham had the pox and he had gotten it from me. She went on some strange tear about Hampstead Heath and the swimming ponds. She *might* have said something about gardening in diamonds. She laughed hysterically for several minutes, just giggling like a thief, and raged about fishing in a skiff. Oh, and then she told me I have an average house, which was the most baffling of all because my home is quite distinctive. Anyone who enters notes my audacious use of color and pattern. She was really not in her right mind, and her inconsolable sobs were beginning to grate on my nerves, so I did everything I could think of to try to calm her down. I sang lullabies and gave her books to throw at me and offered her more brandy or tea. I said we could sit down at once and write a letter to dear Twaddle. I told her I have his direction. We could write whatever she wanted. Anything at all if she would just stop weeping for a little while."

"Did it work?" Bea asked, amused by the empty boast.

The only direction anyone had for the rapacious gossip was the *London Daily Gazette* office on the Strand.

Mrs. Taylor shook her head no. "But she eventually wore herself out and began to whimper, which is when I insisted she take a reviving nap in my bed. By then it was almost seven and my head was aching and I realized I would not get more sleep. Plus, I had to send a note to Waltham to make sure he suffered no ill effects from Millie's tantrum. Her response was inappropriate, and I hoped to assure him he would endure no such embarrassments from me. It was the least I could do because I had encouraged the alliance in the first place, thereby exposing him to her abuse."

As Mrs. Taylor described the note she sent to Waltham to consolidate her position as a moral obligation, Bea was struck by how lightly these manipulations sat on the other woman's shoulders. Although every word she uttered was calculated to produce a desired effect, they somehow felt instinctive and spontaneous. And they had a way of creating a conspirational sense, as if she and the listener were devising a scheme together. Men, especially young ones lately arrived to the capital, would find it irresistible, and Bea could see what attracted Kesgrave. As much as he would have been drawn to her beauty, he would have been intrigued by her air of exclusivity—the belief that she had secrets that she wanted to share only with him.

"You tucked Millie into your bed and then returned downstairs to write to Waltham?" Bea asked, seeking to clarify the order of events.

"Heavens, no!" Mrs. Taylor said with a dismissive wave. "My maid Sarah assisted her. But I did send the housekeeper up with a cup of warm milk about ten minutes later. The exhausted lamb was already asleep. After scribbling a heartfelt apology to Waltham, I applied myself to other correspondence and had breakfast. Then I read the newspaper. As I usually sleep until eight-thirty, it was strange to be up so early. We have morning birds in the back garden. I had no idea!"

"How long after the milk was taken up did you discover Miss Lloyd's body?" Bea asked.

Firmly, Mrs. Taylor said two hours, then admitted she felt dreadful about the whole thing because for the majority of the time Millie was sleeping—or, rather, when she *thought* she was sleeping—she had been a perfect beast to her. "In my head, I mean, because I thought it was rude of her to slumber so long in someone else's bed. I could not stand it any longer because I was eager to begin my day properly, so I went upstairs to wake her up and found her. Then Piddly arrived and now here we are."

Piddlehinton, appearing to resent the reminder, glared at her.

Thoughtfully, Bea contemplated how the change in victim would alter the crime, deciding the biggest shift would be in the suspects. Potential murderers included people who wished Mrs. Taylor harm, not her friends. Making this observation, she was surprised to see the courtesan nod approvingly.

"We are also of one mind, your grace," Mrs. Taylor announced, pulling a note card from the depths of her reticule. "Here are several men who bear me a grudge."

The magistrate startled at the announcement and leaned to the side to read the slip of paper over his friend's shoulder. "When did you have time to draw that up?"

"While Sarah was helping me dress and arrange my hair," she explained as she handed the sheet to Bea. Then she took another rout cake. "I knew it would be helpful for the duchess to have a place to start, but I must admit that the idea of any of these men sneaking into my bedchamber while I was sipping tea and reading about Parliament's latest efforts to rein in the Luddites strikes me as impossible. I simply cannot imagine it. But it is even harder to conceive of one of the staff hating Millie so much they would kill her, so it must be either one of these four men or a stranger."

Having conducted several investigations, Bea was well familiar with the theory of the shadowy outsider bearing an unknown motive. He was usually cited as a diversion to draw attention away from a particular suspect, and she gave it the same consideration now as she usually did—which was to say, very little. It was always possible, of course, but certainly not probable.

She examined the list of suspects: Baron Debenham, Earl of Audenshaw, Dudley St. Ives, Viscount Barlow. Then she handed the note card to Kesgrave and asked Mrs. Taylor about the name at the top. "You mentioned Debenham earlier in relation to meeting Waltham. You and he were together in December you said?"

"That is correct, your grace," Mrs. Taylor affirmed, selecting yet another rout cake before presenting the plate to Piddlehinton, who took the last one. "I was with him for eight months, from August to April, which I thought was a delightful interval, just enough time to develop a sincere affection for him and not enough for his quirks and habits to begin to wear on me. Debenham disagreed and has been sending me threatening letters ever since. They are most troubling in their vehemence, are they not, Piddly?"

In this assertion, the magistrate had no trouble providing his support, noting that the violence in Debenham's missives had taken him by surprise. "You would think a woman had never given him his congé before, but I find that impossible to believe. Every man is shown the door eventually."

The courtesan hailed the truth of this observation as Bea asked next about Audenshaw.

"He is a scoundrel!" Mrs. Taylor cried. "His lordship owes me a great deal of money, which he tried to worm his way out of paying like the lowest rogue! I gave him the most satisfying month of his life and in return he gave me paste! My solicitor sent him a letter this week demanding settlement at once or the matter would be referred to Hawes."

"Hawes?" Bea repeated, resisting the urge to look at Kesgrave, who would almost certainly bristle at the mention of the infamous crime lord who ruled over the worst rookery in the city with an iron fist. "As in Hell and Fury Hawes"?

"Is there any other in London?" Mrs. Taylor asked with a rhetorical flutter.

Obviously, no, there was not, Bea thought. "What does he have to do with you?"

"Usually nothing. All my business is conducted via my solicitor," she explained. "Sometimes, however, I encounter an intractable problem and then I enlist Hawes's help personally. The threat of his involvement is frequently all that is required, although on occasion the situation has called for a more creative solution. Either way, seeking his assistance always puts me in a foul mood because I prefer to solve my own problems."

Bea did not have to ask how Hawes convinced delinquent debtors to settle their bills because she had learned all about his methods firsthand while investigating a previous murder. Although he presented himself as an affable businessman, he employed fear and violence to achieve his ends.

Hoping the investigation did not lead them to cross paths with the crime lord again, she asked about St. Ives.

"He is a fly that refuses to be swatted!" Mrs. Taylor said with ardent frustration. "I told him when he first applied for my favor, in February, that I was not interested in puppies, but he refused to believe me. He decided I was being coy and sent gift after gift. They were lovely, of course, but not enough to persuade me because I find so many of these young men to be deadly dull. They swarm around me at the beginning of every season, callow youths looking for something on which to cut their eyeteeth. Eventually, St. Ives gave up his pursuit, but then he asked for his presents back and began to pester me anew when I refused. The presents were freely given and thus I was under no obligation to return them. Furthermore, he had made a pest of himself for months and it seemed only fair that I be compensated for the nuisance of having to contend with his obstinacy and disappointment. If he had accepted my refusal after the third or fourth time, I might have seen my way toward graciously returning *some* of them. But he simply would not relent."

"This is the younger St. Ives?" Kesgrave asked. "The boy is scarcely twenty."

"Yes, Dudley. Although he behaves as though he is two, squalling and throwing tantrums when he cannot get his way, he is actually three and twenty. Last week at the theater he made an awful spectacle of himself," Mrs. Taylor said, recalling the incident with a shudder. "He was deep in his cups and insistent that I return the pearl earrings he gave me because he had taken them from his mother's jewelry box and he had changed his mind: I was no longer worth the trouble he would get into for stealing them. I told him that is not *my* problem but was kind enough to suggest a jeweler in Darrow Street who makes excellent reproductions."

"And that leaves Viscount Barlow," Bea said, recalling the last name on the list. "Is that Lord Barlow, who fled to the Continent to escape his creditors two years ago? Has he returned?"

"Regrettably, it is not," Mrs. Taylor said with a tired shake of her head. "It was his brother who inherited the title when Barlow died in a duel last summer."

"It was in Dieppe and was over an accusation of cheating at cards," Piddlehinton added, although he could not say who stood as the accuser and the accused. "The reports were incomplete."

"Regardless, his brother blames me because I introduced Barlow to Redfern, with whom he formed a fast friendship and discovered the delights of the faro table," Mrs. Taylor explained. "It is a ridiculous charge, for I did not encourage him to wager eight thousand pounds over the course of one evening at Mrs. Arnold's. And even if I did, Barlow was soon to turn thirty, old enough to take responsibility for his actions. But the younger Barlow refuses to be reasonable about it, glaring at me whenever we cross paths in public and making snide comments to anyone who will listen. Several of his nastier remarks have been printed in the broadsheets by intrusive gossips who do not understand half of what has happened. He has become intolerable since the duel, warning off potential suitors. I do not understand why he is taking such an aggressive stance against me and not Redfern or Mrs. Arnold. I am the most blameless! Truly, I do wish the man could bring himself to settle down and enjoy the advantages of a title that he had little expectation of inheriting like Waltham. *He* is delighted to have a cousin clumsy enough to fall off a cliff. We should all have such graceless relations, he says."

Although Bea imagined there was more to the story of Barlow's downfall than just the one evening of ill-advised gambling, she could not believe Mrs. Taylor was solely responsible. If Redfern had taken his friend to Mrs. Arnold's establishment, then he shared some of the blame. The fact that the new Lord Barlow was unduly focused on the courtesan as the instrument of his brother's destruction indicated that the man's critical faculties were not fully intact. If he possessed an unhealthy fascination with her, then it was possible that he had mistakenly killed Miss Lloyd in a fit of rage.

Begrudgingly, Piddlehinton admitted that Barlow's anger did indeed seem out of proportion to the circumstance. "Penny is a tempting handful, but she is certainly no Delilah to lead a man to his destruction, and Redfern has a history of corrupting young men. It is a shame he cannot be brought to see reason. Even so, I cannot see him stabbing a woman repeatedly with a hatpin. It is too gauche."

"And yet you can see me?" Mrs. Taylor asked heatedly.

"The hatpin was in your hand!" he replied with weary indignation, as if he could not believe he had to repeat the information yet again. "Your dressing gown was covered in blood, and Millie was in your bed! When those conditions apply to Lord Barlow, then I will revise my opinion of his gaucheness."

But Mrs. Taylor, finding his lack of trust after so many years of friendship deeply wounding, advised Bea to add a fifth name to the list. "Sir John Piddlehinton. His determination to see me hanged for murder makes me wonder if he has an ulterior motive."

Beatrice duly complied.

Chapter Four

Although aggrieved by Mrs. Taylor's cruelty, Piddlehinton nevertheless agreed to escort her back to her home. He would never allow his hurt feelings to stand in the way of his duty, and his obligation now was to lend his friend support until the moment he secured her imprisonment at Newgate.

"On the state side, dear," Mrs. Taylor reminded him with a cheerful lilt, which the magistrate took as a personal affront. If he was distraught at the prospect of delivering her to the miserable prison, the least she could do was be distraught at the prospect of being delivered. She further gave offense by insisting the matter would be resolved swiftly and they would resume tattle time before a full week was out. "By Wednesday at the latest, you will be doing your excellent impersonation of Mrs. Drummond-Burrell gushing over the lemonade at Almack's while I recount exploits from my sojourn in Newgate. Perhaps it will be the very thing to spur me to write my memoirs. As you know, I already have so many outré tales to tell."

The duke, who had offered his arm to help his former

mistress into the carriage, displayed no alarm at this statement, although he could reliably be expected to figure in the
project. He simply watched her settle on the bench with a
placid expression and stepped back to allow Piddlehinton to
ascend the step. Then he slammed the door shut with a loud
clap.

As soon as the horses were in motion, their hooves clat-
tering against the cobbles of the drive, Kesgrave said, "I owe
you an apology."

Bea exhaled sharply, her heartbeat, which had never quite
subsided, pounded again as she anticipated an explanation for
the Great Fabrication. It was gratifying, the urgency he
displayed in broaching the subject, for it meant that it had
consumed his thoughts as well. While they were politely
serving tea in their drawing room, while they listened to
Piddlehinton's scorn and Mrs. Taylor's unlikely defense, he
had been worrying about the lie as well.

He perceived the gravity.

He understood the enormity.

She was not alone.

As Bea struggled to contain her relief, for it would never
do to grin before he gave his explanation, Kesgrave continued. Hands clasped behind his back, he looked down at her
from his superior height and said, "Although our marriage
does not conform in many respects with the expectations
imposed by society, there are some conventions with which I
must hold firm, for they align with principles I myself hold
dear. One's wife should not be subjected to one's former
mistress in her own home, and I am sorry to have put you in
that position. You may be assured it will not happen again."

Bea felt like an ant.

Standing there, in the drive of Kesgrave House, the rattle
of Piddlehinton's carriage fading as the horses turned onto
the street, she had the eerie sensation of being back in the

library at Lakeview Hall, Otley's slain body before her and the arrogant Duke of Kesgrave flicking her away like a bothersome insect that had the unmitigated presumption to crawl onto his picnic blanket.

It was a curious thing, disconcerting and strange, to feel herself returned to that place, so distant in months and miles. An entire relationship removed, she thought, marveling at how much could be conveyed by his tone, which was knowing and aloof, as if he were reciting the ships in the Battle of the Nile by rote memorization.

Beneath the coolness, however, she detected a thin vein of irritation, as if annoyed to be held to account—not by her, no. By himself. The duke had violated his own standards, which were considerably higher than hers, for she had just one requirement: Do not lie.

A simple thing.

And yet!

Determined to shield herself from the charge of female irrationality, she did not reply immediately. First she wanted to make sure her voice could match the indifference of his. Then she said, "That is what you are apologizing for, your grace?"

Oh, but it did not work.

Her tone was the opposite of apathetic.

And then, driven by nerves and fatigue and an insidious terror that it had all been too beautiful to last anyway, she asked with withering contempt, "*That* but not the Great Fabrication?"

He regarded her with confusion.

By all that was holy, the Duke of Kesgrave drew his brows together in bewilderment as if he had no idea what she was talking about, and Bea contemplated the horror of living in a universe where his lies to her meant so little he could not even recall telling them.

Softly, then, because she felt as though she were falling, Bea said, "The dowager visited yesterday to congratulate me on the cherub."

And still nothing.

His expression did not alter.

Remarkable.

Closing her eyes as if to absorb the blow, she tilted her head down and turned on her heels to walk back to the house.

Jenkins, she thought.

He was supposed to bring the carriage around to take them to Balfour Place and had yet to appear. She would find out what was keeping him.

Yes, precisely, she had a task to perform.

And a murder to solve.

A woman's life was at stake!

She was not running from Kesgrave's evasion but toward Mrs. Taylor's salvation.

But her rushed movements and agitated manner must have looked like flight to the duke, who strode after her, his tone gentle now with worry as he asked what had caused her distress. "If my grandmother took you to task for not informing her of your condition yourself, then you may be assured that I took full responsibility. She knows you are blameless. I should have realized Tilly would blab it at the first opportunity, but I was too befuddled by the news to consider the consequences."

At the foot of the stairs, Bea forced herself to stop. Holding her arms tightly at her side, she turned to look at him, his golden curls gently tossed by the breeze, and marveled at how innocent he appeared. All she could see was concern for her, and that unsettled her further because she did not know how the two things could exist side by side. "You spoke with your grandmother *last night?*"

Struck by her emphasis, he nevertheless began to answer in the affirmative, only breaking off midway through his reply in a flash of comprehension. "Oh, yes, I see, the Great Fabrication."

Bea laughed, a hollow sound. "You lied to me, Damien. You said you were spending the afternoon interviewing physicians with the dowager, only you did not have the presence of mind to tell your grandmother not to call on Berkeley Square. Then you stayed away for the rest of the evening, despite implying you would be home for dinner, and don't you dare insult me by claiming it was a misunderstanding. I am not in my dotage. I know what you told me. And then when you did finally saunter in at God-knows-what-o'clock, you left me to sleep in our bed alone. I do not know what game you are playing, but I want no part of it. You will deal with me honestly or not at all!"

Lightheaded with fury and panic, fearful she might swoon, she stepped sharply around the duke to march to the stables to discover what in the devil was keeping Jenkins. It never took him more than a few minutes to bring the carriage around. Piddlehinton was probably back in Balfour by now. At the rate she and the duke were progressing, the beloved counterpane would be scrubbed clean by the time they contrived to arrive.

Bea began to run.

Kesgrave called after her, the crunch of gravel under his feet growing louder as he drew nearer. He was behind her, then next to her, then several paces in front of her, halting her progress, his lovely blue eyes alight with impatience and pity.

Unable to bear his expression, her heart choking her with every painful beat, she looked down at the ground, her clenched hands trembling despite her efforts to still them, and ordered herself to think of something calming.

Miss Lloyd's freshly murdered corpse.

Mrs. Taylor's blood-soaked bedclothes.

A list of vengeful suitors.

Sadly, these pleasant thoughts did not have their usual salutary effect.

Indeed, her agitation increased as she imagined the nature of his reply.

He would deflect, she was sure of it, by insisting her response was out of proportion to the situation at hand. One missed dinner was not a betrayal, and it certainly did not warrant the wholesale reevaluation of their relationship.

You are making mountains out of molehills, you ridiculous girl!

But Kesgrave did not take issue with her rationality, instead pointing out with snapping anger that she was increasing. "You are increasing and not getting enough rest, as evidenced by the fact that you were fast asleep when I returned home last night at ten, which is not an ungodly hour. And then this morning you slept until nine-thirty. Nine-thirty, Bea, when you usually rise at seven! Lily told me how pale you were yesterday, and Mrs. Wallace fretted that you must be coming down with a cold or something worse because you were listless during dinner and hardly touched your meal despite it being one of your favorite dishes. The physician said rest is vital for a heathy pregnancy, and I did not want to wake you up, so I took myself off to my lonely old bed and had a pitiful night's sleep without you."

The irritation in his tone was wonderful.

Kesgrave was genuinely annoyed at her for failing to take into account both her health and his consideration for her health, and although his response did not address the Great Fabrication, it still provided some relief.

What he said was true.

Lily and Mrs. Wallace *had* clucked over her the night

before, chastising her for doing too much. Her lessons, for example, were a trifle excessive for a woman of her gentle nature, and she begged them to recall that she had driven a magnifying glass through an assailant's eye when he attacked her in that very room only a few weeks before. Which of the two points the reminder was meant to illustrate—that the lessons were not excessive or her nature was not gentle—she was unable to say.

Even so, at no time during the conversation had it occurred to her that the servants would share their apprehensions with Kesgrave, but of course they had, for he was their employer. Despite their fondness for her, they were answerable to him first and foremost, and their concern for her health was genuine.

Endeavoring to steady her breathing, she conceded that she had not looked at the matter from that perspective—and why would she, for she was not such a light sleeper that his sliding into bed next to her would disturb her. In two months, it had never happened once. "You do not need to treat me with kid gloves just because I am increasing. Indeed, I must insist that you do not. It is uncomfortable for me."

"Ah, but you do not understand," Kesgrave said, a smile teasing the corners of his lips as he reached out to brush a stray lock from her forehead. "When I said *wake you up,* I meant *wake you up.* I had the most remarkable and extraordinary afternoon and all I wanted to do when I arrived home was tell you every single detail. It took all my self-control *and* confinement to another room not to shake you awake. And it was no better this morning, pretending to attend to business with Stephens when all but a narrow sliver of my mind was focused on talking to you. I am pretty sure I agreed to overhaul the plumbing at the Daventry property because I was not paying attention. Mrs. Wallace had just informed me that you were awake when

Penny arrived at our door. Her timing could not have been worse."

"Poor Stephens, bracketed in his office with a duke who would not give the midlands estate proper shrift," Bea said, the knot of dread in her stomach beginning to ease. She had noticed, of course, how he had neatly side-stepped the matter of the lie, and although she would raise it again soon enough, she allowed him a temporary stay.

"Poor Stephens nothing," Kesgrave said with an emphatic shake of his head. "He has been trying to gain my approval for the project for six months. He took shameless advantage of my inattention."

It was, as always, irresistible, his ability to laugh at himself, and Bea marveled at it now, as she had marveled at it then, at Lakeview Hall, during the country party that had altered the course of her life. Absurdly grateful for it, she took a step closer and murmured consolingly about hapless dukes who were at the mercy of their Machiavellian stewards. Unable to withstand such impertinent provocation, he tugged her into his arms and pressed his lips against hers.

Her ardor heightened by relief, she returned his kiss with an enthusiasm that was not appropriate for the front drive— or even the back drive—and moaned softly as the duke pulled her more tightly against him.

Engrossed in the activity, neither one noticed the clomp of the horses until the team was standing next to them. Jenkins, accustomed to such displays, waited patiently on the bench, his expression blank and yet somehow amused.

"Timely as ever," Bea said by way of greeting.

The groom tipped his hat.

"In fact you are," Kesgrave announced as he opened the carriage door. "The duchess was distracting me again when I have very important information to impart."

Settling on the bench, Bea allowed that his explanation

regarding his behavior last night made sense. "But I was only pale and unable to eat because I was so worried about the Great Fabrication. Why did you lie to me, Damien?"

"I had my reasons, and once I tell you them, I am certain you will understand. But that is part of a larger conversation and I have something more pressing I need to say to you now because the transgression is greater," he said earnestly. "You rebuffed my attempt to apologize earlier, but you must permit me to issue it again. You should not have to stomach the embarrassment of my former mistress in your own home, and I am sorry that I was unable to intercede. I had been about to turn her away when you appeared."

But of course it was not her embarrassment that was under discussion but his.

He was deeply mortified for himself.

Calmly, she insisted that an apology was unnecessary. "Opportunities to investigate murders are not so abundant that I can afford to refuse one on the grounds that it is improper. It strikes me as absurd anyway given that the act of investigating itself is already an inexcusable faux pas. In light of that, what does more indiscretion matter?"

"But are they so rare?" Kesgrave asked dryly, the curt press of his lips an indication that her excusal had not pleased him. "I am convinced if you refused this murder another one would knock on your door tomorrow. In only a few months, you have become a one-woman rotation office."

It was not a compliment.

The Duke of Kesgrave was incapable of saying *rotation office* without a slight sneer in his tone, and Bea felt her breath catch at the surprise of the rebuke. Then she chastised herself for the naive reaction, for she should have known to expect it. No man wanted a Runner for a wife.

It was among the first rules of matrimony.

She fluttered her eyes closed, allowing herself a moment to feel the pain, then she opened them again and smiled amiably. "I am sorry if that is a problem for you, your grace. I was given to understand that you did not mind my investigations."

Kesgrave swore under his breath and thanked her not to be deliberately obtuse. "I am not objecting to your habit of identifying murderers. I have not uttered a single word against it since the day we wed. But Penny is not Russell's sparring partner, Bea. She is my former mistress, which is a damned sight different! And you know it! Please do me the courtesy of acknowledging that rather than belittling my concern."

"You want me to acknowledge it, your grace?" Bea said softly, all but swallowed whole by the waking nightmare quality of the moment, the way she inexplicably found herself in the thick of a conversation she had only vaguely conceived the night before as she watched him sleep in an unfamiliar bed. "Very well, I will acknowledge it. Do you plan to take a mistress?"

Kesgrave's expression turned blank.

Frustration, exasperation, anger—all were gone in a blink of an eye, and he regarded her with bland interest.

More than ever, Bea felt like an ant.

Had she wanted to goad him into anger?

No, of course not.

Well, perhaps.

He had pressed this conversation on her, compelled her mind to go to the one place from which she had intentionally kept it, walling it off like a prosperous city in a hostile land, and she resented him for it. For years, she would have squashed her misgivings and abided by the self-deluding covenant of an aristocratic woman.

But now there they were, at the heart of the citadel, and

there was nothing she could do but lay down her sword. She gave up.

Time lost all meaning as she waited for a response, and although she could not say if one minute had passed or a hundred, she knew it was more than enough to arrive at a response. If the duke intended to answer, he would have done so by now.

Coolly, she said, "I do not know what to make of your silence, your grace. I would appreciate it if *you* would do *me* the courtesy of a reply."

"I am trying to figure out how you can ask me that," he said flatly.

It was a knife.

Sharp and long, it drove right through her, eviscerating what little control she had left and tears pricked the corners of her eyes. The statement was so simple and yet it echoed with the sound of five hundred years of breeding clamoring to restore decorum. The question itself was an impertinence too far; the duke would not endure the indignity.

It was a struggle for Bea not to succumb to her grief, for the matter-of-fact response felt like a nail in a coffin. He did not even feel obliged to imbue his voice with a modicum of outrage.

"For I cannot understand how you can doubt the depth of my affection," he continued, the sadness now evident in his face, his lips turned down in a sorrowful frown, his eyes troubled. "I have done everything humanly possible to show you how much I love you, and if that is not sufficient to overcome your insecurities, then I do not know what is."

Bea could not breathe for the boulder that lodged painfully in her chest, for his words were a devastating mix of consolation and capitulation. Relief that she had misunderstood him clashed with anxiety that he had done the same to her.

Wiping away the tears that had begun to fall, she tried to explain that she was not suffering from anything as facile as insecurity. The sobs, alas, undermined her entirely, as did the breathlessness of her voice, and she said it again, with significantly more insistence. "It is not insecurity. It's not!"

But it sounded like too much protesting to Kesgrave, who shook his head with doleful regret and replied gently. "You have made yourself wretched after one conversation with Penny, and yet you mocked me for apologizing. I am sorry for it. I am sorry for all of it, but mostly I am sorry that in allowing her into our house, I unwittingly exposed you to your deepest fears. But you have nothing to worry about, Bea. You must believe me."

"No," she said.

He flinched.

And it was heartbreaking for her, to see him recoil in surprise and doubt and fear, and she darted across the carriage to sit next to him on the bench, her shoulder pressed comfortingly against the solidity of his.

The contact helped.

With it, the unbearable pressure in her chest subsided and she found it easier to speak. "That was thoughtless of me, and I am sorry. What I meant was: No, it was not the conversation with Mrs. Taylor that has undone me entirely. It was last night, watching you sleep in your own bed and knowing that is the normal arrangement for married couples of our class. Your sharing my bed—that is the anomaly. Everything about our relationship is anomalous, and it is possible only because you are the exception to so many rules. But the problem is, I do not know *how many* rules for which you are the exception or *which ones* in particular. You yourself said it only a few minutes ago: Our marriage does not conform in every way with the expectations of society, but there are some conventions you value.

Most men—and I am pretty sure all dukes—take mistresses and it has no bearing on their affection for their wives. How will I learn where you stand on the matter if I do not ask you?"

Kesgrave reached for her right hand and threaded his fingers through hers. "We are en route to my former mistress's home so that you may examine the slain corpse of her rival with an eye toward identifying her murderer, and *I* am the exception?" he asked in a curiously light tone. "All I did was love a bright particular star and think to wed it. Is that really so extraordinary?"

Well, yes, obviously, when that so-called bright star was in fact a drab spinster with no conversation and six lackluster seasons to her credit. The *ton* understood that he had made a wildly inappropriate choice even if he did not. It was the reason Mr. Twaddle-Thum had taken an intense interest in her and why Aunt Vera—

No, Bea thought, determined to deny herself the solace of self-pity.

She had long recognized that her negative thoughts undercut her own confidence, but she had never considered how they might affect Kesgrave.

Why would she?

He seemed so impervious to the pinpricks that kept ordinary humans writhing in discomfort, but now she realized he felt the jabs. Her insecurity had cast a pall over their marriage, and she resolved to reject it altogether.

Going forward, she would allow only positive thoughts.

Oh, yes, your grace, she thought in amusement. You will have no trouble holding to that resolution.

Kesgrave, his thumb making gentle circles on her palm, added her asking him forthrightly if he planned to keep mistresses to the list of ways in which she was exceptional. "I am certain that if that question has been put to a husband before, it was with considerably more fury. Your icy detachment was unsettling."

She employed that same cool tone now as she corrected him by pointing out she had used the singular: a mistress. "In my gloomy imaginings, you were unfaithful to me one woman at a time."

Raising his chin to an imperious angle, he reminded her that he was a duke. "That threadbare arrangement may be suitable for a baron or even an earl, but a man of my consequence requires excess. I believe Wickford keeps four mistresses."

"Four?" Bea repeated, cocking her eyebrow to display what she hoped was the proper amount of awe. "Do they come as a matched set like a team of bays?"

Kesgrave owned that he did not know but promised to find out later in the week, when he saw Wickford at his club.

"No, you must not," Bea said on a laugh. "Twaddle would assume you are setting up a stable and spend weeks speculating about all the ways I am failing you as a wife. I shall strive to live with the disappointment of never knowing."

"Your forbearance is inspiring," he murmured, leaning forward to press a kiss against her cheek. "And to answer your question with the same straightforward candor with which you posed it: No, never, not even if hell froze over. I trust that puts your mind at ease but if it does not, I am happy to discuss it further."

Bea sighed, gorgeously at peace. "It does, Damien. Thank you."

"And I am sorry for the way I responded," he said. "I have extolled the benefits of a frank conversation on several occasions, and the first time you attempt to conduct one, I bristle defensively. You were entirely correct to raise the issue and satisfy your curiosity. In response, I can say only that I was unnerved by the situation. You may be nonchalant about meeting my past lovers, but for me it is a deeply uncomfortable experience."

"Well, hardly nonchalant," Bea replied. "Did you not notice the extravagant trim on the gown she wore? All those rosettes! I was keenly aware of my plain muslin dress and how upset Lily would be that she had allowed me to meet your former mistress without ribbons and that ridiculous diamond-encrusted bandeau you insisted on buying over my protests."

"Even so, I want to apologize for taking that discomfort out on you," he added solemnly. "It was wrong of me and I will endeavor not to do it again."

She smiled at his earnest determination to seek absolution that had already been granted and shook her head. "You are set on apologizing for something today, aren't you? In that case, your grace, I advise you to start with the Great Fabrication. If you have done anything in the past twenty-four hours that you should be sorry for, it is that."

Immediately chastened, he recognized the accuracy of her observation and duly apologized with lavish contrition but insisted she really would forgive him once she knew everything.

"Ah, yes, your remarkable *and* extraordinary afternoon. I can only assume it was indeed astounding, as you are not usually given to redundancy, only pedantry," she said with an impish grin, her anger over the lie somewhat mollified by his ready acknowledgment of it. She would have been irate all over again if he had made some attempt to deny or excuse the behavior.

Incapable of resisting her teasing look, he brushed his lips against hers and quickly pulled back despite her efforts to deepen the kiss. "Taunt me all you want, brat, but you will eat your words, for you will be struck dumb with astonishment," he said as the carriage came to a stop in front of Mrs. Taylor's house. "It begins at Fortescue's."

Of all the things Bea expected to hear, the name of the orphan asylum that had featured in their previous investigation was the very last. "It does?"

Before he could say another word, however, the door swung open and a flushed Mrs. Taylor waved her arm, urging them not to dawdle. "Thank goodness you are finally here! Piddly is on a rampage, saying that he must ready the body because the coroner's man will be here soon to collect it and ordering my footmen to bring Millie downstairs. He knows you are en route and is being deliberately cruel, and although I added him to the list only as a poke, I now cannot help but wonder if he is trying to destroy evidence before you arrive. You must come at once. My staff are listening to him! I reminded them that Piddly is not their master, I am, but he told them I cannot pay their salary from Newgate and so they are doing as he says. Do hurry, please!"

As much as Bea wanted to know how their visit to the orphanage earlier in the week had led to the Great Fabrication, the prospect of examining a dead body in situ was more alluring and she climbed down from the carriage. Walking toward the house, she noted its pristine condition: the Doric pilasters, the elegant cornice, the decorative frieze above the fanlight. Geraniums spilled out of the window boxes on the first floor, and if some of the delicate petals were crushed, their rumpled appearance did nothing to diminish their cheerfulness.

The interior of the home was more elaborate than the facade, but it exuded a welcoming warmth, with dark-painted walls balanced by brightly colored vases set in niches. As she mounted the steps, Bea was struck by the rich mahogany of the handrail, which was supported by cast-iron balusters.

Mrs. Taylor had spared no expense in turning out her home.

As if to demonstrate the level of care she took with her residence, she stopped halfway up the staircase and picked up a black button-like article that was lying on one of the treads. "You see, Millie and her Pomfret cakes," she said with an exasperated shake of her head. "She was always chewing on these horrid little things. I detest licorice."

Unfortunately, she did not have time to indulge either emotion, for Piddly's voice could be heard from the room above as he directed the footmen to lift the body. "Come on, now, lads, do not be shy! James, you take her shoulders, and Marcus will take her legs."

"Don't you dare, James!" Mrs. Taylor called, her skirts rustling as she dashed up the last few steps to prevent the removal of the corpse. "The duchess is here! Step away from the bed—both of you. The duchess is here and will examine Millie as I found her. If you confuse the scene by moving things around, I shall be very cross!"

Bea could not hear the footmen's murmured replies, but their looks were abashed as they trotted past her on the landing. Piddlehinton, standing to the left of the doorway, pressed his lips together in ardent disapproval as she entered the bedchamber and got her first glimpse at the slain woman.

Chapter Five

The victim did indeed bear a striking resemblance to Penelope Taylor, and Bea could only imagine what an unnerving sensation it must have been for the latter to see a version of herself lying lifeless on her own bed, lips slightly open, fragile features empty and pale. Presumably, that was the reason she did not enter the room, preferring to hover by the entrance, one hand clutching the doorframe as she gestured toward the body with the other.

"As you can see, it's all quite revolting," the courtesan said.

Bea could see, yes, her eyes sweeping the bedchamber, which was decorated with the same sumptuousness as the rest of the home. The walls were covered in alternating stripes of rich celestial blue and vibrant gold; giltwood mirrors with Prince of Wales's feathers hung on either side of the bed, its posts brightly gilded; and green verditer curtains in lush velvet and navy tassels flanked the windows. Lively patterns decorated everything: the chinoiserie urn next to the door, the Persian rug under the bed, the floral sofa against the far wall.

And at the center of all this colorful opulence: Millicent Lloyd.

The scene was pretty much as Mrs. Taylor had described, with the victim lying supine on the bed, her head turned to the right, away from the door, toward the window, where weak sunlight stretched through a thin layer of clouds. The vibrant yellow of her dress clashed with the deep scarlet of the counterpane, adding an unsettling gaiety to the ghastliness, and splatters of blood adorned her face in a gruesome pattern.

Her understanding of physiology incomplete despite recent efforts to fill the gaps in her education, Bea concluded that the artery that had been hit—the carotid if she was recalling her *Physiological Anatomy of Man* correctly—spurted blood upwards for a few seconds before enough of the artery was severed to lessen the spray. Piercing the skin several times, the killer had made four or five punctures in her neck, presumably driving the hatpin through the flesh in a controlled frenzy before realizing he had carried out his mission successfully.

Miss Lloyd died quickly and with no sense of what was happening to her. By the time her mind had recognized the presence of pain, it was already over. She had had no opportunity to fight back, a conclusion supported by the lack of blood on her hands and the clean entry points of the wounds. These developments meant she was asleep when the killer struck, lending credence to Mrs. Taylor's argument that she would not have noisily complained about her guest sleeping too long only minutes before dashing upstairs to murder her. If she wanted to take advantage of her rival's vulnerability in her own home, she would have done it without fanfare while the staff were engrossed in their duties.

As the victim was unconscious, the killer did not have to

act with any particular speed or urgency. He had an opportunity to think through the steps of his attack and settle on the best approach. The use of Mrs. Taylor's hatpin indicated one of two possibilities: He did not have a murder weapon when he arrived or he had a murder weapon when he arrived but decided the hatpin made a better one. Perhaps he had realized upon entering the room that using one of Mrs. Taylor's possessions would make it appear as though a member of her staff were the culprit.

Alternatively, his original intent might not have been to kill her. If he was a former lover or an aspiring one, he might have sneaked into her room to attempt a seduction and something about the scene changed his mind.

It was possible, Bea thought, but unlikely.

To be sure, love frequently teetered on the edge of hate, but she did not believe the equilibrium could be so frail as to tip into murder at the drop of a hatpin.

She examined the jewel-encrusted accessories now as she walked from the bed to the bureau where they lay amid an assortment of silk ribbons and combs. As Mrs. Taylor had noted, the hatpins were several feet away from the corpse, well beyond her grasp if she had reached out for something with which to stab her rival in the heat of an argument.

"Are the hatpins always there?" she asked the courtesan, noticing for the first time how well suited the ornate little device was to murder. In essence, it was a two-inch spike.

"Those hatpins in particular are not," Mrs. Taylor replied, tightening her grip on the doorframe as if to stop herself from drawing closer. "All my pins are kept in a tin in my dressing room, but my maid usually leaves some out either because she has just removed them from my hat or she plans to use them again soon. There are typically three or four on the bureau."

If the killer had been in her bedchamber before, then that was something he might know.

Bearing this thought in mind, Bea returned to the bed and studied the puncture wounds again. Removing the grisliness from consideration, she wondered about the strength it would take to make the holes. Could Penelope Taylor, with her hummingbird arms, drive a hatpin through skin with enough force as to make clean, meticulous holes?

She wondered what the duke thought.

"And you were in the drawing room the whole time Miss Lloyd was up here sleeping?" Bea asked.

"The whole time, yes, and it was very difficult for me, I assure you, for I was restless and impatient after the first half hour," she replied testily.

"You mentioned hearing birds in the garden," Bea said. "But the windows in the drawing room do not overlook the garden."

Mrs. Taylor tsked with amusement at what she described as her grace's attempt to find an inconsistency in her story. "The privy is next to the garden, and I did in fact use it after finishing a third cup of tea. But you are correct in your implication. I did leave the drawing room. I am certain that is the lone occasion, but do confirm my story with the staff. They will tell you the same thing. They were constantly in and out as I tended to my correspondence at the escritoire. As I rarely arise before eight-thirty, breakfast had yet to be started, and I nibbled on toast while Sarah and Mrs. Booth prepared eggs, gammon and muffins. It was so early, everything seemed difficult, and I thought it would be easier if breakfast was served in the drawing room. Then I read the newspaper, but it was no use because I kept imagining Waltham greeting me with my curls in disarray. As Damien knows, I take great pains with my appearance. And then there was the brewing worry that Waltham would arrive earlier than anticipated and encounter Millie. That would be awkward for everyone. I had to wake her."

"What time was that?" Bea asked.

"A little before nine-thirty, I should say," Mrs. Taylor replied.

"You came upstairs by yourself?" Bea asked.

"Yes, although not before complaining about it to Sarah and Mrs. Booth, for it really was the height of impudence to sleep so long in someone else's bed. And then I saw *that*"—she practically spat the word—"and knew what it meant for my life and poor Millie's. I stood there, staggered, unable to move, and then I sort of woke up with a start at the bang of the door downstairs. I rushed over to the bed to see if I could do anything to help her and found the holes in her neck, which were horrifying in a whole new way. I leaped back, stepping on the hatpin, which I picked up. And that is when Piddly entered the room, gasping in shock and staring at me as though I were the devil incarnate. I swore I did not do it, but he would not listen to a word I said, insisting instead that he always knew this day would come. He went downstairs to send a note to the coroner, and I summoned Sarah to help me dress, for I knew what I must do, which was call on you, your grace, and beg for your help. I knew my prior relationship with Damien might prejudice you against me, but it was my hope that you were not so small-minded. I am relieved to see that you are not."

Bea acknowledged this observation with the dip of her head as Kesgrave lowered himself next to the bed and retrieved something from underneath it.

A swath of lavender.

Silk, she thought, noting the luster.

Mrs. Taylor began to grumble over her maid's negligent

treatment of the delicate garment before realizing it was spotted with russet splatters.

She gasped.

Holding up the robe for Bea to inspect, Kesgrave said, "Given where the stains are concentrated, I believe he put it on backward to protect himself from the blood. With its voluminous folds, it must have just barely fit over his clothes."

His conjecture aligned with her understanding of the murder as an unhurried event. The killer had time not only to figure out the best way to murder Miss Lloyd but also to take measures to protect himself against the worst of the spray.

Piddlehinton, who returned in time to hear the duke's conclusion, thought his grace was grasping at straws. "If anything, that dressing gown is even more damning, for purple is Penny's least favorite color. She says it is lowering to her spirits because she feels as though she is in mourning. If she had to choose any one dressing gown among the many she owns to ruin, it would be that one."

Mrs. Taylor, finding this unfavorable critique of her person devastating when she had responded to all his other charges with cavalier disregard, began to cry. Slowly, ineffably, fat tears began to roll down her cheeks, and unable to speak easily, she choked out a few incoherent words and scurried down the stairs.

James arrived in the hallway then and informed the magistrate that the man from the coroner's office had arrived to oversee the removal of the corpse. Piddlehinton dashed off to greet him, and Bea, closing the door to the room, asked Kesgrave if he thought his former mistress was capable of this —she gestured to the bloody scene.

Folding the dressing gown into a neat square, he said, "Physically, yes. But only because Miss Lloyd was asleep and could not defend herself. If she had been able to offer resistance, even the smallest amount, then it would have all been much messier. There would be cuts or bruises on Penny, I am certain, and the stabs on Millie's neck would not be limited to the ones that broke through. There would be marks where Penny tried to drive in the hatpin, although I feel compelled to add that I am not sure how, when or where she would have acquired information about arteries in one's neck. If she were to end someone's life with a dagger-like object, then she would be far likelier to ram it into her heart."

It was, Bea thought, a reasonable argument, as that was where she herself would aim—and precisely where Lord Pudsey's killer had struck.

"In terms of the mental fortitude required to kill a rival who was also a friend, I am certain Penny possesses that," he continued as he placed the bloodied garment at the foot of the bed. "She is fundamentally unsentimental and would never permit affection or warmth to stand in the way of achieving an objective. It is why she is able to discuss her friend's murder with the cool detachment Piddlehinton finds so unnerving and incriminating. But it is also why I cannot convince myself she had a hand in this. As the situation stands now, I cannot fathom how Miss Lloyd's death benefits her. It appears only to harm her. Even if her goal is to make trouble for someone else such as Piddlehinton, going about it *this* way still does considerable damage to her reputation, and a woman like Penny relies on her reputation. If she wanted to strike back against Miss Lloyd—and I do not think any cause has been suggested yet to support such enmity—then she would have done it in such a way that the blame fell on someone else, most likely one of the servants. Additionally, I believe her concern for her possessions is sincere and if she had wanted to kill someone, she would have done it in a manner less ruinous to her linens."

The duke's assessment struck Bea as accurate. Although

she could not pretend to know the courtesan nearly as well as he, she recognized the other woman's sensible outlook. Her willingness to exploit her forthcoming internment at Newgate spoke to a preference for sober-minded expediency. Seeking to eliminate a rival, she would do it in such a way that nobody would even suspect murder. Poison, for example, was rarely detected.

As always, Bea allowed for the possibility that there was a deeper game afoot than she could conceive and that the seeming messiness of the scheme hid a malevolent tidiness.

Nevertheless, Kesgrave's comment about the linens rang true.

She asked him what he thought of Mrs. Taylor's claim that she was the intended victim. "Does that register as plausible to you after examining the scene?"

"Well, it does not register as *im*plausible," he replied, drawing his brows together pensively. "She was in Penny's bed at an hour one would expect to find Penny, the light was dim because the curtains were drawn, and murder is frequently a rushed business. I find it difficult to imagine the killer feeling the need to confirm the identity of his victim without a particular cause. If he were in a crowded assembly room, then it would be incumbent upon him to make certain he had the correct neck before administering the hatpin."

Of course, yes, the drapes, Bea thought, as she walked across the room to inspect the weight of the fabric. It was quite heavy indeed, and pulling the velvet swaths together, she noted how dark the room grew. It would be easy enough to mistake one black-haired woman for another in the shadowy murk.

Kesgrave, walking around the bed to stand near the entrance, confirmed his own theory. "From here, I cannot tell the difference. Unless I knew better, I do not think it would occur to me to question the identity of the figure in the bed.

And I am not apprehensive about the prospect of committing murder or being caught in the act."

"That is true," Bea said as she joined him by the door so she could judge the effect of the drawn curtains for herself. "But the evidence indicates the culprit was not especially worried about getting caught. He took the time to find an object suitable for murder in the darkened room and to put on the dressing gown like an apron to protect his clothes."

"Because the killer knows Penny's habits," the duke replied with an affirming nod. "One of the former lovers on her list? Debenham or Audenshaw?"

A din of voices carried in from the staircase, with Piddlehinton swearing he would brook no further interference and Mrs. Taylor insisting that she would not allow her own servants to overtax themselves. They had already had an unduly fatiguing day, what with it starting a full hour earlier than normal, and a cup of tea was precisely what they needed to restore their flagging spirits.

"Codswallop," the magistrate cried, his voice drawing nearer. "You have never shown such consideration to your servants before and are only doing so now to thwart me."

Mrs. Taylor admitted it was true. She had been quite thoughtless in the past to her staff's needs but that was all changed now. "Millie's death has given me a new appreciation for the fragility of life, and I must insist that my footmen take care of themselves."

Before Piddlehinton could reply, Bea stepped out of the room and directed the magistrate to enter with a wave of her hand. "You may do as you wish, Sir John, as the duke and I have finished our inspection. We appreciate your patience. Now I would like to speak with the staff. We shall start with the maid and housekeeper, as the footmen are enjoying a break in their labor."

Having argued for her servants' repose only as a ruse to

delay Piddlehinton, Mrs. Taylor now insisted they return to their duties and offered the tea to her guests. "I would appreciate a soothing cup myself, as the morning has been very upsetting and hectic."

Given the look of exhaustion on the courtesan's face, Bea believed it was true. Her eyes were rimmed with red, and her skin had taken on a pallid cast. Declining the invitation, she said she and Kesgrave would interview the servants below-stairs to allow her an opportunity to enjoy her drink in peace.

Mrs. Taylor owned herself satisfied with this arrangement as she contemplated the comforts of her drawing room, noting how much she would miss sitting on her settee in the quiet of the early evening. Then she sighed and admitted she was not quite as sanguine about her stay in Newgate as she had endeavored to appear. "I have some trepidation about the quality of the accommodations even on the state side. But there is nothing for it! Better to stay there briefly than die brutally in my own home like Millie. Poor, poor Millie. Second best to me in everything, even in her death. At the very least she deserved to be viciously slaughtered for something she did, not as a mistake for my sins," she said, a lone tear rolling slowly down her cheek. Then she strove to collect herself with a shake of her head. "Here, let me give you the letters from Debenham. There are a dozen in all, some more threatening than others. There is one where he longs to chop off my head."

Bea grasped the neatly tied packet as she descended the stairs to the kitchens. There, she was met by the fretful housekeeper, who could not believe the goings-on. Sir John and Mrs. Taylor had always been as thick as thieves and now he was going to arrest her for the murder of Miss Lloyd.

"I can't wrap my head around it!" she said, her fingers working the dough as she rolled it out on the table. "And the mistress saying she will be back in a few days. I have no idea what to think. What will happen to us, I don't know."

Bea murmured in sympathetic acknowledgment of these unanswered questions. She had no idea what would happen to Mrs. Taylor's servants in the event that she was found guilty of murder other than to suppose Piddlehinton would compensate them for their work and try to place them elsewhere. Mrs. Taylor had the funds to cover their wages and would have little use for them.

Considering the events of the morning, Mrs. Booth shook her head and said Miss Lloyd's behavior was beyond shameful. "All that yelling and shrieking on the doorstep before decent people have awakened! We brought Miss Lloyd inside as quick as a wink before the neighbors could hear. They do not like the mistress one bit. They say she lowers the quality of the block, which is why Mrs. Taylor insists on keeping a tidy home. The exterior is freshly scrubbed, and the flowers are carefully tended so they remain bright and perky. Mrs. Marshall next door cannot say the same, with petunias so straggly they look as though they had been tended by a three-year-old child."

Ah, yes, Bea thought, the prim Mrs. Marshall, who would have been put to blush by Miss Lloyd's swears. "What happened after you brought her inside?"

"I tried to take her down to the servants' hall to pour some tea into her to sober her up before sending her back on her way, but the mistress said she would take care of it and took Miss Lloyd into the drawing room," she replied.

"And you returned to the kitchens to begin cooking?"

The color rose in Mrs. Booth's cheeks as she admitted she had not. Then she lowered her voice as she added, "I listened at the door. The mistress and Miss Lloyd have had their squabbles over the years, but it was the first time she had shown up drunker than a wheelbarrow—and before breakfast!

I was curious. And so were the others! Sarah and James were right next to me."

Although the housekeeper spoke in a confessional whisper, there was nothing particularly shocking about her revelation. Servants were notorious for listening at keyholes, and Bea could hardly blame them. The machinations of the ruling class were fascinating. "What did you hear?"

"So much shouting and yelling and crying. It was hard to understand because the door is thick and Miss Lloyd was drunk. I know she screeched, 'My first lord! My first lord!' over and over again. And she said something about the French pox, which was indecent, and I covered Sarah's ears so she couldn't hear. Then there was lots of thumping as Miss Lloyd threw books across the room. I do not know what the mistress said because she kept her voice low and smooth, but at one point she did cry out, 'Here. I have paper. Let us write to him at once. What do you want to say?'"

As the housekeeper's account aligned with Mrs. Taylor's, Bea assumed the *him* in the statement referred to Mr. Twaddle-Thum. "Where were you while Miss Lloyd was upstairs sleeping, from seven to nine-thirty?"

Mrs. Booth's reply was unhelpfully vague. "Here and there. I don't stand still for long. One minute I'm fetching flour from the pantry for the muffins and then next I'm in the scullery cleaning the griddle."

Sarah offered a similar response, citing the long list of responsibilities she had before the mistress arose for the day. "And I did not get through half of them because she was awake and required my attention. Her walking gown has yet to be ironed."

In their busyness, neither had noticed anything unusual, let alone an intruder tiptoeing through the hallway. Looking around the kitchen, with its high windows along the north-facing wall, Bea asked if they had any idea how someone could get into the house. "All the doors and windows were locked? Even the front door, after Miss Lloyd entered?"

Both women said yes at almost the same time.

"James locked it," the housekeeper continued. "I saw him do it. The only window open this morning was the one in the drawing room because Miss Lloyd complained of being hot and the mistress opened it to give her some air. But I closed it as soon as Sarah brought her upstairs because it was chilly. It might be June, but there is still a nip in the air, especially at that hour. And those are the only ways into the house that have been opened today."

"And the servants' entrance," Sarah added, which elicited a confused look from the housekeeper. "Don't you remember? You pointed to the slop bucket and said it smelled as though something had died in it, and I didn't have time to give it a good scrub, so I put it outside to let it air out. I intended to clean it soon enough, so I did not bother to lock it again. I didn't think it mattered because the gate at the top of the stairs is secured and we usually keep it open during the day."

"So someone could have entered the house that way," Bea said.

But the housekeeper swore it was impossible. "Sarah and I were right here. We would have noticed a stranger in the corridor."

The maid, however, was not as certain, for they were concentrating on their tasks, their heads down and minds focused. "If someone was sneaky about it and moved silently, I wouldn't have noticed, and neither would you have. I've seen the way you concentrate on the frying pan when you are making eggs."

"I still think I would have noticed, but Sarah is right," the housekeeper replied. "Eggs require my attention."

"And the muffins!" Sarah interjected. "You say they are very easy to overcook."

The housekeeper, her tone slightly defensive, insisted that they were. "Leave them on the fire a minute too long and the bottoms will burn."

Bea thanked the women for the information just as the water in the pot began to boil, and the housekeeper ran over to the hearth to remove it from the heat. Sarah dropped into a deep curtsy and returned to the scullery.

As most London townhouses shared the same general design, Bea was not surprised to find the servants' entrance at the end of a narrow corridor interrupted by two doors. The one nearest the kitchens was locked, presumably to ensure the safe storge of the wine, but the second was open and equipped with a sink, two tables and a small oven. Stalking the hallway silently, the murderer could have hidden in the stillroom if he heard someone approaching. From there, it was only a brief run to the staircase.

If an outside intruder killed Millie, then he almost certainly entered through the servants' entrance, she thought as Kesgrave opened the door to the belowground area between the building and the street. It was narrow, with a hole for coal delivery, a planter with a small cherry tree, and shallow steps leading to the pavement. Next to the door, under the window boxes bursting with color, was the bucket Sarah had mentioned, its opening pressed against the gravel.

Bea looked up at the wrought-iron gate, its ornamental foliage dauntingly sharp, and wondered how difficult it would be to surmount. The height presented a challenge, but it was the spiked rosettes that served as the real deterrent. Even so, it was not impossible, and she imagined a determined villain could find his way over the barrier with comparatively minimal damage. The time and caution required would subject him to the curiosity of passersby, but the block was quiet and appeared to draw little foot traffic. If anyone had noticed him at all, it was likely to be a neighbor from across the square peering out of their window to check the weather for the day—although there was a thicket of trees in between that would surely impede the view. Nevertheless, calling on the houses directly across the way and asking a few questions might be worth the effort.

It would certainly be worth it to Mr. Twaddle-Thum, who would compose scathingly gleeful odes to her seemingly never-ending impertinence.

As she contemplated the fresh humiliation at the hands of the infernal gossip, Kesgrave climbed the steps and examined the gate. "The lock is fairly standard and would not be difficult if one had the correct tool."

"And skill," Bea added as she trotted up the steps to study the latch over his shoulder. It looked like every other one she had ever seen. "Most people do not possess your remarkable ability to open secured doors."

"It is actually more common than you think," he declared modestly.

"Oh, I am sure," she said, lifting her gaze to examine the windows across the square. Even without the copse, the view was imperfect, as the distance between the houses was considerable. Having noticed a figure scraping over the gate, the neighbor would be hard-pressed to provide a description. "Presumably, it is a course of study at Eton, for when young lords are taught that no doors are locked to them that is meant to be literal."

"In fact, it is nowhere on the curriculum," he replied.

"As always, you are in a class of your own," she murmured archly as she returned her attention to the gate and realized its decorative blossoms were sharper than they had appeared from below. Tiny spikes darted out of the petals, and as she wondered how the killer avoided tearing his flesh—leather driving gloves, perhaps—she perceived something ... a flutter ... a flicker ... out of the corner of her eye. Intrigued, she turned sideways to slip past the duke and drew closer to the movement.

It was fabric.

A torn scrap was flapping gently in the breeze.

Carefully, she removed the ragged square from the spoke of the wrought-iron flower and held it up for Kesgrave to inspect. It was less than a half inch wide, more dangling threads than actual weave. "Our killer was kind enough to leave us some helpful evidence. It is a piece of his clothing."

Pressing the fibers between his fingers, the duke identified the garment as a morning coat. "This particular shade of green—bottle green—is the favored color of the season, and broadcloth is generally popular. If the fragment belongs to the murderer, then we may safely say he is a gentleman."

"Piddlehinton's coat is green," Bea observed thoughtfully.

Kesgrave smiled as he slipped the loose strands into his pocket. "As I said, the bottle green morning coat is a fairly standard article of clothing. Most male members of the *ton* own at least one, including the suspects on Penny's list. It is a helpful clue, I am sure, but by no means decisive. That said, yes, we should inspect Piddlehinton's coat for a tear. I do not doubt Penny added his name only out of spite, but there's no harm in being thorough."

In fact, there was grievous injury, for the magistrate took great offense at the request. "How dare you! Implying in this roundabout manner that I had anything to do with Millie's murder—it is abominable! Only a cad goes around murdering women, and I am not a cad. I am a pillar of the community! So, no, I will not lower myself to prove what you should know already. I have read tales of your impudence, your grace, but this exceeds anything I had imagined."

Although Bea had not anticipated his outraged response, she was not entirely surprised by it and regarded him with amusement. "As you have followed my exploits in the *London*

Daily Gazette, then I cannot believe my asking to see the inside of your morning coat is the worst you can imagine. Mr. Twaddle-Thum has me regularly barging into strangers' houses to examine their decapitated chefs. Now do please show us so that we may eliminate you from the list of suspects."

Piddlehinton darted a glance at the drawing room door, as if weighing the value of storming out, then sighed peevishly and removed his morning coat. "I will not forgive this insult, your grace. No, I will not. As a magistrate, I am due a certain amount of deference, which is sorely lacking from this encounter. And I question the conclusiveness of the inspection, for how do you know I do not have another green coat at home and *that* is not the one I tore climbing over the gate?" he grumbled, effectively making a case for the other side of the argument, which forced Bea to ask the inevitable follow-up question regarding a second coat matching the description.

Having invited the query, he promptly dismissed it as imbecilic, for why would he waste funds he scarcely had on securing duplicate items. "I am no spendthrift or a dandy! A dozen coats in the same color might be suitable for Brummell and where is he now? Dashing around the Continent in his shirtsleeves, I do not doubt," he said contemptuously, holding out the garment, which his fingers continued to grasp tightly despite Bea's efforts to take it from him. Finally, he let go and walked across the room to the window, as if unable to bear the sight of it in her hands.

Confirming that the morning coat bore no holes or tears required very little time, and only a few seconds later, Bea returned it to him with a solemn thank you. He huffed with annoyance as he put on the garment, his face growing red as he struggled to secure the buttons across the generous expanse of his belly. His fingers tugged the fabric sharply, stretching it as far as it would go, and just when the endeavor seemed doomed to failure, he managed to close the one at the bottom.

Huzzah, thought Bea, keeping a respectful silence as the loud clatter of shattering glass carried in from the hallway.

Chapter Six

In the entryway, amid a wreckage of broken glass and pink carnations, stood a blond-haired gentleman of average height, sporting a fashionable haircut and scuffed Hessians. His face—sharp and lean and most likely handsome when not twisted into an expression of sweeping horror—was devoid of color. Shaking his head, as if trying to erase a terrible thought, he appeared oblivious to the destruction: the glass shards, the seeping water, the crushed flowers. He held his hands out before him, as if still grasping the vase that had slipped from his fingers.

"Waltham is here," Mrs. Taylor said unnecessarily. "In all the hubbub over Millie's murder and my own imminent imprisonment, I forgot to send him a second missive rescinding my earlier invitation. So he is here to spend the afternoon with me. Look at the lovely arrangement he brought me. Pink is such a happy color. It is ruined now, but we all know it is the thought that counts. Come, let us repair to the drawing room, so Sarah can clean up the mess and Waltham may have a glass of wine. He is quite undone by the news."

Undone, however, was an inadequate description, for he appeared utterly dumbfounded and could not bring himself to move from the corridor, despite his host's repeated assurances that a few bracing sips of port would go a long way to restoring his senses.

"But ... but ... but I *just* saw her," he said weakly when he had finally gathered his wits enough to express a coherent thought. "This morning. Only hours ago. She was vibrant and alive and beautiful. To say that she is gone is beyond astonishing and then to tell me it was by your own hand, Penelope. I cannot believe it. I *will* not believe it."

"Good, do not believe it," Mrs. Taylor said matter-of-factly. "Because it is not true. It is only what Piddly thinks, and he is not very clever. Delightful company, to be sure, for there is nobody with whom I would rather have a light gossip. He is so snide and amusing! You really should hear his impersonation of Mrs. Drummond-Burrell. You would swear she was in the room. But I would not trust him to figure out which cat killed the mouse even with its tail dangling between the feline's jaw. That is why the Duchess of Kesgrave is here. You must know her, for she is famous for her detecting skills. The duke is a dear old friend of mine, and as such cannot bear the thought of my going to the gallows. Together, they have kindly agreed to find out the truth. Until then, I shall be safely tucked away in Newgate, for it is obvious to everyone involved that Millie was killed in my stead. I am the true victim and must hide away lest the murderer decides to rectify his mistake."

Waltham shook his head, either to deny a familiarity with the duchess's work or to reject the soundness of a plan that involved the worst prison in England. "I hear the words, but I cannot understand any of them," he said softly as he tilted his baffled eyes downward and noting, seemingly for the first time, the wreckage at his feet. Color returned to his cheeks as he stuttered an apology for making such a mess in her entry. "I do not mean to add to your troubles."

Mrs. Taylor dismissed his concerns with an airy wave and insisted he could not make anything worse even if he tried. "You are delightful company, and if I regret anything about this desperate situation—other than Millie's death and my own imprisonment for it—it is that we must end our association before it even begins. I cannot allow your name to be connected with a murderess's, however fleeting the designation. But before I push you out the door, do let us have that drink together so that I may answer your questions. I am sure you want to know how Piddly could be such a dunderhead as to suspect me, but please do not judge him harshly. I *was* holding the murder weapon when he arrived, and the poor darling has such a limited imagination."

Piddlehinton did not appreciate this tepid defense of his intelligence and had just begun to protest ardently when his presence was requested in the bedchamber. He contented himself with scowling viciously in his host's general direction and then trotted up the stairs. Mrs. Taylor thanked the footman for sparing them all a lecture with his impeccable timing, and Waltham stepped gingerly around the rubble. Sarah darted forward with a broom to sweep up the debris as the marquess held out his arm to escort Mrs. Taylor to the drawing room, determined to observe the proprieties despite the misery of the situation.

Although Bea was disinclined to linger over port, she wanted to discover the details of the victim's early-morning confrontation with her lover and followed the pair into the other room. She waited until Waltham was settled in an armchair with a glass of wine before asking him to recount their argument.

He flinched at the description of the encounter and swore it was nothing so contentious. "Millicent was upset with me for severing our connection. The dear girl was naturally devastated. She had grown fond of me in the months we were together, as I had grown fond of her. But it is the nature of these arrangements to be fleeting, which I am sure she understood. So while she grumbled about my deserting her, I resisted the urge to defend myself and allowed her to vent her spleen. That is why I would not call it an argument. She was rightfully vexed with me. To be candid, I should have told her last night of my decision rather than this morning as I was leaving."

"At five o'clock," Bea said pointedly.

The marquess had the grace to flush and said, "Yes, at five o'clock, damn it. I *did* try to sneak away to avoid a scene. I readily admit to the shameful cowardice. But I was not going to be a complete scoundrel. I planned to send her sapphire earrings with a highly complimentary note explaining how much I have enjoyed her company. Unfortunately, she woke up as I was putting on my shoes and asked for an explanation. I had no choice but to tell her about my decision to end our relationship. As I said, she was devastated and refused to accept my decision. She promised to do better by me and when I remained unmoved, she resorted to name calling."

"You are lucky, then," Mrs. Taylor interjected. "With me, she threatened to start a rumor that I had given you the pox."

"My darling!" Waltham said, reaching out to clutch the courtesan's hand. "I am sorry you were exposed to such ugliness. It is my fault. I should have handled the matter better. I will admit that I hoped to avoid a confrontation, but you must know your name did not pass my lips. I cannot say how Millicent figured it out. She made a similar threat to me. But the dear girl was instantly overcome with remorse and apologized so sweetly. She and I parted on the best of good terms, and I am startled to hear that she came here. When I left, she was planning on going back to sleep. I had thought to do the same but when I returned home, I discovered I was famished, so I had an early breakfast and read the paper."

Although Bea found it difficult to believe Miss Lloyd had mastered the surge of emotion long enough to make a pleasant good-bye, she supposed the ability to overcome her natural responses was part and parcel of her profession. "If you did not mention Mrs. Taylor, what reason did you give for ending the relationship?"

"Nothing!" he replied tersely. "I did not think I owed her an explanation. It was enough for her to know that my life had undergone a drastic change and I was reevaluating many of my decisions and habits."

"You are referring to the marquessate," Bea said.

"Dreadful business that," Waltham replied, drinking deeply of the port. "It is difficult to accept one's good fortune when it comes at the expense of someone else. I neither wanted nor needed it. I am comfortably set without the estates, and my poor cousin-in-law is left with four daughters to raise on her own. I have told her that she must stay at Waltham Castle as long as she wants. It is more her home than mine. The thought of uprooting her is unbearable, although I wonder if getting away from the site of so much misery is better for her. To see those cliffs every day! And what the weeks leading up to Christmas will be in that house but an endless reminder of the illness that took her son away on that most holy day. As I said, the whole business is dreadful and after a few weeks of settling the estates, I was grateful to return to London. And yet now there is this new tragedy. Poor Millicent! She brought much sparkle and joy to my life, and I cannot believe she is truly gone. I keep thinking it must be a mistake."

Mrs. Taylor, her features drawn in concern, reached out her hand, clutched his forearm and squeezed sympathetically.

"As I said, it *was* a mistake, for the killer meant to end my life, not Millie's."

This reminder did little to cheer the marquess, who swore savagely at the notion of her suffering the torment of Newgate for something she did not do. He seemed determined to drown his sorrow in the wine, taking several deep sips, but then he raised his head and resolved to be useful. "You must speak with Barlow. He nurtures a most violent hatred of Penelope and has been lobbying the prime minister for an act that makes it a crime for a woman to corrupt a man who is younger than she. It is errant nonsense and stands no chance, which Barlow must know. He will be looking for revenge by other means. You should talk to him, your grace."

"You may be assured she will," Mrs. Taylor said soothingly. "I have drawn up a list of all the men who wish me harm and included him."

But the notion that there were so many men who fit that description distressed him further, and he finished his port in one large gulp. Then he grabbed her hand and pressed a kiss against her palm. "My poor darling girl!"

Mrs. Taylor cooed.

Noting the intimacy, Bea decided it was time she and Kesgrave left. They had interviews to conduct, starting, it seemed, with Lord Barlow, and Mrs. Taylor would no doubt appreciate the opportunity to say goodbye to Waltham. The courtesan probably had other affairs to set in order before submitting to Piddly's authority. The circumstance was very strange, and Bea could not imagine what going to prison entailed.

Mrs. Taylor rose with her guests to escort them to the door, but Kesgrave assured her it was not necessary. They could find their own way out. She agreed with reluctance, reminding them to keep an eye out for broken glass. Tiny shards had an annoying habit of escaping the broom regardless of how diligent one's staff was!

In the entrance hall, they encountered Piddlehinton, who was thanking the footmen for helping the attendant from the coroner's office remove the body to the cart. He gave them each two shillings for their efforts as Sarah placed a vase with the rescued carnations on the console near the doorway.

It was, Bea thought, a lovely if futile gesture.

Piddlehinton did not share her opinion and ordered the maid to take the flowers away immediately, claiming they set the wrong tone for Penny's leave-taking. "It will do her frame of mind no good to think of going to prison as the same as popping off to Harding Howell to buy an umbrella. The blossoms will be dust long before she sees the light of day again. I suggest you put them in the servants' hall, where you may enjoy them."

The maid scurried off with the vase, and Piddlehinton, sighing deeply, turned to Bea and said that he hoped she was not actually going to spend her valuable time investigating Millie's murder. "I understand the impulse to humor Penny, as I myself did the very same thing in bringing her to your home. You are to be lauded, your grace, for your kindness. Few wives would conduct a civil conversation with their husband's convenient, let alone console her in her hour of need. But I assume you have more important matters to which to attend, and even if you do not, then the duke does. My estate is but a tiny fraction of the Matlock holdings, and I find caring for it consuming. Do not worry that Penny will find out. I will not say a word to her, so she will continue to reap the comfort of believing you may save her."

Although Bea allowed that his concern for the ducal schedule might indeed be sincere, she nevertheless found his efforts to dissuade them puzzling if not suspicious. By his own account, Mrs. Taylor was a dear friend, and she would think that he would want to do everything within his power to ensure she did not hang for the crime of murder, whether she committed it or not. That he was so determined to see her held accountable made Bea wonder if he did in fact have a second bottle green coat—a bottle green coat that he would now promptly discard lest it be used against him as evidence.

Even as she contemplated how he would dispose of the garment or how she would locate it if he did, she realized his attitude most likely had a far more mundane explanation. Mrs. Taylor, for all the entertainment value she provided the magistrate, was a lightskirt. The Duke of Kesgrave owned thousands of acres, possessed incalculable wealth, and traced his family back five centuries to the Peasants' Revolt.

Inevitably, Piddlehinton's sympathies lay with his peer.

Better that an innocent woman swing from the gibbet than a man of rank and breeding squander a single afternoon on a fool's errand.

Piddlehinton had no qualms, however, about wasting the duke's time with speeches about not wasting the duke's time, and it was fifteen minutes before he permitted them to leave the house.

Extricated from the magistrate's officiousness, Bea stepped outside the house and immediately spied the marquess's curricle standing in the road, with a tiger attending the horses. Seeking to confirm Waltham's story, she hailed the liveried groom, introduced herself as the Duchess of Kesgrave, and asked if he had accompanied his lordship to Miss Lloyd's residence the night before.

He had, yes, and although he did not want to complain about having to wait several hours in the dark for his employer to appear, the interval was longer than he had been advised to expect.

"But milord's plans are changeable," the tiger added with an air of acceptance. "When I drove him home, he thought to go to bed but realized he was famished and sat down to breakfast instead."

As this aligned with what the marquess himself had said, Bea nodded, thanked the groom for his assistance and strode to her own conveyance, where Jenkins held the door open for her. As Kesgrave helped her into the carriage, she returned her focus to Piddlehinton, about whom she was of two minds. As she settled onto the bench, she said she could see him as both the murderer and a sycophantic magistrate wanting to spare his betters needless exertion. "He appears genuinely troubled by the prospect of your chasing a murderer who does not exist. But it could simply be that after listening to Mrs. Taylor plead her case to us, he realized he was vulnerable to discovery. I am sure he only agreed to bring her to Kesgrave House because he did not expect to get through the front door."

It was, Bea noted, a reasonable assumption to make, as the duke himself had been in the process of turning the pair away when she appeared in the entry hall.

Kesgrave, sitting on the bench opposite her, noted with amusement that the question of Piddlehinton's guilt seemed to have driven all thoughts of the Great Fabrication from her mind. "I expected you to demand an explanation as soon as we stepped out of the house."

It had not, no, Bea assured him firmly. "I cannot pretend to know how your estimable brain functions, although I imagine it like a library constantly collecting and cataloguing minute facts, such as the name and order of every ship in the Battle of the Nile. But my own is capable of holding several ideas in it at once. I was merely allowing you to settle comfortably before asking you to resume your narrative, as a courtesy. We left off at Fortescue's. Please proceed when you are ready."

But he could not begin at once, not when she was looking

at him with such impish condescension, and before he could satisfy her curiosity, he was compelled to list all fourteen ships.

Well, not *all* fourteen.

Generally capable of controlling her impulses, she could not withstand the provocation for more than a few seconds and she cut off the recitation at ship number ten—HMS *Majestic*—by pressing her lips against his. He responded at once, his hands tugging her across the aisle of the carriage to settle her on his lap, but when she sought to deepen the kiss, he pulled away.

"Your attempts to distract me will not work," he said sternly, sliding her onto the bench next to him. "I am determined to tell you why I lied to you yesterday whether you care to hear it or not. Now, Fortescue's."

But he got no further with his explanation this time than the last, for he had barely mentioned the name of the orphan asylum before the door to the carriage opened and Mrs. Taylor climbed in. She sat on the bench across from Bea, smoothed her skirt and folded her hands in her lap. "Please take me with you," she said calmly.

Stunned by her sudden appearance, Bea looked at Kesgrave, who congratulated Mrs. Taylor on an excellent performance. "I believed you were resigned to your fate."

"But that is the remarkable thing, Damien, I was," the courtesan insisted. "I *was* resigned to it! I was going to be stoic and brave and endure every horror, from lice to gruel, without complaint. I thought I *would* be safe there. But Waltham—he was being so lovely and dear, trying to bolster my courage by finding little bright spots about prison, and he suggested that it might improve my figure. My hips, he said, were perhaps a little too lush, and it would not be awful if I lost an inch or two there. I know he was grasping for whatever he could, the darling man, for there is no such thing as being too lush, but it made me realize the true horror of Newgate is I would lose weight. I must not allow that to happen because it always goes from my chest first, and my bosom is my best attribute. Without it, I would still be milking cows in West Snettisham. You know it is true, Damien. You remarked upon its magnificence yourself. You wrote a sonnet extolling it, or was it a haiku? I cannot recall all of it, but I am certain you rhymed *handful* with *man full.*"

Kesgrave was aghast.

In all the months that Beatrice had known him, she had never seen his face contorted in such a way—the granite jaw set stubbornly, his cheeks stained with embarrassment, the sculpted lips tightened with repressed fury, his eyes glittering with cold irritation.

Bea laughed.

She could not help it.

In all her imaginings, in all her wild fantasies of the humiliation she would impose on the poor duke, in all of her dark nightmares about the indignities he would be forced to endure in taking a drab spinster with an impertinent curiosity as his wife, she had never once considered the possibility that it would be he himself who delivered his greatest mortification.

But there he was, in a carriage with his former mistress, his youthful sentimentality exposed to his wife, the air of restrained urbanity that he carried about him lightly undermined by the lavish excesses of his juvenile self.

She could not conceive of anything more perfect.

Only Mrs. Taylor then added pensively, "Or perhaps it was a limerick," and Bea's laughter redoubled at the notion of his resorting to the famously bawdy form to make his case.

He must have been adorable at twenty, Bea thought.

As it was precisely this sort of conclusion that likely horrified him the most about the revelation, she was not at all surprised by his effort to change the subject.

"We cannot take you with us," Kesgrave said, his tone cool despite the intensity of his expression. "We will abide by our original agreement to look for the true murderer while you await word of our efforts in prison. We have no authority to overrule a magistrate. It is his decision to make, not ours."

"You are not making the decision, Damien," Mrs. Taylor insisted. "I am. But really I have no choice, for I cannot sit in a cell wasting away to nothing. I have tried to remain optimistic about the matter. You know I have! It is my nature to imagine the best possible outcome for everything, and that optimism has served me well in life, allowing me to acquire shares in many profitable companies as well as a comfortable home. But Newgate will destroy me. It will turn me into a shadow of my former self—literally! I cannot allow that to happen."

Bea's laughter trailed off as the courtesan pleaded for clemency, and she found herself in sympathy with her plight. Newgate was a hellish pit, an ungodly abyss of misery and despair, and she would not wish confinement there on her worst enemy. Even if Mrs. Taylor was guilty of the charges against her, she deserved a more humane punishment.

Every murderer did.

And yet it was only the nobility and the landed gentry who had the luxury of absconding to the Continent or devising thin pretexts with which to persuade their cronies.

The way England distributed justice was patently unfair, and while Bea was in no way advocating for the abolition of the country's carceral system, especially not as it pertained to the men who had tried to kill her, including but not limited to Bentham, she was inclined to permit Mrs. Taylor a little leeway.

Consequently, she pointed out the benefit of bringing her

A MURDEROUS TRYST

with them to their interview with Barlow. "If he is the killer, then he is under the mistaken impression that he murdered Mrs. Taylor this morning in her bed. Imagine how unsettled he will be by her sudden appearance and the realization that he murdered the wrong woman. I am certain we could use that to our advantage."

Mrs. Taylor eyed Beatrice with a new respect as she turned to the duke and exhorted him to use her. "I shall make a most convincing ghost, and while Barlow is stupefied with fear at my imminent haunting, the duchess will swoop in to extract a confession. It is a brilliant plan, and I must confess, Damien, I did not expect you to do so well for yourself. Few men of your ilk marry clever women. They seek intelligence in their mistresses, for they cannot spend *all* their time in bed, but a wife is for procreation, not conversation, so the quality of her mind does not signify."

It was an insult wrapped in the pretty paper of a compliment, for it indicated that the young duke had done nothing to distinguish himself from the dozens of other peers she entertained, but if Kesgrave felt the slight, he gave no indication as he conceded the plan had merit. He tapped the roof, and the carriage jerked into motion.

Bea waited for him to caution Mrs. Taylor against further fond remembrances, but he held his silence, as did his former mistress, who no doubt recognized the tenuousness of her position. Antagonizing the duke would be folly.

As the two other occupants were determined to remain silent, it fell to Bea to make conversation, and she asked the courtesan questions about her relationship with the previous Lord Barlow to better understand his brother's resentment. Mrs. Taylor answered haltingly, her gaze darting frequently to Kesgrave to make sure she was not saying anything too outré or shocking. Although Bea's experience with such matters was limited to what she had read in books and scathing remarks Aunt Vera made, she could not identify anything remarkable about their affair. The previous Lord Barlow— Richie, as his intimates knew him—sought the usual excitements available to a young lord in the metropolis, and Mrs. Taylor supplied them. She might have been a bit more judicious in whom she introduced him to when they were at the faro table, but the Red Corner House possessed a tattered respectability. Bea herself had visited the gaming hell in the company of Nuneaton and suffered no harm to her reputation.

Arriving at the residence, Kesgrave asked Bea how she intended to proceed. "Barlow will not come to the door to greet a woman who refuses to give her name, nor is there a name Penny could give short of her own that would pique his interest. And if I present my card, I would be invited in and brought to the drawing room to await his presence."

As the finer points of her scheme had not occurred to her, Bea allowed that these were reasonable questions and proposed that she herself would knock. "Then I will introduce myself, explain that I am investigating a murder, and insist on gaining approval from Barlow before setting foot in his home. As I am generally known to be a bit strange, the butler will not even blink twice at the eccentricity. He will simply toddle off to fetch his master, and while he is gone, Mrs. Taylor and I will switch places, so that she may greet him first and we can gauge his culpability by the expression on his face."

While Mrs. Taylor hailed the plan's inevitable success, Kesgrave observed that it greatly underestimated the ability of a high-ranking title to counter a wide range of bizarre behaviors. "You will be plied with tea and cakes with the same alacrity as me," he added with amusement.

Chapter Seven

A lthough the duke's prediction did not come to pass, thwarting it required a great deal of effort on Bea's part and she all but held on to the doorjamb to resist the butler's efforts to draw her inside. "It goes against my conscience to enter a home where I cannot be sure I am welcomed. No, I must stay here while you inform Lord Barlow of my arrival. Do not give it another moment's thought, my good man."

Alas, that was impossible for the servant, and he compelled her to at least wait in the entry hall, just on the other side of the threshold. Seeing no recourse, Bea agreed and he gratefully darted off to inform his employer of her visit. As soon as he disappeared down the short corridor, she gestured to Mrs. Taylor, who trotted over to stand beside her in the entrance. A moment later Barlow appeared at the far end of the hallway, a welcoming smile on his face that promptly turned to confusion as he regarded the two women. Recognizing both, he seemed incapable of assimilating the oddity of their appearing together and he looked from one to the other with utter bafflement.

Notably absent from his expression was fear or apprehension at the resurrection of the temptress whom he had slain only hours before. As he drew closer, his perplexity turned to anger and he snapped furiously to his visitors, "How dare you darken my doorstep!"

But in fact he took issue with just one of the callers, and a moment after seething wrathfully at Mrs. Taylor, he greeted Bea with a cordial good day. Realizing the duke was with her as well, he welcomed him amiably and apologized for the unfortunate coincidence that had him arriving at the same time as the infamous trollop. "Allow me to clear this bit of rubbish from my doorstep and then you may tell me your business."

"Oh, but you see, this bit of rubbish *is* their business," Mrs. Taylor explained with admirable reserve, displaying none of the delight she must have felt at forcing him to endure her company. "They are investigating my murder."

Barlow blinked several times and then said with wonder, "Why, you are mad as well as immoral. It does not matter! They can hang you from Bethlem as easily as from Newgate."

Mrs. Taylor turned to Bea with a knowing look. "And this is why he is on my list of suspects. He wants me dead and would go to any lengths to attain it."

"That is a bald-faced lie!" Barlow cried.

"You just consigned me to the gallows," Mrs. Taylor said with exaggerated patience. "You see, hanging from a gibbet ends in death. It is science."

"What does a harlot like you know of *science?*" he snarled.

"I know how gravity works," she replied.

Clearly tempted to say something nasty in return, Barlow smothered the impulse with a stern shake of the head and addressed himself to Bea, comprehending enough of the situation to realize some defense of his own morality needed to be made. "What I was taking issue with in my denial was the idea that I would go to any length to attain this ... this woman's death. I would never condone murder, not even for the most depraved among us, which is why I am conferring with Liverpool to enact a law that would see women like her punished for corrupting helpless young men."

"He was *twenty-nine*," Mrs. Taylor said pointedly. "Well past his majority."

Barlow ignored the interruption. "The last thing I seek for my brother's corrupter is an easy, quiet death. I want her to endure the misery of a public trial. I want her to be held up as an example of all that is corrupt and evil in the world. I want newspapers to write about her conviction and execution as a warning to all women who would ruin young men and the young men who would be ruined by them. That is why I am working with Larraby to draft legislation that would make what she did to my brother a crime."

"It will never be introduced," Kesgrave said coolly. "Larraby is humoring you. I do not know why, other than to suppose he has a connection with your family. Most likely, he is a friend of your father's and feels an obligation. But the bill you are proposing is errant nonsense and will not be brought to the house, let alone debated and voted on. And I think you know that—just as you know that grown men are responsible for their own actions. Your brother gambled too deeply, which is an all-too-common affliction of young men among the *ton,* and I am sure you feel guilty about not interceding in any appreciable way to help him overcome his problem. Rather than accept responsibility for that, you would rather flail about and assign blame indiscriminately in an attempt to absolve yourself. That is your prerogative. You are free to waste as much of Larraby's time as his lordship will permit. We are here only to ascertain where you were this morning between seven and nine-thirty. Kindly give us your details and we will leave you to your smoldering resentments."

"And to inspect his bottle green morning coat," Bea reminded mildly. "That is the other reason we are here."

Although it was the duke's set-down that incensed him, for it both demeaned his efforts and trivialized his rage, Barlow vented his spleen on this final affront: the assumption that he owned a green morning coat. "How *dare* you think that I am so faint-hearted in my sartorial choices that I would wear the same banal morning coat as every other gentleman in London," he said, launching into a lengthy speech regarding the excessive originality of his wardrobe, which was made per his own specifications by a tailor in Pine Street, of whom Barlow was the sole client.

Bea was happy to accept the premise of his argument and would never dare to imply that any article of clothing he possessed bore the slightest resemblance to anything she had ever seen at Almack's or in Hyde Park. As his current outfit lacked the attention-grabbing flair of Viscount Ripley's high shirt points or the Golden Ball's colorful waistcoats, she could not perceive for herself the difference between his morning coat and the duke's other than his was an unusual mustard shade. Nevertheless, she assumed he spoke the truth. Even so, she still needed to confirm his whereabouts for the time of the murder.

"What murder?" Barlow shrieked. "She is right there—alive and well!"

"This morning a woman who was sleeping in Mrs. Taylor's bed was murdered," Bea explained. "It is her killer we are trying to identify, operating under the understanding that Mrs. Taylor was the intended victim. Now, for the third time, will you please tell us where you were from seven to nine-thirty."

"For God's sake, I was here, in my home, doing all the sundry things I do every morning such as eat breakfast, read the newspaper, converse with my wife, review my appointments, plan my wardrobe, discuss current events with my sons, and look over the accounts," he said testily, then he called for his butler, who promptly appeared in the hallway, and told him to assemble the staff. "And the family! I want every single member of the household in a line in the west corridor right now. Do not forget the boys."

"Yes, my lord, at once," the servant murmured, undaunted by the unusual request.

As the butler strode away, Barlow turned back to Bea and said, "It might seem excessive to gather everyone in the house, but I will not allow that … that … hussy to cast aspersion on me when she destroys men's lives."

Bea rushed to assure him that his response was perfectly in keeping with the situation. "I wish that every suspect I interviewed was as thorough in proving their innocence. It makes the process of elimination so much quicker."

The description irked him, for he had done nothing to deserve being lumped with a group of dubious characters, and yet he could not hide his pleasure at the recognition of his forthrightness. It was true. He handled all business affairs as straightforwardly as possible and refused to waste time dithering or dawdling. He set multiple goals for himself each day and met them with an ease that was intimidating to others.

He demonstrated his efficiency, leading them to the west corridor and ordering each servant in their turn to provide three pieces of information for the duke and duchess: his location, activity, and time. Even his children were subjected to this treatment, and while the eldest two were able to answer cogently, the youngest—barely three—could only reply with two lines from "Three Blind Mice" before bursting into tears.

"I trust you are satisfied, your grace, now that you have made a small child cry," Barlow said peevishly.

"Thank you, I am, my lord," Bea replied mildly, declining to respond to his provocation. "Your cooperation is greatly appreciated. We will get out of your way and permit you to return to your day."

Unwilling to allow his butler the pleasure of ejecting them from his home, Barlow insisted on seeing them out personally. As he escorted them to the door, he grumbled about the violence their visit had done to his well-ordered day. Now he would accomplish only half the things he had set out to do— and all because the duchess had dared to suspect him of murder. "It is the greatest affront! Meanwhile, a vile temptress is left free to lead ever more young men down the garden path. Take that young puppy St. Ives. Falling into the Serpentine in an attempt to lure her attention away from Debenham. And in April! He might have caught a chill and expired! I sent his father a missive alerting him to the issue and he returned a grateful if curt reply. I am certain he will support my bill."

Barlow seemed to remember his manners as they arrived at the entrance and thanked the duke and duchess for calling. After ascertaining that they planned to attend Lord Kempton's ball the next evening, he announced that he would make an appearance as well and looked forward to discussing more amiable topics. Then his expression turned stormy again as he looked at Mrs. Taylor. "I will see you on the dock if it is the last thing I ever do!" he growled, closing the door with a crisp snap.

"I want to thank you, Damien, for your defense," Mrs. Taylor said with an earnestness previously absent from her conversation. "I am used to contempt, but his vitriol is unnerving. I swear I did not introduce Barlow to any entertainment that is not widely enjoyed by the vast majority of the *ton,* and I never encouraged him to behave in a particular way. In everything, I followed his lead."

"You do not have to explain yourself to me," Kesgrave replied kindly.

"I know. And that is what makes you unique," Mrs. Taylor said with a hint of sadness. Then she shook herself slightly and turned to Bea. "What is next, your grace?"

Bea, meeting the duke's eyes over the courtesan's head, said, "St. Ives?"

"St. Ives," he agreed as he hailed Jenkins, who was walking the horses.

Mrs. Taylor grimaced and wondered if it was absolutely necessary to call on St. Ives *quite* so soon. "Audenshaw is higher on my list and he does owe me all that lovely money. I should think my appearing on his doorstep in your illustrious company will be more than enough to persuade him to settle his account, especially if he believes he murdered me earlier this morning."

Mounting the carriage step, Bea darted an amused glance at Kesgrave as she observed with cynical comprehension that there was no point in paying Hell and Fury Hawes for what the Duke of Kesgrave could do for free.

"Precisely, your grace," Mrs. Taylor said approvingly. "I cannot claim to ape Lord Barlow's level of efficiency, but I do like to kill two birds with one stone whenever possible. And in this case, it would be three because it would postpone the interview with Dudley. In truth, I dread the meeting heartily. I would rather be berated by a dozen Barlows than listen to that grating puppy complain even more about his mother's pearl earrings. He is so young and tedious."

Kesgrave sat down on the bench next to Bea and said, "Nevertheless, we will visit Dudley St. Ives next."

Mrs. Taylor contented herself with a weary sigh.

The duke, deeming the elaborate ruse employed to gain entry to the previous home needlessly complicated, knocked on the door and requested an interview with the young master. Then he stared with blank incomprehension when the butler looked pointedly at Mrs. Taylor. Without further comment, the servant led them to the drawing room and invited them to take a seat.

As the butler left to fetch Dudley, Mrs. Taylor thoughtfully inspected the space as she figured out the best place to stand to optimize the effect of her presence. "I felt constrained by the doorway at Barlow's, although it could not be avoided. But what about here?" she asked, draping herself on the divan and drawing her arms over her head. "Is that more shocking than if I stand against the windows? I think the sunlight gives me a heavenly quality, very much like a halo in a Renaissance painting. It is so hard to choose! It is just that one gets so few opportunities to rise from the dead, one does not want to waste any."

Lying on the couch, its deep green brocade brightened by threads of gold, the courtesan tilted her head away from the door and contemplated the ceiling. "If only we could attach twine to the chandelier and then I could dangle like an angel."

Her disappointment at being earthbound surprisingly keen, she pursed her lips and asked if various items could be used to suspend her. "I think the cord on the drapes has the most potential. I do not mean for us to throw something together now. I mean so that we could have a plan the next time," she explained, rising to a sitting position just as Dudley entered the room.

Mrs. Taylor frowned at the new arrival, whose wide brown eyes were set in a narrow face, and darted to her feet, all thoughts of appearing ethereal forgotten as she said, "Aha, you are shocked to see me!"

"I am not," he said, striding across the floor to take possession of her hands. "I always knew this day would come. You are too beautiful and kind to withhold yourself from me forever. I do not even care about the pearl earrings if it means

I shall have you. My mother has so many pairs she will never notice the loss. Here, goddess, let us have some champagne to celebrate this glorious occasion. We shall be so happy together. I will worship you every minute of the day. Do give me a kiss so I may begin at once!"

Mrs. Taylor, making every attempt to free her hands from Dudley's grasp, dodged her head to the left to evade his lips. "A little help would be appreciated, your graces."

Startled to discover the room was further occupied, he swung around and noted the Duke and Duchess of Kesgrave standing next to the settee. Although they were surely a disconcerting sight, he did not allow confusion to lessen his joy. Nor did he find their presence chastening. In his youthful exuberance, he insisted they share in the celebration of his profound happiness. "We shall have a toast," he announced, tugging Mrs. Taylor to the doorway, where he called for someone to bring him champagne. "I shall recite one of my poems, shall I? Which one is your favorite, goddess? The ode to your shoulders or the meditation on the melodiousness of your singing voice?"

"You have never heard me sing," Mrs. Taylor snapped peevishly, finally managing to extricate herself from his grip.

"Just one of the many delights in store," he said with a radiant smile as he leaned into the hallway and called again for champagne. "I shall have my solicitor contact your representative at once so that we may settle the negotiation as quickly as possible. Do not fear that I mean to be clutch-fisted. I shall be as generous as the moon. Do you like emeralds? My sister has an emerald necklace that would look stunning on you. I am sure she will not mind if I give it to you, as it would suit your coloring much better than hers. Furthermore, I have never seen her wear it. I am sure she does not even like emeralds."

Although Mrs. Taylor's eyes glowed avariciously at the

mention of the jewels, she flatly declined the offer, having no wish to embroil herself further with his family. The pearl earrings were enough, thank you very much!

Her efforts to communicate her lack of interest clearly, however, were thwarted by Dudley's giddy transports, which were in turn overcome by an angry bellow in the hallway demanding silence.

"Not another word about champagne," the man said, storming into the room with a fierce scowl, his overly large ears making the familial connection plain. "I told you to stop wasting my money on that doxy!"

He pulled up short, however, when he saw Bea and intuiting her identity from either Twaddle's reports or Kesgrave's presence, he hastily apologized for the misunderstanding. "I meant *that* doxy, not you," he clarified, pointing to Mrs. Taylor, who had resumed her position on the divan. "I have nothing but admiration for your accomplishments, your grace. Anyone who can knock Lady Bentham down a peg has my enduring respect. Please, sit down and tell me how I may help you. I would also appreciate if you could explain to me what is happening right now. I am confused."

"She is not a doxy," Dudley said, his face turning red at the insult. "She is a goddess walking among us and she has consented to be *my* goddess. Nothing you or anybody can say will change that. We are fated!"

Both Mrs. Taylor and the elder St. Ives protested, the former insisting that she had not and would never accept his proposal and the latter reminding his son that he held the purse strings. "See how long she tolerates your adulation after the accounts are empty."

Affronted, Mrs. Taylor swore there was no amount of money that would induce her to spend more than ten minutes in Dudley's presence, a claim St. Ives regarded with justifiable cynicism. His son asserted that he had enough scratch to cover expenses for almost a year, after which he could sell an assortment of cherished items, such as the Gainsborough hanging in the hallway at the top of the stairs.

"That is mine," he said petulantly. "I can do with it as I please."

"It is a portrait of your mother," St. Ives said, aghast.

"I see her every day, don't I?" the wretched child replied. "Why do I need her likeness when I have the real thing before me at the breakfast table reminding me to wipe my fingers on the serviette, not my trousers? Besides, she wants me to be happy, unlike you, who has desired nothing but my misery from the moment I drew my first breath. I hate you!"

Although the boy stamped his foot in a particularly juvenile display, his father revealed no embarrassment, only fatigue. Turning to his visitors, he said, "This nonsense cannot be why you are here. Nor do I believe the doxy would stride boldly into my house to accept my asinine son's offer. Say what you will about her decency, but she knows the correct way to soak greenheads for every farthing they've got and it is not under the auspices of his parents. Something else is afoot. Do kindly explain."

"You see, this is why I try to steer clear of callow youths," Mrs. Taylor said wearily. "Everything you do is regarded with suspicion. It is simply not worth it."

"You mean their pockets are not deep enough to warrant the effort," St. Ives replied tersely.

Before his son could rush to Mrs. Taylor's defense and set off another round of arguing, Bea stated their purpose. "This morning, a young woman was stabbed to death while sleeping in Mrs. Taylor's bed—in her stead, we believe—and we are trying to identify the killer. To that end, we would like to ask your son a few questions."

St. Ives took no offense at the implied insult to his son and said, "I am certain Dudley had nothing to do with it.

There is no malice in him, only inanity, which I am confident he will outgrow. Tell me what you need to know to bring this matter to a close."

Dudley, however, was greatly aggrieved by the suspicion and wheeled around to confront the object of his affection. "You wound me with your distrust, goddess! I am your most ardent admirer, your most devoted servant, the man who is willing to drop to his knees to beg for a crumb of your attention. I would never harm you."

While his father muttered, "Oh, for God's sake," Mrs. Taylor cited his treatment of her at the theater the week before as evidence to the contrary.

"You punched me in the shoulder and then tried to tackle me to the floor."

"That does not count!" Dudley cried. "You were wearing my mother's pearl earrings and I was trying to get them back, but you would not stand still. How could you be so brazen as to wear them to Drury Lane?"

"You gave them to me!" Mrs. Taylor replied.

St. Ives inhaled sharply and stared at his son aghast. "You gave her your mother's pearls?"

Although Dudley flinched at the harsh censure in his father's voice, he raised his chin and confronted his sire forthrightly. "Well, I had run through my allowance for the quarter and needed to give her some present to gain her attention."

Appalled, St. Ives muttered, "I should let you hang."

"I did what I had to," Dudley said stiffly, which elicited a defeated sigh from his father.

Bea, addressing St. Ives, said, "The first thing we would like to know is where your son was this morning at the time of the murder, from seven to nine-thirty?"

Frowning darkly, St. Ives replied, "He goes riding every morning in the park regardless of the weather. I assume he did the same today as well."

"You may be certain that I did!" Dudley huffed.

Ignoring him, his father asked what evidence Bea required. "Will the word of my groom be sufficient? He accompanies St. Ives most mornings."

She assured him that it was. "And we would like to look through his wardrobe."

St. Ives calmly agreed as his son cried out in protest.

"You aren't even going to ask why?" Dudley asked, aghast.

"It is not difficult to infer the answer," St. Ives said, rising to his feet. "And I want this matter resolved now. If allowing the Duchess of Kesgrave to paw through your belongings proves your innocence to her satisfaction, then I will allow it. I think it is for the best if you stay down here. I do not want to be accused of influencing the process."

Some of Dudley's annoyance dissipated as his gaze slid to the object of his affection and he imagined the two of them alone. Mrs. Taylor, her thoughts drifting in the same direction, promptly stood up and waved her arm in an elegant sweep before St. Ives. "After you, sir."

Wasting no time, St. Ives tromped up the stairs to his son's bedchamber and led them into the dressing room, which was neatly organized, with items grouped by kind and color. Four bottle green morning coats were arranged in a neat pile on the top shelf.

"He has only the four in green?" Bea asked, running her fingers under the lapel as she unfolded one.

"Only?" St. Ives repeated scathingly. "How many more do you want him to have? It is already three too many."

"Fair enough," Bea murmured as she handed the first to Kesgrave to examine. "We are looking for a rip or tear, as strands from a bottle green morning coat were found in the gate in front of Mrs. Taylor's residence. So I am trying to ascertain if there is a green coat missing from this assortment."

"In that case, yes, it is just the four," St. Ives confirmed. "If I did not impose strict limits he would have a dozen morning coats in every color. I drew the line at four. I blame his mother for his tendency toward excess. She indulges all his whims, finding his capriciousness entertaining. I believe maturity will temper the worst of it, but it has been a slower process than I had anticipated and I will admit that I grow tired of bailing him out of scrapes. If only all of them were as easy to resolve as allowing strangers to look through his clothing."

Bea inspected a second coat as the duke selected another one. Neither she nor Kesgrave found any defects in the garments. They were pristine.

Dudley was not the killer.

St. Ives received this information impatiently, insisting that he did not need her to tell him that about his own son, but he was also visibly relieved. His jaw loosened, and he wore a faint smile. He even gestured politely for Mrs. Taylor to precede him out of the room.

Kesgrave thanked him for his assistance as they proceeded down the staircase, at the bottom of which Dudley waited with a sullen air, which did not lighten when Bea pronounced his innocence.

"Yes, I know!" he replied waspishly before inviting Mrs. Taylor to visit with him in the drawing room. "We have some unfinished business. If you are going to walk out of my life, goddess, I would like the opportunity to say goodbye properly."

Despite the dignified morosity with which this request was made, Mrs. Taylor refused it coldly, insisting that she had never walked *into* it. "We have no unfinished business because we have no business. Good day to you, Dudley, and thank you for not trying to kill me," she said graciously. As soon as she stepped outside, however, she bemoaned his innocence because it meant that she was still on the hook for the murder. "I do wish you would stop eliminating suspects, your grace, and start finding culprits. It is growing rather uncomfortable for me. I can practically feel the noose tightening around my neck and it is not a pleasant sensation. Shall we visit Audenshaw next?"

Bea observed that they were closer to Debenham's residence, and Kesgrave said they would be returning home, as it had been a long day for the duchess, who had been deprived of a proper morning meal by Mrs. Taylor's unexpected call.

The courtesan received this news calmly, compelling the duke to add that he and Beatrice would return to Kesgrave House while she would have to find lodgings elsewhere. Although her expression darkened, she did not protest, as she knew perfectly well the untenability of such an arrangement. It was scandalous enough that the duke's wife was traveling around London in the company of his former mistress. Allowing that same mistress to share a roof with his wife would do irreparable harm to the latter's reputation, and there was no justification for that.

Having anticipated this very outcome, Mrs. Taylor instructed Jenkins to take them to Culross Street. In yet another display of her practical sensibility, she noted that it had not occurred to her to send around a note to Millie's housekeeper informing her of the dreadful turn of events. "And I am willing to wager that Piddly did not think of it either. If Millie and I looked enough alike for her to be killed in my stead, then we look enough alike for me to me to pretend to be her. I shall keep my head down, say little and complain of the headache. Nobody will be the wiser."

Although Bea did not share her confidence, she kept her peace because she did not have a better solution. Taking Mrs. Taylor to her own home was impossible, and she was too elegantly dressed to disappear into the dingy backroom of a

London inn. She would draw undue attention to herself. But to stay at a respectable hotel like Grillon's required a lady's maid and luggage.

Kesgrave likewise took no issue with the suggestion, simply tweaking the plan slightly by instructing Jenkins to stop the carriage at the corner before the address. "We do not want Miss Lloyd's staff to wonder why the Duke of Kesgrave escorted her home."

"La, you think of everything, Damien!" Mrs. Taylor said with an admiring flutter of her lashes. "You are so much more impressive than I remember. Or perhaps it is just that you are older now and have the wisdom that comes with age. You were only a puppy yourself when I knew you, so determined to cut your cousin out. Or was it an uncle? I must confess the details are a little hazy."

"Do not strain yourself trying to recall," Kesgrave replied coolly.

But it was too late.

Of course it was.

The words had been said and they could not be unsaid, leaving Bea to ponder their meaning. Obviously, the uncle was Lord Miles. His father had just the one brother, and his mother's relations were not a consideration in his life. The implication, then, was stark: The duke's only interest in the courtesan had been in thwarting his uncle.

Well, not his *only* interest, Bea thought wryly, watching the other woman purse her lips in a coy smile as she acceded to the duke's wishes. Mrs. Taylor was still beguilingly gorgeous and invitingly lush, and even if Kesgrave had cultivated an appreciation for other traits in the intervening decade, the young lord would have been satisfied by her beauty alone.

Foiling Lord Miles's plans was merely a bonus.

Mrs. Taylor held her tongue for the rest of the drive and

climbed down from the carriage with a cautious affect, as if expecting Piddlehinton to burst from behind the horses to apprehend her. When nothing so dramatic happened, she straightened her shoulders and thanked the duchess for rushing to her rescue. "I am not insensible to the discomfit my presence creates, and I am grateful that you would not allow it to influence your behavior. You are a credit to Damien, which is something I could not have imagined saying even yesterday. Like anyone who keeps abreast of the habits and actions of the *ton,* I was baffled by his decision to take you as his wife. It simply did not conform with any known logic. But I understand it now."

"Thank you," Bea said gravely, endeavoring to smother a smile at the courtesan's earnestness, which may or may not have been more fluff. "And you are very sure you can fool Miss Lloyd's staff? Even if they do not see your face clearly, won't they notice you are wearing an unfamiliar gown?"

"This plain thing?" Mrs. Taylor scoffed, lifting the skirt slightly, with its veritable garden of rosettes, and then dropping it abruptly. "It does not possess enough interest even to be called bland. It will not register with the servants at all. And here"—she reached into her reticule and removed a cloth square—"I will hold this handkerchief over my mouth and cough profusely. It will cover my face and encourage them to keep their distance. All will be well. I shall see you tomorrow, then, for our visit with Audenshaw."

Kesgrave said they would not return the next morning to collect her, and Mrs. Taylor waved her hand breezily, indicating the information did not worry her. Presumably, she had her own scheme in mind. Bea laughed, but the sound was immediately swallowed by a yawn, and the duke bundled her into the carriage, laying her head on his shoulder. "You may begin whenever you're ready."

Bea rubbed her cheek against his coat as she settled

comfortably into the crook of his arm and made the same assertion. "For I have nothing to say."

"Because you already know it all?" he asked with droll amusement.

"Unless your interest in Penelope Taylor was sparked by something other than aesthetic perfection and personal malice, I think I do, yes," she replied.

The duke brushed her cheek with his left hand, then entangled his fingers with hers. "It was petty. I had no intention of setting up a mistress during my first season, at least, but the moment I heard my uncle was pursuing her, I felt an intense compulsion to cut him out. So I made an offer, which she rejected on the grounds that she was already entertaining a proposal. I offered more money, a bigger house, a larger staff, and she consented. It felt wrong almost immediately, for she was a human being and I treated her like a thing, like a shiny trophy I could hold over my head in victory. It soured the experience for me. And then a month later, I passed my uncle on Bond Street and he smiled at me with so much smug triumph I understood it all in a flash. I had been played like the veriest greenhorn, which was readily apparent once I realized the truth because dear Uncle Miles never wasted his blunt on highflyers. He preferred brothels and dark alleyways. I had known that about him but failed to consider it in my eagerness to score a niggling point against him."

Bea closed her eyes and tried to picture him a dozen years earlier, freshly arrived to London—a wealthy young duke with every possible advantage. How easy it all must have felt, the world itself splayed at his feet, and his uncle deftly maneuvering him.

It was, she did not doubt, a significant blow.

"You were how old?" Bea asked. "Twenty? Twenty-one? The age Viscount Ripley is now? Considering the damage that young man did in an effort to establish himself, I should think you would take comfort in knowing there are far worse sins than fairly compensating an underling for services rendered. And I say 'fairly' in the belief that it is impossible to pay a woman too much money for the use of her body. Regardless, Mrs. Taylor does not seem to harbor any resentment over the affair. I assume you apologized to her."

Kesgrave's fingers tightened, for a moment almost painfully, before he raised her hand to his lips and pressed a soft kiss on her palm. "Indeed, I made a clean breast of it in a most noble fashion, giving myself no quarter in the retelling, and she laughed. It struck her as genuinely funny that I had allowed myself to get so worked up over a trifle. She *was* a prize—the most glittering one in all of London, she assured me—and it was that admission that made the situation intolerable for me, for then I knew she also perceived herself as a thing. And no matter how many times I told myself it altered nothing, the illusion had been pierced and I could not pretend otherwise. She had been bought and paid for like any other item in my possession. I ended the association a few days later, barely after the two-month mark, which also made me feel like a cad."

That there could be any illusions to pierce in an arrangement based on financial negotiations over lease payments and monthly stipends fascinated Bea. Marriage, of course, was not so very different, with its dowries and settlements, and she supposed the problem stemmed from the lack of options generally available to women. Few professions were open to them, and it was difficult to achieve financial security without a man conferring it in one way or another. It was precisely this quandary that her mother had confronted with her treatise on female equality that had so horrified Aunt Vera.

There had been no easy answer twenty years ago when Clara Hyde-Clare sought to address the issue, and there were no easy answers now.

"I can only assume the severance you provided was equally generous," she said blandly. "Did you allow her to keep the house?"

"Yes, as well as the servants, carriage, and horses," he admitted with a deprecating smile. "But only for another seven months, until the lease expired at the end of the year. One of the greatest advantages of inheriting a prosperous dukedom is the ability to expatiate one's guilt with cash."

"Like buying indulgences from the Catholic Church," she teased, realizing then that the gossips had gotten it wrong. The duke had kept Mrs. Taylor for only two months, not the nine that was cheerfully bandied about.

"Only my soul was not at stake," he replied.

"Oh, but was it not?" she wondered softly, brushing her lips against his jaw before allowing her lids to drop closed and succumbing to the lulling sway of the carriage. There was still so much she did not know—why he had lied, where he had gone—but even as she told herself to request an explanation now, she sighed and drifted off to sleep.

Chapter Eight

Bea held her patience—as Joseph laid the plates, as Marlow poured the wine, as Mrs. Wallace fretted over the placement of the table in the library, worried that her grace might catch a draft if she sat too close to the eastern exposure. Even Joseph lingered as he arranged the cutlery in an even row: seafood fork, meat fork, dessert fork, fish knife, dinner knife, soup spoon. Never in the history of dinner preparation had a footman taken so much care folding a serviette.

It was all Bea could do not to sweep them briskly from the room.

As it was, she kept her hands clasped loosely behind her back as the servants fussed over the meal and darted sympathetic looks in her general direction. They were all so concerned about the poor duchess, forced to entertain her husband's former mistress in her own home, and even the butler, whose respect for his employer was all-consuming, could not help pressing his lips in a vaguely disapproving frown.

It was a stunning rebuke, considering the source, and Bea

could not decide if she wanted to defend Kesgrave or laugh at his predicament. It was so thoroughly absurd.

The one thing she knew she must not do was make an attempt to assuage their distress. Any effort to convince them she was untroubled by Mrs. Taylor would have the paradoxical effect of deepening their compassion, for they would just assume she was protesting too much. It was far better to endure their pity with heroic stoicism.

Finally, Joseph, seeming to realize he could dawdle for only so long, shifted the position of the butter knife a fraction of an inch and left the room. As soon as the door closed, Bea furrowed her brow and asked the duke if he needed a moment to recover. "Perhaps you should sit down? I know how highly you value the servants' good opinion, and now you have given them a perfect disgust of you—introducing your wife to your convenient! What will you do next? Invite Mother Needham to tea? Obviously, I cannot say anything in your defense because that would undermine my standing in the household, but I could ask Mr. Twaddle-Thum to put in a good word for you. I know the staff are among his most devoted readers."

"Thank you, brat, but no," Kesgrave said firmly, his lips twitching. "I shall suffer their condemnation silently and subtly coerce the restoration of their good opinion by purchasing new chairs for the dining hall belowstairs. I understand from Stephens that some of the current ones squeak horribly. But enough about the servants! Come, sit, you must be famished."

Although highly entertained by the notion of the Duke of Kesgrave bribing his own staff, she refrained from making a teasing comment. She was too eager to hear an explanation for the Great Fabrication to allow a distraction. "I trust you are not going to change the topic of conversation yet again."

"As I have spent the entire day champing at the bit to tell

you about the utterly astonishing events of yesterday, I am not going to allow *you* to distract *me* by addressing that provoking comment," he said, offering his arm to escort her to the table. "But if I were, I would point out that it was Penny who repeatedly changed the topic by inserting herself into every conversation we had today. I have acted in good faith."

"I am not sure blaming your former mistress is the high-minded defense you think it is, your grace," Bea replied with amusement as she settled into the chair. "But that is neither here nor there. The topic is the Great Fabrication. You may begin your explanation. You said it relates to Fortescue's?"

Nodding, he sat down across from her. "As we arrived at the asylum, there was a woman leaving. She stood in the doorway for a moment and then walked up the path."

Bea recalled the figure perfectly. "She did not acknowledge us in any way, which I thought was in keeping with the cold menace of the building. I would have been disconcerted had she smiled warmly and bid us good day."

"She looked like my mother," Kesgrave said.

Bea, who had been in the process of ladling pea soup into a bowl, nodded matter-of-factly as if this statement were unexceptional, then halted suddenly as the meaning of the words struck her. It was indeed a startling claim, and she wondered what precisely he was attempting to say. "As in she shared your mother's coloring?"

"As in, she was an exact replica," he replied.

Well, that was certainly an unanticipated reply, Bea thought, placing the ladle on the table. "An *exact* replica?"

He confirmed with a nod, his expression oddly aloof, and she fluttered her eyes closed as she summoned a picture of the woman. She had caught only a fleeting glimpse before the matron tilted her head down and scurried up the path. Even so, Bea had seen enough to know she differed from the previous duchess in one significant way: She was tall. The figure at Fortescue's filled the doorway, while Kesgrave's mother, a former courtesan known as La Reina, had barely reached five feet.

Like Mrs. Taylor, she possessed a delicate beauty.

In the painting of her that hung on the first-floor landing in Kesgrave House, she stood next to a stallion, a gleaming black beast that could easily trample her tiny frame. The contrast between her vulnerability and the large steed's power heightened her fragility, making her seem almost fairy-like, and yet there was something authoritative in the way the horse simply stood there, as if yielding to her command.

All in all, Bea thought it was a silly portrait, excessively dramatic and needlessly portentous, and she wished the artist had simply posed the duchess against a Roman column with some shrubbery in the background. She was not a Spanish king, for goodness' sake.

But the disparity in height did not signify, for it was only one of several traits that could be passed down from parent to child, with physical appearance being the most revealing. If the woman's resemblance to Kesgrave's mother was as close as he described, then she had to be related to him as well.

That one of the most successful courtesans of her age had borne a child out of wedlock was hardly a remarkable event. Pregnancy was a significant hazard of her profession, and the far more shocking turn would have been if La Reina had managed to avoid the pitfall altogether.

But of course she had not, for it was the conception of Kesgrave himself that spurred the fifth duke's marriage proposal. The prospect of embarrassing his family while thwarting his brother and horrifying society was irresistible to him, and he wed his mistress with all due fanfare, insisting on St. George's in Hanover Square and an announcement in the *Times*.

Pensively, Bea observed that the woman from Fortescue's must be his sister, and then, hearing how strange those words sounded to her own ears, amended it slightly. "Your half-sister, I mean."

The duke dipped his head in acknowledgment, his expression revealing no particular interest in the development, and Bea wondered if that was what it meant to be raised in the aristocracy—to live in constant expectation of encountering one of your parents' by-blows around a random street corner. It was certainly a common enough phenomenon, and the duke had to have supposed there was at least one baseborn child out there, if not the issue of his mother, then the product of his father. Adultery was de rigueur among the *ton,* whose marriages were frequently transactional, and seeking comfort in the arms of another was an acceptable solution to an unhappy situation—and even a happy one, as she had spent much of the past twenty-four hours worrying.

And what could it really mean to Kesgrave anyway, to suddenly discover an illegitimate half sibling? What bearing would such a revelation have on his life? Despite its much-vaunted viscosity, blood was only slightly thicker than water, and neither substance was strong enough to form a bond. Love did not work like that, embedded in the foundation, like the brick walls of a cellar.

The woman was nothing to Kesgrave.

And yet even as that thought darted through her mind, Bea pictured the wispy limbs of the barely formed baby in her mother's womb whose life had also been snuffed out by a murderous lord driven half-mad by jealousy.

The child never existed, and yet Bea mourned it.

Was that not love?

Despite the maudlin turn of her own thoughts, she resolved to keep emotion out of her response, for she did not want to introduce a note of sentimentality into a conversation where there was none. Her growing mawkish about something for which he felt only indifference would embarrass them both.

Dispassionately, then, she sought to learn the facts of the situation[1]—and just the facts. "You returned to Fortescue's yesterday to find out who she is. Presumably, you spoke to Mrs. Caffrey. How many buckets of water did the capable head matron make you dodge before providing you with the desired information?"

A ghost of a smile appeared on his lips as he admitted he had been spared further evidence of the building's decay, as Mrs. Caffrey was too smart to flog a thriving horse.

Comprehending at once, she asked how much he had donated to the asylum.

"A modest sum, given its state of disrepair," he replied, returning the ladle to the tureen. He did not, however, serve himself soup or anything else from the half dozen platters on the table, which Bea found notable. If he did not possess an appetite, then perhaps he was more unnerved by the situation than his manner indicated.

"I am certain Mrs. Caffrey will be able to fix far more than the leaky roof with your contribution, as your definition of *modest* differs greatly from everyone else's," she noted dryly. "What did she tell you about the woman?"

"Her name is Verity Lark, and her brother, Robert Lark, writes for the *London Daily Gazette,*" he replied.

It sounded twice as daunting, the prospect of *two* illegitimate siblings, but Bea did not react sharply to the revelation. The customary practice was to place unwanted children with a kindly farmer on the ancestral estate, and in all likelihood, the couple already had children of their own. It was one of the things that recommended them for the assignment.

"Is Robert a foster brother?" she asked.

Kesgrave shook his head, causing Bea to gape at him for a

full second before he added almost carelessly, "She does not have a brother."

"But did you not say only a moment ago that Verity Lark has a brother who writes for the *Gazette*?" she asked, certain she had not misheard him, for it had been a fairly simple statement.

"I did not, no," he replied unhelpfully. "Mrs. Caffrey said it. According to her, Robert Lark is the author of a series of articles exposing the deep well of corruption at the heart of Fortescue's former board of supervisors. I have read those articles myself, as Stephens found them when I asked him to research the asylum, and the abuse they detail is troubling. Mrs. Caffrey's predecessor was quite rapacious."

Naturally, this information did not surprise Bea. Possessing a decades-old terror of institutions devoted to the care and maintenance of orphaned children, she expected them all to be hotbeds of squalor and exploitation. "But Mrs. Caffrey's understanding was wrong? The man who wrote the articles is not Verity Lark's brother?"

"A man did not write the articles," he explained. "Miss Lark herself is their author."

"Oh, I see," Bea said slowly, not at all shocked to discover that a woman born on the wrong side of the blanket would ultimately be required to make her own way in the world. "Miss Lark has an alter ego."

This observation amused him as well, and his lips quirked up at the corners. "*An* alter ego? No, not at all."

Perceiving yet another semantical distinction dear to his gorgeously pedantic heart, Bea rushed to correct herself. "Is *alter ego* the wrong term to describe Robert Lark? Should I have said nom de plume?"

Now he grinned as he explained the problem with her reply was its use of the singular. "She has *dozens* of alter egos. It is the damnedest thing, Bea."

He spoke mildly, as if discussing the quality of the pea soup, and yet the look that swept across his face was the opposite of equability.

It was utter befuddlement.

Unnerved by it, she decided the arrangement would never do. A whole table between them—her sleeve would be soaked in sauce if she tried to grasp his hand.

"Come," she said, rising to her feet as she gestured toward the settee in the quiet nook near the hearth. "Let us adjourn to a more convenient location where I can provide physical reassurance without risking the wrath of my maid. I understand allemande is very difficult to wash out of silk, and given how much care Joseph took laying the table, he would be devastated to find out he had placed the poulet aux champignons in the wrong spot."

Although he submitted to the treatment without protest, he did observe with droll amusement that she would never get a proper meal at this rate.

"As you and every reader of Twaddle-Thum know, I do not require proper meals," she said, crossing to the sofa. "Only a regular supply of rout cakes."

"Of which you were also deprived today," he said with an uncharacteristic sigh as he sat down next to her. "I am sorry, Bea."

Oh, but it was funny, how Mrs. Taylor and the magistrate had gobbled up all but the plate, leaving her only crumbs, and she refused to allow him to feel bad about it. "It is precisely the thing that will burnish my reputation when Twaddle recounts the tally later in the week: one rout cake for Her Outrageousness, seven rout cakes for her guests."

"I know you would happily serve tea to a dozen of my former lovers if it meant more murder mysteries for you to solve, but Penny's visit here was an egregious breach in etiquette. I should never have allowed it to happen," he said yet again.

"Is that a dozen former lovers all at once, your grace, or in succession?" she asked with a thoughtful tilt of her chin. "Because as much as I relish the challenge of identifying murderers, the prospect of dealing with a full complement of Mrs. Taylors does give me pause. Were all your mistresses as capricious and whimsical or only the ones from your salad days?"

But Kesgrave shook his head and replied with stern authority that he would not allow her to lead him into further indiscretion. "I still retain some sense of decorum despite your efforts to corrupt me."

"*My* efforts?" she asked, raising an eyebrow with arch curiosity. "Do I need to remind you whose former lover required tea service today?"

"Well, you did not *have* to serve her tea," he replied.

"The only thing worse than serving tea to your mistress would be refusing to serve tea to your mistress, which I am sure you know. Twaddle certainly does. I can just imagine his cooing with pleasure," she said, then shifted slightly so that her arm brushed his against the back cushion of the settee. Comfortably situated, she urged him to continue with his narrative. "And now when you get that look of utter befuddlement on your face, I can clutch your hand without splashing pea soup everywhere."

"Is that how I looked?" he asked, seemingly taken aback by the description. "Utterly befuddled?"

"Presumably, your instruction in impassivity at Eton—or is stolidity something they teach at university—failed to account for half-sisters with full repertoires of characters," she said consolingly.

"In fact, that was the one lesson my father deigned to teach me himself," he replied lightly, demonstrating how well he had mastered the subject. "It was impressed upon me at a very early age that emotion was weakness and the display of emotion was a tactical error. He viewed every interaction as a contest from which only one participant could emerge as victor, an outlook that made being in his company excessively unpleasant. Fortunately, I was able to hide my discomfit by the time I turned five. But that is neither here nor there. We were discussing Miss Lark."

"Miss Lark, yes," Bea said firmly as if untroubled by the further revelation of his father's horribleness. But she laced her fingers through his. "Given how much you appear to know about her, I assume you arranged an introduction."

"I got her location from an editor at the *Gazette*," he said.

Bea could not suppress a giggle at the image of the Duke of Kesgrave striding into the office of Mr. Twaddle-Thum's employer. "He must have been delighted to see you."

"As the entire staff believed I was there to demand Twaddle's head on a platter, they were more than happy to hand over Robert Lark's address," he replied with a grin. "I can only assume they do not know the truth of his identity."

"It cannot be a very well-kept secret if you managed to figure out he was Miss Lark on your first meeting," Bea pointed out. "Or was she so overwhelmed by your august presence that she admitted everything in an instant?"

"It was the latter, but not in the way you think," he said, shaking his head as a bemused look flitted across his face. "Nothing about the meeting happened in the way you think, Bea. Nothing. It truly was the damndest thing."

"All right," she said, her heartbeat ticking up slightly, although she could not account for the strange increase in her anxiety. His words alone were not concerning.

And yet the bemusement and befuddlement.

It all felt a little too momentous.

"I knocked on the door," he said[2]. "It is a nice enough

house, neat and tidy, in Bethel Street, and a footman answered. He was dressed in full livery, which was striking in its formality for such a modest residence, and then he spoke. And it was a female voice. It was she, Verity Lark, and it was as though she had been expecting my call. I swear, Bea, she greeted me so calmly, so coolly, as if butter would not melt in her mouth, and said that her name was Verity Lark and she was dressed as a footman because she was on her way to the Home Office to try to meet with one of the under-secretaries to stop a terrible tragedy that was about to unfold. And then she requested my help—again, as cool as you please."

Well, naturally, yes.

That was all Bea could think having heard this remarkable turn of events—well, naturally, yes, Miss Lark sought the Duke of Kesgrave's assistance. With some unspeakable horror bearing down on her and the slim likelihood that any of the bigwigs in the Home Office would allow her entry, let alone consent to listen to her concerns, his sudden appearance on her doorstep must have felt like a godsend.

"Did she know who you are?" Bea asked, then shook her head at the poorly worded question. "I mean, did she know who you are to her? Or, rather, who she is to you?"

"She did, yes," he replied.

Bea called up the image of the woman in the poke bonnet again and strained to extract useful details from the memory. She had been too shaken by the fears of her childhood to notice anything in particular about her. All she could recall was a lithe figure and arrow-straight shoulders, which indicated that the woman was not yet in her dotage—hardly a stunning insight.

Even so, she decided the woman must be older than Kesgrave. Hiding a pregnancy from the *ton* was simply too difficult without going into full seclusion, and by all reports, La Reina rarely missed a social outing, keeping to a rigorous schedule of salons, routs, garden parties and balls. Furthermore, presenting the duke with another man's child struck Bea as the sort of antic the famously malevolent courtesan would delight in.

An older sister, then, who wrote articles for the *London Daily Gazette* under a male pen name, assumed false identities from a large assortment of personae, and uncovered terrible tragedies that she sought to avert with visits to the Home Office.

It was a lot to digest, and she imagined Kesgrave silently struggling to make sense of it all en route to Whitehall.

That he agreed at once to lend his support Bea did not doubt for a moment. He was too decent to refuse a sincere request for help, and even if he suspected he was being gulled or led on a merry chase, he would have acceded out of a sense of curiosity.

"I assume you went straight to Sidmouth," she said, unable to conceive of him wasting his time with some mid-level functionary. She could not even summon the name of the under-secretaries, of which there were two, and she had a habit of remembering everything she read. "What time was this? Was he still in the building or did you have to visit him at home?"

Kesgrave replied that he could not recall the precise time, but it was late in the afternoon, most likely after five, and then he tightened his grip on her hand and asked if that was really what she wanted to know. "You do not have a single question about the interrogation to which I subjected her or the horrific tragedy she claimed was about to transpire? You are content to jump straight to the home secretary? *That* is where your fine investigative mind goes?"

Bea shifted, tugging the silk of her dress under her knees as she settled her legs on the cushion so that she could look at him directly. "My fine investigative mind—and I remain humbled, your grace, by your enduring faith in my abilities—was keeping to the facts of the case to allow you the opportunity to decide how much or how little you wish to share about your inner turmoil on the drive from Bethel Street to Whitehall. I know you agreed to help because that is who you are, Damien, and I know you succeeded because that is also who you are. What I do not know is how much of your consequence you had to exert to convince Sidmouth, who strikes me as something of an autocratic fool, to take her seriously, and if you plan to see Miss Lark again. You are encouraged to answer these questions in the order with which you are most comfortable, although I am significantly more interested in the latter."

The duke smiled faintly during the length of this reply, and although he opened his mouth as if to calmly submit with her request, he abruptly shut it as the befuddled look returned. He stared at her for several long moments and then said with a sort of baffled amazement, "She picks locks, Bea."

"Does she?" Bea murmured, intrigued by how that bit of information was revealed during their brief encounter. She was fairly confident the doors to the Home Office were not locked against them, but if by some strange occurrence they were, she knew Kesgrave would have been able to open them easily.

"We were at this ramshackle house in Glensdale Road and the door was locked, and she pulled a snake rake from her pocket and opened it," he explained with the same air of bewildered wonder. "She opened it with a speed and agility equal to my own, and I cannot say why that drove a spike into my heart, but it did. Something about knowing we shared a strange, obscure talent created an ache I could never have imagined."

Bea thought again of the tiny life that had barely taken form in her mother's belly and understood precisely how he

LYNN MESSINA

felt. The ache was absence. It was the hole where the other person was supposed to have been. Of course seeing Miss Lark pick a lock had moved him to an unbearable degree: It was a snippet, a fleeting scrap, of an alternative history in which the lonely, besieged dukeling was not left to wander the halls of a massive, desolate castle on his own.

Her own heart overwhelmed by the lost expression on his face, she smiled sadly as she ran her fingers over his golden curls. "And that is the answer to the second question, whether you realize it or not. I agree it is remarkable that you both developed the same skill, and although presumably her need for it differed from yours, the reason for its acquisition was the same. Neither of you would accept that a room was locked to you. I think that is a solid basis for a relationship. Many siblings have far less in common. Flora and Russell, for example. The only overlap between them is a desperate desire for their father's approval."

But Kesgrave shook his head, and Bea knew it was not in denial of her cousins' bond. What she was proposing was inconceivable to him, and she waited for him to explain why the prospect was untenable.

It did not take long.

"Although you consider picking a lock to be a highly complex undertaking, it is in fact fairly easy to master, requiring only tenacity and repetition," he said with a deprecating smile. "As a topic of conversation, it would sustain Miss Lark and me for fifteen minutes at most. And then what shall we discuss? Our childhoods? She could tell me about the hardships she endured at Fortescue's, and I will tell her about the army of servants employed to satisfy my every need?"

The answer was yes, Bea thought, yes, precisely that. Without question, the disparity in their upbringings was huge, and it would be ridiculous to argue that the miseries the duke suffered were equal to those of Miss Lark's. He was the heir to a massive fortune, and as such enjoyed every material comfort known to man. Even so, his own uncle tried to murder him on multiple occasions, giving him some insight into the terror and adversity that could haunt a child. It was another point of commonality between the siblings.

But his objection was not about a lack of drawing room conversation, not really. Whatever awkward silence might slip into the exchange, the sixth Duke of Kesgrave was more than adept at filling it with an appropriate observation, for that was what it meant to be a noble whose lineage stretched back almost half a millennium. The ability to speak intelligently on any number of topics was bred in the bone like deportment and elocution, and by the time he turned six he would have been able to conduct a cogent discussion with his governess on her favorite novels.

No, what Kesgrave feared was the awkwardness itself, the unnerving sense of uncertainty and unease that came from not feeling quite at home in one's own body. Firmly in control of every situation he encountered, he had never stood partially hidden by a ficus in a ballroom wishing he could disappear completely or clasped his hands in a tight ball as his aunt prattled on about porridge to a withering Mrs. Ralston. His steadfast composure was one of the most reassuring things about him, for nothing disconcerted him, neither being entombed in the basement of a theater nor receiving a proposal of marriage while sitting on the chest of a murderer. All situations were subordinate to his command.

Except an unknown sister who could pick locks.

Nothing in his education addressed the unlikely event of finding one's mother's by-blow endearing. The proper way to respond had not been taught alongside stolidity and Homeric archaeology at Eton, and now he was foundering for a reply.

His reticence was in itself endearing, for Bea had never known him to be anything other than utterly assured in his next move. Even so, she had no wish to increase his discomfort by drawing attention to it and she skirted the issue by speaking only to his stated concern. "Sidmouth," she said.

Although it was not a non sequitur in the strictest sense, it veered enough from the topic to cause confusion and he repeated the name with his brows drawn.

Smoothly, Bea reminded him that he had wondered what he and Miss Lark could talk about after they had exhausted the subject of lockpicking. "I am proposing the home secretary as an answer. It is reasonable to assume she shares your contempt of him. As a reporter—I believe you said she writes for the *London Daily Gazette*—she probably has all sorts of opinions about him that predate their meeting. And that is another subject: the newspaper. It is highly unusual for a woman to find employment as a journalist, and you could ascertain how she came to join the profession. I am sure it is a very interesting story. Then there is the matter of her colleague, Mr. Twaddle-Thum, about whose habits you would not mind hearing a little something," she said, then allowed that the last suggestion might apply more to herself than him. Nevertheless, speculating about the gossip's true identity had to be worth a good quarter-hour's worth of chatter. "These are merely the thoughts that occur to me in the moment. If I had the opportunity to give the question proper consideration, I am sure I could come up with at least a dozen ideas, which I could jot down in descending order of weightiness. I know how fond you are of numbered lists, your grace."

Presented with this practical solution, Kesgrave smiled faintly and offered his own ambiguous reply, conveying to her Sidmouth's regards. "He looks forward to seeing you tomorrow night at the Kempton ball and hopes you will save him a dance."

"Does he?" Bea murmured, abiding by the duke's desire to change the subject. She had no wish to compel a conversation he was not yet prepared to have. "I supposed that answers my first question, for you must have stood on all your consequence if Lady Diana's come-out managed to enter the discussion amid concerns of an imminent tragedy. Did you also discuss the inferior quality of the port at Boodle's?"

"No, but the condition of the racing track at Ascot did arise," he said mildly.

"Well, it *has* been a wet spring," she conceded.

"These hefty matters were not raised until after someone had been sent to confirm that the spy who had provided the inaccurate information had moved out of his lodgings without telling the Home Office of his plans to leave London and Sidmouth served tea while we waited for his return," Kesgrave explained. "However, you are correct in your conclusion. I did have to exert some authority, as my presence was not well received. The under-secretary—his name is Kingsley—tried to eject me as soon as I stepped into his office, and General Jentleson praised my recent public spiritedness but warned me against meddling in matters I could not understand."

Having never set foot in the building, Bea nevertheless found it remarkably easy to picture the scene: the duke striding confidently into the room, an air of purpose and privilege resting lightly on his shoulders as he took the measure of its occupants. His entitled assurance would have been galling to the two men, whose influence had been amassed only through years of striving and hard work. Naturally, they would resent the interference of a man born into power. "Did the general advise you to take up your seat in the House of Lords?"

"It was, Jentleson assured me, the best route if I wanted to try my hand at governmental affairs," he replied gravely.

It was impossible not to admire such exquisite condescension, and Bea clapped appreciatively. "What I would not have paid to witness that speech! I trust you thanked him for the advice, then assured him you had already done your duty and considered the many weighty issues before Parliament as you polished your coronet or walked the rows of your pinery."

"Oddly, no," he said amiably. "I kept my attention focused on the more pressing concern of convincing Sidmouth that the informant Kingsley hired to spy on the Society of Yarwellian Philosophers was unworthy of the trust placed in him. A mass meeting with a well-known orator was taking place last evening in St. Dunston's field, and although the event was a peaceful gathering of reform-minded laborers, the informant reported that the men would be armed. He said they planned to march to the Tower of London and seize it in the first strike of a civil war that would ultimately consume the nation."

Although there were aspects to this explanation that Bea did not comprehend—what, for example, was a Yarwellian Philosopher?—she knew enough about the way the British army conducted its business to see at once the threat. Soldiers positioned around the perimeter of the field would not hesitate to shoot into a crowd of hundreds if they believed the stability of the country was at stake. Peace was worth any number of dead bystanders.

If Miss Lark had discovered that the Home Office's spy was determined to start an insurrection, then she must have been very frantic indeed to make herself heard.

Bea's heartbeat increased slightly as she contemplated the tragedy that would have inevitably transpired had Kesgrave not presented himself so opportunely at the Bethel Street address. "It did not matter how Miss Lark was dressed, the under-secretary would never have listened to her, not with Sidmouth and the general there. He would look like the veriest fool for being duped by his own underling and his ego could never have supported it. She is fortunate you appeared when you did, as are all the men and women who gathered in the field last night. It is impossible to say how many lives would have been lost had you not interceded."

It was the only reasonable conclusion to draw, and yet Kesgrave insisted Miss Lark would have succeeded without him. "She had already settled on a plan by the time I arrived at her door and merely adjusted it when she realized it would be more efficient to make use of me. Her ingenuity is endless. After she convinced Sidmouth that the mass meeting would be peaceful, she dashed to the headquarters of the Yarwellian Society to apprehend Fitch—that is the alias the spy used in London—and rescue her associate, and she pulled off both feats by pretending to be an entire regiment of the army."

It was impossible to miss the hint of respect in his voice. "You like her."

Kesgrave shook his head as if to deny it, then sighed heavily and pressed his shoulders against the back of the settee. "It really is the damndest thing, Bea, but I do," he said, looping his fingers through hers again, although his grip remained light. "She surprised me. I do not know what I thought would happen when I knocked on the door in Bethel Street. The truth is, I had not considered it deeply because I felt like a lackwit just being there. Because why *was* I there? The woman could not be who I thought she was, and even if she was it had nothing to do with me. Still, I had spent the better part of a day tracking her down. It was perverse! And then all of a sudden she was standing before me, dressed as a footman and requesting my help, and before I knew it I was miles away, in the dingy basement of a ramshackle house, stamping out the flames of a growing conflagration while Miss Lark fired her pistol in the air and Colson Hardwicke wrestled the lying informant to the floor."

It was back in his voice, the note of befuddlement, but his expression remained clear. He was not as flummoxed as before, and Bea, observing the difference, opened her mouth to make a frivolous remark about the horrendous abuse of his Hessians. If Hoby could condone such flagrant mistreatment of his precious boots, then surely he would not cavil at a woman donning a pair? But the final part of his statement drove the comment from her mind. "The Marquess of Ware's scapegrace son who was disinherited years ago for accruing gambling debts so massive he stole from his own father to try to settle them—he was there too?"

He laughed at her astonishment. "It is like a dream, is it not, with all these seemingly disparate elements appearing together. Yes, *that* Colson Hardwicke was there, and I do not think he is quite the ne'er-do-well he would have the *ton* believe. Either his reputation was a sham from the beginning or he has redeemed himself by working for the Home Office. Regardless, during the course of the intrigue, he had disappeared, which is why Miss Lark was compelled to seek my assistance. She needed to convince his superior, Daniel Grint, that Kingsley's spy was lying. Grint, you see, is also an undersecretary, so he is a rival for Sidmouth's approbation. Kingsley hired Fitch to spy on the Society of Yarwellian Philosophers, which supports the reform movement, and Grint suspected Fitch of being a secret radical, so he hired Hardwicke to keep an eye on him. Miss Lark was assisting Hardwicke, who had joined the Society of Yarwellian Philosophers to watch Fitch, and she became alarmed when Hardwicke went missing. She thought Fitch had taken him hostage, but Hardwicke was in fact seized by members of the society who thought *he* was the spy. It is all a great tangle. But suffice to say, tragedy was averted and would have been even without my help. I merely simplified the process."

A tangle indeed, Bea thought, unable to believe that the Gordian knot would have unwound so favorably without Kesgrave's assistance. Nonetheless, she did not question his understanding of events and instead teased him about his contribution. "By discussing racing conditions with Sidmouth."

"By observing the proprieties," he corrected affably. "And empires have been lost on less, as the Trojans can attest. But the real value to my being there was to make it clear to Sidmouth that I would not stand idly by should he decide to act on the information despite knowing it was not credible."

That the home secretary would seek to exploit the lie to further his own agenda did not surprise her in the least. By all reports, he was generally without conscience. "Given his repressive stance on the reform movement, I imagine he would welcome any pretext that would allow him to suspend the writ of habeas corpus. He has argued for it several times now, has he not? And he knows that a threat that does not actually exist cannot be proven to be false. Once shots were fired, the meeting would become violent whether that was the intention of the organizers or not. In that regard, Miss Lark is more fortunate than she realizes. There is no telling what they would have done to ensure she could not spread word of Fitch's perfidy."

Kesgrave nodded and said he had had that very thought, which was why he made it clear that he would not hesitate to contact the editor of the *Morning Chronicle* if they proceeded without making an effort to corroborate Miss Lark's intelligence. "That is why Sidmouth agreed to send Grint and Jentleson's aide to inspect Fitch's rooms, which the spy had vacated in his eagerness to leave London. While we waited for their return, Sidmouth served tea and we discussed Ascot and Lady Diana's come-out and sundry social matters until Grint returned with confirmation."

"Forcing the army to stand down," she said. "The general could not have been pleased about that, all those troops ready and eager to put down a rebellion."

"He recognized the prudence of taking a more cautious approach, and Sidmouth allowed him to keep some soldiers at the site, so it was not complete surrender," the duke said. "Kingsley, however, was churlish, and with good reason, I believe. I did not linger, for Miss Lark had dashed from the room and I wanted to catch her before she disappeared, but I suspect Kingsley will soon be relieved of his position if he has not already."

Although Beatrice appreciated his perspective, she found it difficult to believe Kingsley would lose his post over the debacle. In her experience, men of a certain rank and breeding were allowed to make a muddle of things over and over again without consequences. But it was not the under-secretary who interested her. "Miss Lark dashed from the room to rescue Lord Colson from Fitch in the basement of the Yarwellian society?"

"Precisely," he said with a fleeting smile. "She believed Fitch knew where Hardwicke was and assumed Fitch would return to the headquarters to steal the funds the society had raised because he was not a secret radical as Grint supposed. He was just another rapacious thief scheming to get his hands on as much money as possible. Miss Lark did not seek my assistance but I offered it, as my obligation to her would not be at an end until I returned her safely to her home."

How coolly he said it, Bea thought, as if merely discharging a duty.

And that was all it might have been if not for the clever implement known as a snake rake.

Miss Lark did not know it yet, but the course of her life had been irrevocably altered by the possession of one slim little lockpicking device. She would not be permitted to return to her secluded existence in Bethel Street. Allowing her to do precisely that might have been Kesgrave's intention at the time, for he had explicitly stated that she was nothing to him, but he would never be able to hold to it. His interest was already too keen to be satisfied with the lone interaction.

As he himself had said multiple times now: It was the damndest thing.

Bea, for her part, could not wait to meet Miss Lark,

Obviously, of course, she *would* wait.

Despite her history of bounding into situations where she did not belong, especially after promising she would not, this boundary was one she would not transgress. She would never deny Kesgrave the pleasure of introducing her to his sister.

"And you did help by ruining your lovely Hessians while putting out the fire," Bea said, recalling the detail from earlier in his narrative.

Kesgrave assured her he had not. "You failed to perceive the extent of Hoby's brilliance if you think a few flames are enough to destroy his work."

"As you are well aware of how fervently I desire boots from him, you must know that is a particularly cruel thing to say, your grace," Bea replied, only partially in jest. But as she had a scheme afoot to enlist the help of Nuneaton in acquiring her own exquisitely made pair, she did not linger on the subject, instead asking if Miss Lark knew the identity of her father.

"She says she does not," he replied.

Thoughtfully, Bea tilted her head and observed that Miss Lark's ignorance on the matter struck her as a particular choice. "In light of her resourcefulness, I mean. It seems like information she could discover if she was so inclined."

"Agreed. My grandmother found out easily enough," he added with almost casual indifference.

Oh, but he knew what he was saying and did not flinch when Bea lurched forward and clutched his forearms in astonishment. "The dowager knows!"

"She has known all along," he replied smoothly.

And again it was deliberate, the studied nonchalance, for it was a shocking claim whose significance could not be overstated, and she tightened her grip in concern. Having been denied vital information about her parents by her own family, she knew how upsetting it was to discover that something was not as you thought. "*All* along?"

"Well, not from the beginning of my parents' liaison," he amended. "She was aware of the relationship, of course, but had no reason to think his arrangement with La Reina would be any different from any of the two dozen that preceded it. When she learned about the betrothal—via the announcement in the *Times* like the rest of the *ton*—she hired a thief-taker to find out everything he could about her future daughter-in-law. She claims it was out of curiosity, to know more about her grandchild's antecedents, but she admits that she hoped he would uncover something that could be used to compel the end of the engagement. When the thief-taker discovered the baby at Fortescue's, my grandmother thought she had the perfect weapon and threatened La Reina with exposure."

Obviously, the dowager's scheme fell short of this lofty goal. The nuptials proceeded as planned, with Kesgrave entering the world a mere five months after his parents wed. But the question was, how did it fail?

"Did La Reina tell your grandmother to go to hell?" Bea asked.

His lips quivered faintly as he said, "More or less. She dared my grandmother to take out an ad in the dailies and announce it properly, for it meant nothing to her if people knew she had borne a child out of wedlock. Further public censure would only make her more appealing to the duke, she said, because all he wanted from the liaison was the beau monde's revulsion and disgust."

At this harsh sentiment, Kesgrave displayed no unsettled

emotion, and Bea supposed it was because there was nothing revelatory about the ugliness. He already knew his parents were monstrous human beings and there was no new depth to plumb.

He had reached bedrock decades before.

"My mother then said that the only person who would be hurt by the revelation was her own grandchild, who would have to bear the shame of having a bastard sibling," he continued with the same unnerving dispassion. "And, of course, the baby, whose own father knew nothing about her for her own welfare. He was not a good or decent man, and she shuddered to think of the wickedness to which he would expose the girl. It was on her head if he did. Realizing it was futile, my grandmother ended the conversation and never raised the topic again."

A knot of dread formed in Bea's stomach, icy and forbidding, similar to the one that had overtaken her on the lawn in front of Fortescue's, although it was not as alarming.

Of course it was not.

She was in her favorite place in the world, the nook in the library at Kesgrave House, next to the fireplace and opposite eighteenth-century biographies, and a warmth pervaded her limbs, which came not just from the hearth but a sense of belonging. Beatrice Hyde-Clare had never known a greater peace than the gentle crackle of the blaze as she opened a book to its title page.

Even so, anxiety coursed through her at the thought of the helpless baby being consigned to the ominous asylum, with its menacing towers.

Why was she even there?

There was no reason for it.

With her success, La Reina could have afforded to ensure a modicum of comfort for the girl. Placing one's mongrels with a kindly farmer and his wife was a time-honored tradition for a reason—it appeased the conscience while eliminating responsibility—and Bea could not conceive why the courtesan did not avail herself of it. Even if she did not personally know of a suitable family, one of her servants would have been able to point her in the right direction.

Bea refused to believe there were no other options.

Leaving the infant Miss Lark to suffer the callous disregard and offhand cruelty of Fortescue's was a deliberate choice, which the dowager would have recognized. La Reina's gross indifference to her own child's welfare was the greater mark against her, and the Duchess of Kesgrave would have used the threat of revelation as a cudgel. Society's harsh condemnation was an indomitable force that had cowed even the most strident matron, and yet La Reina remained impervious to its effects.

Having failed in her endeavor to rout the ruthless upstart, the dowager presumably abandoned the girl to her fate, as she had never regarded her as anything other than a pawn. The notion that she should expend any of her vast, seemingly limitless resources to ensure her grandson's sister was raised by kind or even loving parents had most likely never crossed her mind.

And why would it?

To many of the people in the ruling class, children had no inherent value. They were worth only what they could achieve: carrying on the family name, ensuring a legacy.

As fond as Bea was of the dowager and as much as she understood the other woman was simply a product of her own pampered existence, Bea felt a smoldering rage toward her. The apathy was unacceptable.

But it was also decades ago and there was nothing to be gained in harboring a resentment against something she could not change. All it did was draw her focus away from Kesgrave, which was indulgent and shabby.

Consequently, she leaned back slightly and raised her chin so she could see his expression more clearly. Then she asked how his grandmother responded to his queries about Miss Lark. "Was she very surprised?"

"She was confused," he replied evenly.

Too evenly, she thought, tensing for the next revelation as she offered a reasonable explanation. "Because she could not fathom how you found out?"

He pressed his lips together as he shook his head. "Because she could not fathom why I cared. It had nothing to do with me. She said that to me several times: 'But why would I tell you, Damien? It had nothing to do with you.' She had no idea what had become of the child—and that is what she kept calling her: the child. The child was none of her business. The child was no better than she ought to be. The child was her mother's daughter. The child had harlotry in her blood."

Although he spoke flatly, with barely any inflection, the duke's answer still carried a wealth of anger, and Bea, who could not smother her own fury over the dowager's pitiless judgment, felt some relief in knowing he shared her outrage. As the daughter of a supposedly depraved woman—Aunt Vera had hugely and grievously misunderstood Clara Hyde-Clare's behavior in the months prior to her death—the course of Bea's life had been governed by the belief that the sins of the mother were visited upon the daughter. Her relative had withheld all information about her deceased parents and took every opportunity to crush her spirit in an effort to overcome the moral decrepitude her mother had inevitably passed to her.

It was a petty notion, the idea that virtue lived in the blood, and Bea had no reason to expect better from her aunt and uncle, whose understanding of the universe was firmly rooted in their place in it. They subscribed wholly to the ethical superiority of their betters.

Nobles were noble.

Kesgrave's grandmother, however, had every reason to know better. She had raised two sons who failed to meet the basic requirements of human decency, and they had either inherited their iniquity from the dowager herself or developed it in response to their personal experiences. Although she suffered wrenching guilt over her children's perfidy, she did not consider herself the source of it.

Furthermore, the dowager had unstintingly accepted Bea into the family. While the rest of the beau monde gasped in horror at the loss of its most sought-after prize to such an unworthy contender, she had deemed it as an excellent match. Hailing Bea's pluck, she insisted it was the ideal foil for her grandson's arrogance, which would grow out of hand without someone to keep it in check.

The generosity of that sentiment, the open-mindedness of that approach, was impossible to reconcile with the close-minded attitude toward the infant Miss Lark. Bea would understand the disparity if the intolerant view was how the dowager had felt then, but she had expressed these ideas only the night before.

Gently, she said, "I'm sorry, Damien. That is a terrible way to speak about anyone."

"I yelled at her," he said solemnly as if admitting to a grave sin. "I do not think I have ever yelled at my grandmother in my entire life. Snapped at her, certainly, and barked when she refused to be sensible about her health, but never yelled. She was so taken aback by it and confused. She simply could not comprehend why I was making such a bother. What was the child to me anyway? She called for Sutton to bring me a tisane to calm my nerves. She thought I was overwrought. The notion that I would care to know about the existence of a sibling was so outside the bounds of her conception that she assumed I had succumbed to a fit of vapors. That is when I left because it seemed futile to remain. I apologized for disturbing her evening and returned home to tell *you* every remarkable detail because I knew you would understand what the bother was about. There was even a moment when my grandmother was instructing Sutton to add chamomile petals to the passionflower to ensure a particularly soothing blend when I looked around the room to find your gaze because it was amusing in such a ghastly way."

Having been dismissed by the duke on more than one occasion during their stay in the Lake District, Bea was intimately familiar with the experience and could only assume the dowager found his cool imperiousness more disquieting than his raised voice. She would want to attribute it to anything other than her own poorly considered choices, and a strange start would strike her as reasonable an explanation as the truth. "I am sorry I was not there, for I could have suggested adding a touch of lavender as well. Aunt Vera finds it very restorative when my uncle is up in arms about one of Russell's something-or-others and he describes him as *your son* in a particularly disdainful way."

A smile tugged fleetingly at his lips. "I am sure my grandmother would have appreciated your input, as she considers you too sensible to care about matters long since passed. She asked after you twice."

"Trying to change the topic of conversation, I expect," Bea replied in a display of the aforementioned prudence. "Although her desire to discuss her great-grandchild was sincere. Once she got over her chagrin at Lady Abercrombie breaking the news, she was quite delighted by the development."

"In fact, I did get an earful about telling Tilly before her, and I think at first she assumed the only reason I mentioned the unpleasant business with the child was to change the subject," he said with a cynical frown. "And now she appears to be sulking because she neither sent a message nor called today. She is probably waiting for me to apologize for losing my temper."

"I am sorry I was not there with you last night or awake when you got home," she said softly. "But I can go with you tomorrow if you would like to try talking to her again. Perhaps after a little time to reflect, she will be more amenable to your point of view."

Kesgrave, allowing for the possibility, observed that ultimately it did not matter. "Nothing can make up for the fact that she withheld information of my sister from me at a time when the knowledge could have made a difference in her life. She writes newspaper articles under a male pseudonym and runs around London dressed as a footman and performs dangerous services on behalf of the Home Office. How difficult must her life have been that she needed to resort to such things to earn money? She was nineteen when I inherited the estates. I could have settled a living on her and never even noticed."

"You could still do that now," she pointed out.

But she had heard the regret in his voice, the awareness of an opportunity lost, and was unsurprised when he said he could not. "Miss Lark is too proud to take a farthing from me. I do not have to know her to know that. And I would not insult her by offering."

No, he would not, Bea thought, struck by the sad note in the admission.

It was so unusual to see the duke forlorn that she almost did not recognize it.

Having identified it, she was at a loss as to how to proceed, for she had no desire to deprive him of his sorrow. Her aunt's determined exuberance whenever Bea displayed any hint of grief over her parents' death had just deepened her pain. The only thing worse than mourning her parents was being made to feel as though she ought not mourn her parents.

Bea hated the thought of adding to the duke's burden by making him conscious of it, and yet she wanted to do something to lighten his mood.

What about gentle cajolery?

Surely, it bore no resemblance to Aunt Vera's aggressive cheerfulness.

With that in mind, she reviewed the conversation for a suitable distraction and recalled his description of the chaotic scene in the cellar of the Yarwellian Society. He said Miss Lark had discharged her pistol, had he not?

It was, as far as Bea was concerned, a highly enviable action.

Treading lightly, she wondered if perhaps Miss Lark would consent to giving her flintlock lessons. "That way, you could compensate her generously for a service rendered and lend her financial support without damaging her pride."

"You are already taking firearm instruction," he said.

Sighing heavily, she insisted she was not. "It has been almost four weeks and I have yet to get off a single shot with a bullet. I am so intimately acquainted with the recoil, I could waltz with it at Almack's three times in a row without raising an eyebrow. We have breakfast together every morning on the terrace. No, your grace, I think it is time we accept the unpleasant truth about Prosser: He is terrified of an armed woman. I am sure the men whom he has taught were out shooting grouse with their flintlocks by the end of their fourth session."

"That is absolutely absurd, Bea," Kesgrave said dampeningly. "One would never take a pistol hunting. One uses a fowling piece to shoot game, which only demonstrates how much you have still to learn."

There was a particular ease to his manner as he made the clarification, an insouciance that indicated she had managed to divert his attention from gloomier thoughts, and she was pleased by the success of her ploy. But his demeanor was also very grave, for it was vitally important that she understood the difference in firearms, and the compulsive seriousness utterly delighted her. Affection for him reared, surging upward like a wild beast determined to snap its tether, and she almost knocked him off the settee in her eagerness to express it.

He regained his balance with very little effort, shifting slightly to the left to press Bea's back against the cushion and then gently sliding her beneath him. As he deepened the kiss, as Bea felt the spikey heat of desire pervade her body, she reevaluated her earlier judgment and realized she had been wrong.

This was her most favorite place in the world.

Chapter Nine

Bea was in no rush to start the day.

Waking up next to Kesgrave, her stomach obligingly calm, her mind blessedly still, she marveled at the contrast with the morning before, when her muscles had tightened at the first sign of consciousness, her whole body keenly aware of an impending horribleness before she even opened her eyes.

Now she lingered, stretching indolently and brushing languidly against the duke, who agreed that breakfast could be delayed a little while. Lily was sent away for another hour, although only after she placed the tray with tea and rout cakes on the table next to the settee.

The early-morning activity ensured that Bea was late for her fencing instruction, and to compensate for making Carlo wait a full fifteen minutes, she applied herself to her lesson with unprecedented vigor. By the end of the session, she had mastered the appel and performed a balestra with such grace and precision her instructor let his guard down long enough to compliment her skill, allowing her the rare opportunity to make contact.

As a consequence, she and Kesgrave did not climb into the carriage to resume their investigation until well after eleven. Although it might appear as though they were displaying a regrettable lack of urgency in their quest to identify the culprit who had ruthlessly slain Millicent Lloyd, it was in fact an act of prudence. Debenham would inevitably be surly when he found out he was a suspect in a courtesan's murder, especially when they confronted him with the damning evidence from his own letters, and Bea thought he would be less standoffish if he had digested a proper breakfast first.

Mrs. Taylor, throwing herself in front of the carriage as Jenkins directed the horses through the gate at the bottom of the gravel drive, begged to disagree. Indignantly, she announced that she had been perched behind a shrub at the end of the path since half past nine and could not believe they were so negligent in their duty as to allow half the day to pass.

Jenkins, insulted on his employers' behalf, ordered her to step to the side or risk being trampled underfoot as Kesgrave climbed out of the conveyance. He begged the groom not to shed any blood on the gravel, as it would be the very devil to wash out, and invited Mrs. Taylor to join them in the vehicle.

"Gladly, thank you," she said, darting Jenkins a smug look.

As the courtesan settled on the bench across from them, Bea noted that her appearance was much different from the day before. Her hair was in disarray, with tufts and strands flying in various directions, and the ill-fitting dress did not flatter her figure.

Actually, that was incorrect. The gown's tight bodice flattered her figure to an almost indecent degree. Her cleavage heaved over the silk trim, and Bea feared her bosom might spill out completely if she breathed too deeply.

"Well, you stare!" Mrs. Taylor said crossly. "I have had an extremely trying morning. I would like to see either one of you attempt to get dressed in another woman's home while evading her servants. All of them wanted to be so helpful, especially after they had watched me stumble from the home at daybreak. They had no idea what was the matter, for they were all asleep until they heard Millie knock over the table at the top of the stairs. Their concern for my well-being was torture! And everything Millie owns is just a little too small for me. This gown was the best I could do and still I can barely breathe it is so tight. Despite my tribulations, which were considerable, I am here now! Tell me what the itinerary is for the day. I assume we will start with Audenshaw and proceed from there."

Although the bodice held despite the many deep breaths required by this speech, Bea asked if it would not have been helpful to don a shawl or a pelisse.

Mrs. Taylor stiffened her shoulders in affront, further straining the already tightly stretched fabric, and said, "Again, your grace, I would like to see how you fare in the circumstance. It was all I could do to get dressed and have breakfast without any of Millie's infernal staff growing the wiser. I was certainly not going to linger in the home, rooting through her drawers to find a shawl! I ate my eggs quickly and dashed from the house—only to cool my heels in front of Kesgrave House for almost two hours. I am relieved, Damien, that you do not consider my pending death by way of noose to be a dire circumstance, for I would hate for my execution to disturb your slumber."

Bea assured her that she and Kesgrave took the matter of Miss Lloyd's murder very seriously, which was not, the courtesan was quick to note, quite the same thing. Nevertheless, she rallied at the information and asked what their tactic would be for Audenshaw. "Shall I greet him at the door like a specter?"

"We are calling on Debenham first," Bea said.

Mrs. Taylor frowned and narrowed her gaze at the duke. "You are deliberately putting off Audenshaw just to spite me, Damien."

"It is a matter of geography," he replied mildly. "Debenham's lodgings are en route to Audenshaw's."

Although she clearly did not find this explanation persuasive, Mrs. Taylor was too clever to press the issue. Instead, she forced a smile and recounted her struggles to evade Millie's staff. Donning a black veil to hide her features, she invented a rarely mentioned cousin whose death had devastated her, which had the unfortunate effect of making the situation worse. "Because they kept feeding me those horrible candies that Millie loved as consolation. I was besieged by them everywhere I turned, for she kept them in charming little dishes scattered throughout the house. It was horrible because I do so hate their flavor, but the scent also reminds me of Millie. I am, you see, keenly aware of Piddly's harsh judgment of my response to her death, but I *have* been so consumed with concern for myself that I have scarcely had a chance to comprehend what her loss means to me. I fear I will miss her dreadfully, even her constant imitation. It was wearying, I am sure, but she also worshipped me. That part was nice."

On this reflective note, she fell silent and did not speak until they reached Debenham's home, which was on a tree-lined crescent. Impatient to interview Audenshaw, she did not waste time with a strategy to disguise her presence and simply marched up to the door to make her presence known.

Curling his lips faintly, the butler urged her to be on her way before noticing the august company. Stammering an apology, he explained that he had been told not to admit Mrs.

Taylor under any circumstance, and foundering over how to proceed, asked the duke if he would mind very much waiting in the entrance as he informed Lord Debenham of his visit. "I would never ... it is merely that I was told not to admit her on threat of termination of my employment."

"You see, this is why I wished to interview Audenshaw first," Mrs. Taylor said as the butler disappeared down the narrow corridor. "Debenham hates me so much he wants to erase me from the face of the earth. He is obviously the murderer, and once her grace proves it, we will have no reason to call on Audenshaw."

"I should think being saved from Newgate and the noose would compensate you sufficiently for having to seek the assistance of Mr. Hawes," Bea observed wryly.

Mrs. Taylor readily agreed, then added with the sort of airy calculation that had troubled the magistrate that as the duchess would prove her innocence either way, she had hoped to derive an additional benefit from the miserable experience. "As compensation, you see, for so much of this enterprise has been distressing."

Before Bea could reply, a roar echoed throughout the hall and she turned to see a large bull of a man charging toward them, his face red with fury. "How dare you come to my home, where my *children* live, and flaunt your charms! You brazen hussy! Are you entirely without shame? Put Magnificent and Spectacular away at once. Higgins! Higgins!" he cried, calling for the butler who was only two steps behind him. Realizing it, he stopped abruptly and turned. "Get the Taylor chit something to cover her indecency. Any old thing will do. And be quick about it, man! Go! Go!"

As the butler ran down the hall, the courtesan fluttered her lashes and said with affecting modesty, "Why, Debby, I didn't know you still cared."

Turning purple, he squealed that the only thing he cared

about was removing her from the premises as swiftly as possible just as Higgins returned slightly out of breath. He clutched a dark-colored coat that had seen better days and held it out to Mrs. Taylor, who turned her delicate shoulders toward Debenham and insisted he have the honor.

Debenham yowled in fury.

Mrs. Taylor accepted the coat from Higgins with an elegant shrug and said with affable chagrin, "All right, then, I guess I have to do everything myself."

As there was little to be accomplished from provoking their host, Bea sent her a quelling look and apologized to him for interrupting his day. "I know your patience has been tried already, but if you could manage to hold on to it just a little bit longer, we have some questions we would like to ask you. I promise we will keep it brief."

In a genial tone that belied the high color of his cheeks, he thanked the duchess for her consideration and owned himself delighted to meet her. "I have followed your recent exploits and am curious as to how I may be of assistance," he said, inviting her and the duke to sit down in the drawing room. As he turned to lead the way, he peevishly added, "I suppose the she-devil can come, too."

"Charming," Mrs. Taylor murmured, her small frame dwarfed by the tailcoat, which gave her an alluring vulnerability. If Debenham had hoped to reduce her appeal by covering up Magnificent and Spectacular, he had inadvertently accomplished the opposite.

As Bea sat down next to Kesgrave on the settee, Debenham confessed that he had lied about the source of his curiosity. He did not want to know how he could help; he sought only to discover why the Duchess of Kesgrave was in the company of her husband's former lover. "Or is the arrangement current?" he asked with a speculative air. "Is that how you convinced him to marry you—by vowing to be open-minded and tolerant of his dalliances? If that is the bargain you struck, then I must encourage you to point him in a different direction. Miss Slater possesses a sophistication beyond her years, to which I can personally attest."

He darted a glance at Mrs. Taylor, suggesting she was supposed to take offense at the comment, but she merely smiled and waved her hand dismissively. "That child? She is barely out of the schoolroom. She could never hold the interest of a man with Damien's breadth of experience. If he is in the market for a new mistress, then I strongly would advise him to consider Miss Whiting or Mademoiselle Mairtine. Both women are adept at sparkling in *and* out of the bedchamber—and to that *I* personally attest."

Mildly, the duke thanked them for their concern. He issued no denial nor revealed any discomfit, and Bea, marveling at his equanimity, wondered how he could endure a frank discussion of his sexual habits without flinching and yet feel unnerved by the prospect of taking tea with an illegitimate half-sister.

Mrs. Taylor simpered at his reply and assured the duke in a husky purr that her concern for him had never waned despite their years apart, which caused Debenham to growl fiercely and call her a brazen wench for daring to flirt with another man directly in front of him.

"Am I flirting?" she said innocently.

Impatient with Mrs. Taylor's antics, Bea announced that her questions pertained to the murder of a woman called Millicent Lloyd. In the process of glowering at his former mistress, Debenham turned abruptly to Bea, his brows drawn in confusion, and asked why the blazes she was bothering him about it. "I am sorry the girl was killed, of course, but I do not know anyone by that name."

"Millie was killed in my place," Mrs. Taylor explained, lowering her lips woefully. "It was supposed to be me. I was the intended victim, Debby. Someone wants me dead, and the duchess has kindly consented to find out who."

Debenham's mouth formed a shocked O, and he rose to his feet as if to rush to Mrs. Taylor's side to provide comfort and protection. Recalling himself, he halted midway, his knees slightly bent, and dropped back onto the cushion. The chair's worn frame creaked from the abuse as he said with studied apathy, "How unfortunate for you, Mrs. Taylor. I am sure I do not care."

"Oh, but you do," the courtesan said brusquely, "which is why we are here. I have given your letters to the duchess, and she agrees you are to be suspected of killing Millie in the mistaken belief she was I."

Debenham gasped. "Given my letters to the duchess! But … but they were meant for your eyes only. I would never have been so candid about my desires if I had suspected for a moment that you would be so callous as to share them. I cannot believe you would expose my most intimate thoughts. It is an appalling betrayal!"

"Not *those* letters, Debby," Mrs. Taylor said with a trace of humor. "The ones in which you threatened to kill me."

Now their host was nonplussed.

For several seconds, he stared at her blankly, then he tilted his head to the side, as if trying to decipher a riddle. "I never threatened to kill you," he said with matter-of-fact certainty before looking at Bea and reiterating it more forcefully. "Your grace, I never threatened to kill her, I swear!"

"'You will not live long enough to sufficiently rue this day,'" Mrs. Taylor said, quoting from one of the missives. "'England is not large enough for you to hide from me. I will find you and then you will regret treating me this way.' That is what you wrote, Debby."

Hearing his words aloud, Debenham flinched and allowed they did indeed seem a bit ominous in retrospect, but nowhere in his statements was an actual threat to end her life. "When I said you would not live long enough to sufficiently rue ending our relationship, I merely meant that you were too dimwitted to ever properly understand the immensity of your decision."

Dubious, Mrs. Taylor cited another damning sentence: "'I long to chop off your head!'"

"*My* head," Debenham corrected fervently. "I meant to say my own head, for I could not bear the thought of you and Pitt—er, that is Waltham now—together, for you had just run off with him. Did you think I did not know? You ended things with me one day, ruthlessly crushing my heart, and the very next day you disappeared with him for a sennight. Do you think I am impervious to pain?"

"Knutsford," Mrs. Taylor said.

Perplexed by the seeming non sequitur, Debenham asked, "Excuse me?"

"I did not run off with Waltham. I ran off with the Earl of Knutsford. His mother was in Italy and he wanted to show me the Knutsford Pineapple. It is a folly in the garden, a hothouse shaped like a pineapple, with an elaborate cupola above an octagonal pavilion with Gothic arches, where they grow oranges of all things. I had expressed amazement when Knutsford told me about the building, as you do when you are being courted by a man and are determined to appear fascinated by everything he says. So when his mother went abroad for Easter, he invited me to his country home to see the pineapple for myself. Ordinarily, I would never have agreed to leave London, but he made such a generous offer," she said, pausing here to look at Bea and explain that Knutsford had provided the funds for two dozen shares in a mining company. "He was such a sweet boy. A bit callow for my taste."

"But easy to manipulate," Kesgrave noted softly.

"Well, yes," Mrs. Taylor agreed amiably. "That was his main appeal. He lacks St. Ives's frivolity, although they are similar in age."

Despite the cogent argument to the contrary, Debenham remained wedded to his original understanding. "But Waltham left town at the same time as you. You both left London on the same day, April tenth. 'Tis a date I can never forget, for my heart shattered!"

"I imagine many others left the capital on the tenth as well," Mrs. Taylor replied. "It is a rather large city, and dozens of people come and go all the time. Tell me, did we also return on the same day? Because I was gone for two weeks, not one."

To that query, Debenham had no reply, for it had not occurred to him to confirm that Mrs. Taylor had also returned after bumping into Pitt ... Waltham ... at his club on the eighteenth. "But he was courting you for months! Every time I turned around, there he was, delivering another towering bouquet of roses. He was determined to have you. He told me so himself, damn his eyes! He wanted you because you were mine. It had been like that since we were lads at Harrow. Everything I have he wants, and now you expect me to believe it is merely a coincidence you and he both left London on the exact same day. I am not a fool!"

Graciously, Mrs. Taylor permitted that perhaps he was not. "But can *you* think of another word to describe a man who believes he holds greater appeal than me? Do allow me to reintroduce you to my chief assets, Misses Magnificence and Spectacular," she said, drawing the tailcoat down over her shoulders, slowly revealing her breasts in the tight fabric of the dress.

It was a remarkable performance, Bea thought, the way she heightened the anticipation by exposing the skin tantalizing inch by tantalizing inch. Debenham's breath hitched as he opened his mouth to chastise her and found himself unable to speak as the bottle green cloth slid leisurely down her arms. No wonder the courtesan had managed to attain a measure of financial security for—

Wait a moment.

Bottle green cloth.

Muddy brown on the outside, the tailcoat was lined with bottle green fabric, and Bea shot to her feet to inspect it. She crossed to where Mrs. Taylor sat in a bergère and pulled on the edge of the left sleeve to remove the garment.

Mrs. Taylor cried out sharply, her right arm wrenching as Bea tugged the fabric behind the other woman's back. As the tailcoat slipped from her grip, she said sullenly, "I was not done making my point, your grace! I am at my most seductive when I am undressing, and I would defy Debby to say that Waltham is only interested in me because of a rivalry with him after watching me disrobe!"

"Oh, I think you have accomplished your goal," she said with a dismissive glance at his lordship, who still appeared glassy-eyed despite the interruption. Then she turned her attention to the lining of the tailcoat, examining it for imperfections. The left side was intact, but on the right, just below the armhole was a gash.

Aha!

Bea tightened her grasp as she turned to show Kesgrave and found him standing next to her. "It is a tear," she said, handing him the garment. "At least two inches long. And threads are missing. You can see how frayed it is."

Mrs. Taylor ceased pouting at once and pointed at Debenham on a trill of horror. "Good God, you *did* kill me!"

Although baffled by the proceedings, their host comprehended enough to deny the charge. "Why would you say that? I did not kill anyone. What is going on? Why are you all staring at my tailcoat like it is an atrocity? There is nothing wrong with it. It is a perfectly fine tailcoat. Give it here," he demanded, extending his hand. "It is mine, and I should like it back."

"Let us sit down," Kesgrave said smoothly, retaining his hold on the garment.

An ornery expression swept across Debenham's face, but he did not argue, lowering himself gingerly into the chair and resting lightly at the very edge. "Tell me please why are you so interested in my tailcoat."

Bea explained that they had found fibers matching its color in the gate in front of Mrs. Taylor's home. "We believe the coat was torn when the killer climbed over the gate."

His lordship received this information calmly. "And because my coat has a tear you think I murdered Miss Lloyd?"

"Well, you *did* threaten to chop off my head," Mrs. Taylor reminded him archly.

For the first time since they had arrived, his lordship ignored his former mistress and addressed himself solely to Bea. "That tailcoat ripped last week while I was taking it off. The fit is a little snug and usually my valet helps me remove it, but I was impatient and handled it roughly, causing the tear. I gave it to Higgins to have one of the maids repair the hole, which is how he was able to fetch it so quickly. You may ask him about it. I will summon him now," he said, waiting for her nod of assent before rising to pull the cord. "If you tell me when the murder took place, I shall consult my schedule and inform you precisely where I was at the time. I had nothing to do with Miss Lloyd's death and regret that my anger at Mrs. Taylor has led me to treat the matter cavalierly. My rivalry with Pitt ... *Waltham* ... is longstanding and does sometimes cloud my judgment. In this case, I have spent nearly two months seething over the way he cut me out. If I have leaped to the wrong conclusion based on the information available to me, then I do most humbly apologize, Mrs. Taylor ... Penny ... my darling."

Although Mrs. Taylor did not think the term of endearment was appropriate in light of their current relationship, she said she would not protest its use. "And I hope you will believe that I did not have contact with Waltham until after he received his inheritance, and even then we only exchanged correspondence. Even at his most charming, he was not charming enough to make me overlook his lack of standing. He was so ordinary compared to you. That is the truth."

Moved by the earnestness of her reply, for there was no hint of her familiar teasing or provocation, Debenham said that he did. "Thank you for that."

A knock on the door signaled the arrival of Higgins, who entered the room with the customarily blank expression of a Mayfair butler. If he thought it was strange that the Duke of Kesgrave was holding his employer's tailcoat, he did not reveal it by look or deed.

Gesturing to Bea, Debenham indicated that she should feel free to interrogate his servant and she wasted no time in ascertaining the salient information. Item by item, Higgins affirmed everything his lordship had said, only with more particulars. The garment had been torn on Wednesday last; the valet had shrieked in dismay at the damage, as the coat was only six months old; the housekeeper had instructed Higgins to leave the torn article in her office; and a new brown tailcoat had been ordered from Schweitzer and Davison in Cork Street on Friday.

In addition, Debenham owned two bottle green tailcoats, both in pristine condition, according to his butler. Higgins blanched at the prospect the Duke and Duchess of Kesgrave rifling through his employer's wardrobe and sighed with relief when the steward was able to prove that his lordship could not have been in Balfour Place at the time of the murder by providing the minutes of their weekly meeting, which had been held at eight-thirty.

Having established his innocence, Debenham rose from the chair with a relieved lightness and insisted on escorting Mrs. Taylor personally to the door. His wife was likely to return within the half hour and it would never do for her to find Misses Magnificence and Spectacular in the drawing room. Then he added on a more sober note how very sorry he was to hear of Miss Lloyd's death and asked if there was anything he could do to help Mrs. Taylor find the culprit. Assured that the duchess had everything in hand, he nodded. "Then I bid you goodbye, Mrs. Taylor. I wish you every happiness with Waltham."

The gracious sentiment was offered with begrudging stiffness, but the courtesan appreciated the effort and wished him well in return, her own voice warm with sincerity. "Now that I know you did not attempt to kill me, I can think upon our time together warmly."

As Mrs. Taylor settled into the carriage, however, she expressed her disappointment at Debenham's innocence. "I really thought he was the villain. His anger against me was so vitriolic, but I understand it better. I had no idea he bore such a deep resentment against Waltham and would have told him about Knutsford if I had thought it would put his mind at ease. I guess this means Audenshaw is the culprit, which is not shocking. A man who is weaselly about money is probably weaselly about all things, for all things *are* money. I suppose I shall never get my payment now," she said with a heavy sigh before asking Kesgrave if he thought she could apply to Lady Audenshaw for the funds after her husband was led to the gallows. Although it might seem as though she was adding insult to injury by making the request, Audenshaw was in fact a clumsy lover, so in that respect she had performed a sort of service for her ladyship by providing her with the opportunity to find a more proficient husband. "That should be worth a few hundred pounds, I should think."

The duke made no reply as Bea turned to glance out the window. It would never do for him to see her grin.

Chapter Ten

The answer was no: Mrs. Taylor should not apply to Lady Audenshaw for the funds, for her ladyship had no intention of settling her husband's debt. Indeed, she insisted that one did not exist, as the courtesan had accepted the compensation on offer and decided it was unsatisfactory only after the transaction had been completed.

"Yes, after I had the diamonds in the ring and bracelet appraised by a jeweler and found out they were paste," Mrs. Taylor pointed out dryly.

"Precisely," her ladyship said amiably. "It required the eye of an expert to reveal the truth. That is the quality of the reproductions Audenshaw gave you, and it is completely in accordance with the bargain you and he struck. It is not my fault you do not have an authority on your staff or even keep a loupe on hand to help you make decisions based on facts, not assumptions. That is a private domestic matter, and I think it is boorish of you to present yourself on my doorstep to pester me about it. A woman of your experience should know better."

Mrs. Taylor met this provoking comment with an amused

smile and said it was boorish of her ladyship to force her to call on Hell and Fury Hawes to seek his assistance in collecting the money. "He lives in Saffron Hill, which is such a noisome place. The smell gets into my hair, and my maid has to scrub it for a full ten minutes."

Although half of London trembled in fear at mention of the notorious crime lord, Lady Audenshaw received the news calmly. "A charming character, I am sure. If his reputation is to be believed, then he is a businessman who appreciates the validity of a well-negotiated contract. You accepted the compensation, and that is the end of that."

"Hell and Fury *is* a businessman, and as such he knows on which side his bread is buttered," Mrs. Taylor said with excessive civility, the tightly clutched fist at her side the only sign of her impatience. "He will do my bidding, as we have a long history of working together and he gets a percentage of all monies recovered. If Audenshaw refuses to see reason, Hawes will have no choice but to do something violent, such as break his legs or chop off a few fingers. It is bad for the crime lord business to appear weak."

A gasp in the doorway alerted them to a newcomer's presence, and Lord Audenshaw strode into the room, his face pale at the prospect of dismemberment. "I say, Louisa, stop arguing with the woman! I told you she cannot be reasoned with! She is not a rational creature!"

His wife disagreed, noting Mrs. Taylor's threats proved her rationality. "Intimidation is always the last recourse of the outwitted. She knows she has no argument to stand on and is resorting to brute force. You have won, my love."

"He has," the courtesan said affably. "And his prize is a thrashing courtesy of the scourge who rules Saffron Hill with an iron fist. Let me be the first to congratulate you, my lord."

Audenshaw's stricken expression grew starker as his wife swore Hawes would not dare harm a hair on his head and

Mrs. Taylor noted the accuracy of the statement as Hell and Fury typically worked from the toes up.

The argument devolved into a squabble, and Bea wondered how long she should allow it to continue before gaining control of the room. Although the bickering was not helpful in finding Millicent Lloyd's murderer, there was something inherently fascinating about the disagreement and Bea found it difficult to look away. Lady Audenshaw had very definite ideas about how affairs should be conducted, a fact that had been conveyed to them when she answered the knock herself. She had happened to glance out her window just as the duke's carriage drew to a stop and noted its occupants with interest. The oddity of the Duke and Duchess of Kesgrave accompanying her husband's bit of muslin anywhere, let alone to her own address, was utterly fascinating, and she darted down the stairs to discover the explanation as quickly as possible.

Owning herself deeply curious as to the reason for the visit, Lady Audenshaw did not allow them to explain. Instead, she led them to the drawing room, a lovely room decorated in bright yellows and blues, and announced that they were wasting their time. The debt had already been discharged, and any efforts to argue otherwise would result only in public humiliation, as her ladyship was prepared to show the contract to Mr. Twaddle-Thum himself if necessary. The esteemed gossip would readily note Mrs. Taylor's signature on the document, which clearly said the debt would be deemed settled on the acceptance of the proffered compensation.

Lady Audenshaw was particularly proud of that language, as she herself had inserted it into the agreement. It was, she insisted, a matter of necessity, as Mrs. Taylor's fee was more than the household could support and yet her husband had been adamant about having her. There was nothing to be done but figure out a compromise.

And the very best paste diamonds did not come cheaply!

They were merely cheaper than the genuine article.

As Lady Audenshaw made this vigorous defense, Bea considered the value of adding her ladyship to the list of suspects. Despite how ardently she defended the wording in the contract, she had to know it was just a trick. Mrs. Taylor had accepted the jewelry in good faith, and revealing the courtesan's naiveté to society would do little to endear her ladyship to it. In many respects, a mistress was but another tradesman, and it was not the thing to deceive the milliner.

Buying bonnets on credit, yes.

Fleeing to the Continent to escape payment for them, yes, too.

But duping the hatmaker was beyond the pale.

Noblesse oblige required one to stint shopkeepers honestly.

If Lady Audenshaw was truly set against giving Mrs. Taylor the compensation pledged to her, then killing her was a plausible alternative. Not yet thirty, she was a sturdy woman of average height whose strident air signaled a willingness to overcome all barriers in her way, including any number of wrought-iron gates. She would think little of donning her husband's clothes and settling the matter once and for all.

Examining Lord Audenshaw now, Bea noted that he appeared equally capable of scaling the gate. A decade older than his wife, he had the same stout frame.

What he lacked, however, was her sense of determined grievance.

Unlike his wife, he did not act as though it was unfair of Mrs. Taylor to complain of unfairness, and it was that blusterous outrage that gave her ladyship the advantage, as far as Bea was concerned. In comparison, Audenshaw seemed hapless, especially as the conversation turned to which body part he would like to lose first.

LYNN MESSINA

"You objected to your fingers, which I understand, for they are very useful," Mrs. Taylor said generously. "Do propose an alternative, and I shall inform Hell and Fury of your preference—as a gesture of goodwill, you understand. I do have fond memories of our time together, which was as intense as it was brief, and would not like that *all* to be tarnished."

Audenshaw sputtered incoherently, his wife called him a lackwit for succumbing to an empty threat, and Kesgrave, reaching the end of his tether, told them both to shut up. His lordship blanched at the duke's disdain, while his spouse, undaunted, proposed his ears.

"Tell your friend Mr. Hawes that he may start with my husband's ears, so that he will not have to listen to your nonsense anymore," her ladyship said.

"Jesus, Louisa!" Audenshaw said, his face growing completely white.

Lady Audenshaw told him to open his eyes to what was right in front of him. "The Duke and Duchess of Kesgrave! They are too sanctimonious to allow a crime lord to chop you up into small pieces. They believe killers should be brought to justice regardless of how justified the murder was, and they arrived with her in their carriage. I saw it from my window. They *brought* her here."

To some extent, her words had the desired effect, for he did indeed open his eyes, as wide as saucers in fact, and then cried, "I didn't do it!"

Scowling irritably, his wife snapped, "What are you prattling on about now?"

"The Duchess of Kesgrave's much-vaunted skill at identifying murderers," he said, lowering his voice as he darted a surreptitious look at Beatrice, as if to hide his interest. "If she is here, then someone has been killed. I am merely stating clearly and for the record that I had nothing to do with it. *I* have not killed anyone."

"And you think *I* have?' Lady Audenshaw replied, stiffening.

Her husband appeared to shrug. "Well, they are here to interview you, not me. I just wandered into the room to see what all the fuss was about. I could hear the disagreement from my study."

"Well, if that is the thanks I get for trying to curb the worst of your excesses, then I shall move home with my mother and allow you to bankrupt the estates within the year," she replied on an angry huff, turning to stamp out of the room. "See if I care!"

Before she had gotten halfway across the floor, Kesgrave exhorted her to sit down. "You too, Audenshaw. You are both suspects in the murder of Millicent Lloyd."

Her ladyship stiffened in insult, her lips tightening as she smothered the reply that rose to her lips, and lowered gingerly to the chair nearest to her. Then when she was settled, per the duke's request, she said with quiet dignity, "I cannot speak for my husband, but I do not know anyone called Millicent Lloyd. I am sorry to hear of her death and am happy to assist the duchess in any way I can. Please tell me what I can do."

Audenshaw, finding something deeply unsettling in his wife's sudden assumption of the social graces, glared at her balefully before insisting that he did not know the girl either. "I have never even heard the name before this moment."

Mrs. Taylor, who had seen the wisdom in complying with Kesgrave's request to shut up, noted that his statement was decidedly inaccurate. "Millie was my dearest friend, and I am certain you have heard me speak of her."

Flinching at the correction, his lordship rushed to explain that he had not realized that Millie was Millicent Lloyd. "You might have mentioned her in passing. Yes, I am certain now that you did. She liked to ape your ways. You found it very irritating, I believe. You wished that she would cultivate her own style rather than stealing yours."

"There, your grace," Lady Audenshaw said airily. "Ralph has identified the culprit for you. It is Mrs. Taylor. I trust that resolves our business and hope that you will call again under more auspicious circumstances."

Mrs. Taylor, lauding the other woman on her newest attempt to avoid her debt, said she could not be the perpetrator of the crime when she was in fact its victim. "The duchess has confirmed that the killer meant to murder me, not Millie, and is here at my request. She knows your husband's delinquency makes him the best suspect. He has the most to gain from my death, and I defy you to prove otherwise."

Although her ladyship's lips curved into a dismissive smirk, she did not offer a cutting reply and instead turned to Bea. "As my husband and I had nothing to do with Miss Lloyd's death, we are eager to prove it. Please tell us how we may do so."

"By establishing your whereabouts at the time of the murder," Bea said simply. "Miss Lloyd was killed yesterday morning sometime between seven and nine-thirty."

"Is that all?" her ladyship asked with a relieved smile. "Then we shall have this minor fracas sorted out in no time. At eight I was sitting at my vanity having my hair done by my maid Beth. She was forming my curls while the housekeeper and I reviewed the assignments for the day, as is my daily habit. You can ask members of the household where I am at eight on any given morning and you will get a uniform answer. I am always at my vanity having my hair done and reviewing assignments."

Naturally, Bea would do precisely that and would keep her

ladyship bracketed in the drawing room while she confirmed the information with the servants. "That is helpful, thank you. And what about you, my lord? Where were you during the stated time period?"

A warm pink suffused his cheeks as he repeated the question, seemingly confused by the query. Then he rubbed his chin with his thumb and forefinger as he considered the answer. "Well, let's see, yesterday at eight I was in Hyde Park taking exercise. It had been several days since I had gone for a ride because the weather has been so nasty, but yesterday I decided I could put it off no longer. And it was actually very nice despite being a bit soggy. My groom will verify that I ordered my horse to be readied at seven and I departed about a half hour later. I had a cup of coffee and toast in the dining room. The footmen and the housekeeper can attest to that as well. But as for someone who could report seeing me on the Row, I cannot name anyone specifically. There were few people out in the damp weather, and I did not speak to anyone. There is always Antigone, I suppose," he added with an awkward chuckle. "But she is a horse and as such cannot give testimony."

Although his wife sneered lightly at this attempt at humor, she remained stalwart in her support and insisted there must be another way to prove his innocence. "I know he could not have done it because he is singularly averse to violence. He refuses to participate in the fox hunt, even with Wellington in attendance. I find it most vexing because he has an excellent seat and it would be an opportunity to shine. But there it is. I am certain he would not kill a woman for any reason and especially not to discharge a debt that does not exist."

Mrs. Taylor scowled but managed to restrain her reply.

Bea told Audenshaw to summon his valet.

Taken aback by the request, he stared at her blankly for

several moments, as if uncertain he had heard her correctly. His wife, however, understood enough to rise at once and pull the cord. The footman, appearing almost immediately, dashed off to fetch Chalmers.

"I say, this is highly irregular, your grace," Audenshaw said, watching the byplay with an expression of concern. "He is the best of good fellows, devoted to my needs and adept with a cravat, but he does not attend to me at the park. I do not believe I have ever left the house in his presence."

Returning to her seat, his wife patted him gently on the head and assured him everything would be all right. "The duchess has a tactic in mind, and I am certain it is to your benefit," she said, then turning to smile brightly at the servant as he perched hesitantly on the threshold. "Chalmers, do come in. The Duchess of Kesgrave would like to speak to you. Should he stand, your grace, or would you like him to take a seat?"

Although Bea had no particular preference, she knew from experience that servants found it discomfiting to sit in her presence. As such, she assured the valet that standing was fine and then asked the last time his lordship had worn his bottle green tailcoat.

Chalmers's eyes darted to Audenshaw.

It was only a moment, a fleeting flit to the right, but it was most definitely meaningful, and Bea wondered at its significance. "Look at me, please, not your employer," she said sternly.

A muscle in the valet's cheek twitched at the instruction as he replied, "Yes, your grace. I'm sorry, your grace."

But still he did not answer.

His reticence indicated something, and although Bea knew better than to assume the implication was guilt, it certainly did not suggest its opposite. "Lord Audenshaw's bottle green tailcoat—when was the last time he wore it?"

Chalmers mumbled a reply.

He was reluctant to answer, which suggested he knew something nefarious indeed. Perhaps the debt to Mrs. Taylor weighed on Audenshaw more heavily than his wife supposed. "Could you please repeat that?"

The valet straightened his back and said clearly, "Never."

Lady Audenshaw gasped.

His lordship lowered his head in shame before stiffening his resolve and saying with defiance, "I told you green is not my color!"

Irked by this explanation, she insisted that it was every-one's color. "That is why it is so fashionable. Bottle green is flattering to all! Even my brother, whose skin is so sallow he looks like a bowl of curdled milk, is improved by it. I cannot believe you have never worn it a single time. It was my birthday present to you last year. Weston made it! Do you not realize how much money it cost? The buttons alone could have paid for that dancer in Van Leeuwen Park for two months!"

Flushing at the nature of the accusation, his lordship nevertheless held his ground, insisting the tailcoat make him look like an evergreen.

His wife scoffed. "Do not be absurd. You are too squat to be a tree."

Audenshaw glared at her with ardent dislike as the valet rounded his shoulders contritely, as if the argument were all his fault. If only he had given a less decisive answer! He should have claimed to not recall or gestured vaguely at the recent past.

As his lordship descended into smoldering silence, Kesgrave asked Chalmers to escort him to the dressing room so that he may inspect the tailcoat himself. The servant volunteered to bring it to him, but the duke demurred, explaining that he wanted to confirm Audenshaw did not possess other garments in bottle green.

Roused from his sulks by the insinuation, his lordship smiled self-righteously at his wife and said, "You see, my dear, my aversion to the blasted color is going to free me from suspicion. Whoever killed Miss Lloyd had some association with bottle green. I have just saved us from being a nine days' wonder, which you will agree is equal to the price of the tail-coat in terms of social currency. Here, your grace, let me show you the way rather than my valet."

Bea told him he would remain here, which drew a grin from her ladyship, who pointed out the imbecility of thinking the suspect would be allowed to examine the evidence. "One does not have to be a devoted reader of Mr. Twaddle-Thum's column to know the duchess abides by common sense."

Even so, one *was* a devoted reader of Mr. Twaddle-Thumb's column, and while the duke was off examining her husband's clothes, Lady Audenshaw sought to get a sense of how terrible it was to have a scurrilous gossip reporting her every move. Although Bea refused to commit to anything more strongly felt than "unpleasant," she persisted in her queries until her husband ordered her to leave their guest alone.

"Can you not see you are making her uncomfortable?" he barked.

In fact, Lady Audenshaw could not, for she was consumed by her own uneasiness in having to play host to her husband's mistress. "I have never been so mortified in my entire life. My mother said you would do this to me."

"Ever so briefly," Mrs. Taylor interjected. "And to whom a debt is still owed. If you want to be embarrassed by something, your ladyship, it should be your parsimony. You are a skinflint, which is worse than being a lightskirt. At least I am honest in my dealings."

Desperate to preempt another argument between the two women, Audenshaw waved at Bea to gain her attention and asked who the other suspects were. "I cannot be the only one you are investigating. There must be dozens! What about Debenham? He hates her with a fiery passion. Just last week he was placing lewd wagers about her in the betting book at Brooks's. Some of them even put *me* to blush! Barlow, of course. He believes she is responsible for his elder brother's death on the Continent, which is a daft conclusion. Anyone who knew the boy could see the wild streak in him. He once ran across burning coals on a dare. Scorched his pants beyond repair! But I suppose we cannot expect a grieving brother to be logical, which makes him an excellent suspect, certainly better than I, who abhors violence. And Netherby! You are talking to that cawker, too, I trust. He stares at Penny's windows from across the road at all hours of the day and night, writing doggerel about the exquisite pleasure of being near her. I was compelled to sit through a recitation of 'To the High Priestess of Love Who Envelopes Us All in Her Glow,' which had eight verses and lacked meter. Listening to it was more painful than poking oneself with a hot brand."

Mrs. Taylor laughed throatily and said Netherby bound his verses—lovely poems, not doggerel—in a little book each week and had it delivered to her home. "It is charming and sweet. The boy is harmless, like an eager puppy."

"There is nothing harmless about a young man's passion, especially if it is thwarted," Audenshaw said. "It can turn to hate in the blink of an eye."

Even so, Mrs. Taylor refused to consider the possibility, insisting with a wave of her hand that his lordship was being needlessly dramatic to remove the focus from himself. "You are the culprit, I am certain of it!"

Kesgrave, returning to the room in time to hear the comment, observed that it was unlikely, as Audenshaw possessed only the one green coat and it was in excellent condition. Although her ladyship was pleased by her husband's exoneration, she could not help grumbling, "Well, I should hope so for the amount of wear it has gotten."

Before Audenshaw could voice the irritated reply that rose to his lips, Bea stood abruptly, thanked the couple for their time and insisted they could find their own way out. She did not add that they should feel free to resume their bickering in private, but of course they did not require her permission. As soon as the drawing room door was closed behind them, she heard the peevish snarl of Lady Audenshaw as she called her husband a bush. Mrs. Taylor snickered.

Once in the carriage, the courtesan lamented the necessity of enlisting Hell and Fury Hawes's help in collecting the monies owed her. It was an option she generally tried to avoid, but Lady Audenshaw would not relinquish a farthing without further inducement. Thus, she would provide it posthaste.

But Mrs. Taylor had no sooner made the declaration than she recalled her situation and realized she could not go haring off to Saffron Hill to secure the crime lord's assistance. Her life still hung in the balance, and the last suspect on her list had just been exonerated.

With her murderer at large, she really would have to check herself into Newgate—state side!—to ensure her safety.

Crestfallen, she stared at Beatrice, who noted that misery only heightened the other woman's beauty. Her pale blue eyes glittered lustrously as tears threatened to spill onto her delicate cheekbones.

Bolsteringly, Bea told her not to despair. "We will discover the truth. It is still early in the investigation—scarcely two days—and we have reason to be optimistic. The swatch from the tailcoat is an excellent piece of evidence, and I am confident it will lead us to the truth. And now we have Netherby. Even if he is the harmless puppy you believe him to be, Audenshaw says he saw him loitering in the square across from your home on several occasions. Perhaps he was mooning about yesterday morning and witnessed something significant. It is certainly worth a conversation, and in the meantime, you can expand your list of suspects, perhaps by adding more wives in the mode of Lady Audenshaw. What about Lady Debenham or even St. Ives's mother? If she found out Dudley gave you her pearl earrings, she might have decided to get them back at any cost. Have you checked to see if they're still in your jewelry box?"

"Netherby," Kesgrave said sharply. "What does he have to do with any of this?"

Although the severity of his tone indicated he found the information disturbing in some way, Bea did not draw attention to his discomfit, merely explaining that he was among Mrs. Taylor's admirers. "While you were gone from the room, Audenshaw observed that the young man was quite smitten with her and frequently lingered on her road simply to be near her. He suggested that Netherby's love might have turned to hate, which would make him a viable suspect."

"I am sure it is nonsense," Mrs. Taylor said firmly. "He is a sweet boy—atrocious poet but very sweet boy. If you think he will provide us with useful information, your grace, then let us do call on him at once. With every name we eliminate, I feel the noose tightening around my neck, and it is a most unpleasant sensation."

As Bea was of the same mind, she raised her hand to rap her knuckles against the roof of the carriage to indicate a change in direction to Jenkins, but the duke forestalled her with a reminder of the Kempton ball that evening. "We will leave Penny at Miss Lloyd's residence as planned and call on Netherby in the morning."

Although Bea had forgotten all about Lady Diana's come-out, she did not think the hour was so late that they had to rush home to dress for it. Kesgrave was merely making an excuse to put off the visit with Netherby for some reason. Curious what that could be, she agreed to postpone the interview.

Displeased by the delay, Mrs. Taylor turned her lips down in an exaggerated pout as she deplored the wretchedness of her situation. Surely, there was some other option available to her, for pretending to be her dead friend was very disagreeable. "Having to give one-word answers to limit your exposure when you really want to explain the importance of attaining the ideal temperature for a cup of tea. Millie's housekeeper serves it much too hot. I actually burned the roof of my mouth. And I could not even yelp in pain, lest they realized Millie never yelped. Are you absolutely certain there is no room for me at Kesgrave House?" she asked, a wheedling note entering her voice as she peered at the duke out of the corner of her eye, as if too timid to look upon him directly. "I am a small woman and take up very little space. I could sleep in a linen closet like a fairy in a children's story. Nobody will have the least idea I am there."

Bea very much doubted it. If restricting herself to single-word answers was difficult for the courtesan, then saying nothing at all would be completely impossible.

Kesgrave, refusing to consider the proposal, suggested she stay at an inn and even offered to stand the expense. Mrs. Taylor's expression, which had brightened at the offer, immediately grew gloomy again when she discovered the duke meant the Swan with Two Necks in Lad Lane, not the Pulteney.

On a heavy sigh, she allowed herself to be returned to Miss Lloyd's residence.

As soon as the carriage resumed its progress, Bea asked

who Netherby was.

"Sylvester is Hartlepool's nephew," he replied curtly. "He *is* a cawker, all bluster and nonsense and poorly considered scrapes. Hartlepool had mentioned the boy was making a cake of himself over an older woman but did not say her name—either out of consideration for me or embarrassment to himself, I see now. Netherby could not have picked anyone more unsuitable if he spent a month thinking about it. I shall have to talk to Hartlepool first. He will not appreciate his nephew being involved in one of your murder investigations. He promised his sister he would look out for the puppy, and it has not been easy. Netherby refused to lodge with his uncle and instead took a ramshackle little house in Lexington Street. Agreeing to pay an astronomical rent for the season was the first of many mistakes he has made."

Although Lord Hartlepool was among Kesgrave's oldest friends, Bea had spoken to him only a handful of times. They had been introduced at Lord Stirling's ball and had conducted a polite exchange, each making banal observations about the duke when the conversation lagged. Her own mind had been distracted by recent revelations regarding her childhood, and she suspected the earl was also preoccupied. Since their initial meeting, they had discussed only the weather and the running conditions at various racecourses across the country.

Hartlepool bred and raced thoroughbreds.

Bea did not doubt that he was capable of conversing intelligently on a wide variety of subjects—and no doubt he was interesting and engaged in all his dealings with Kesgrave—but having found a topic that elicited reliably enthusiastic replies, she was unwilling to risk further awkward silences.

Naturally, his lordship was welcome to ask her questions, but he seemed singularly uninterested in her thoughts.

As it was still early, she asked Kesgrave if he wanted to call on his friend now.

"That is not necessary," he replied. "Hartlepool will be at the Kempton ball tonight. I will speak to him then. He will not be pleased. He has spent three months doing everything possible to cover up Netherby's scrapes so that the boy's mother would be none the wiser, including bribery and minor extortion, if the stories are to be believed and I expect they are. That will all be for naught if Mr. Twaddle-Thum writes a column about him."

Bea nodded and asked if he thought Audenshaw's theory had merit. "Could Netherby's infatuation have turned to infuriation as Mrs. Taylor remained indifferent to his advances? He said he often saw him lingering in front of her home. I find the idea of his hovering like that unsettling, as if he were a hunter stalking a deer. Perhaps he began to perceive her as prey as she rejected his suit week after week."

Rather than respond directly to her query, he recalled that Mrs. Taylor had mentioned something about poetry. "Did the puppy also write odes to her beauty?"

"Several reams apparently," she replied. "He bound them weekly in a little book and had them delivered to her."

"I think that is the best place to start, then," he said firmly. "Men have been using poetry for centuries to give voice to their feelings. If Netherby's adoration had begun to turn to hate, then we may find evidence of it in his odes. Tonight, I will inform Hartlepool of Miss Lloyd's murder and explain our interest in his nephew only in terms of what he might have seen. There is no reason to hint that he is a suspect, especially since we have yet to determine he is a suspect."

It was a sensible course. A more thorough understanding of the situation would permit them to ask questions that were more accurately targeted. There was no reason to rush into an interrogation armed with only half-baked notions. It was better to proceed slowly and with precision.

But even as Bea acknowledged the practicality of the approach, she could not help but feel as though half-baked notions were central to her process. Every investigation began with a niggling sense that something was amiss. Sometimes, such as in the case of Mr. Huzza's exploding steam engine, she could not even articulate her disquiet, and it was only through conversations with various relevant parties that a picture began to emerge. If she waited until she saw the events clearly, she would never figure out what she was looking for. Interviews led to unintended slips, which resulted in unexpected revelations.

Suspects, pressed for answers they had not meant to give, often said more than they planned—and occasionally more than they realized they knew.

Informing Hartlepool of her interest in his nephew would eliminate the element of surprise. Netherby would have an opportunity to arrive at answers before she even posed the questions. It did not matter that the callow youth was not yet a suspect; what she regretted was the loss of an unmediated response. Even if Netherby had nothing to do with the murder, he had to possess some awareness of the inappropriateness of his behavior. A gentleman did not press his suit where it was not welcome, and loitering in front of a woman's home to make her ever mindful of his presence was to exert a coercive effect.

Subtle intimidation was not how one conducted one's affair in a modern society, and to counter the impression that he had comported himself poorly, he might alter the narrative. To evade the judgment of his uncle or even the duke, Netherby might claim to have been far from Balfour. He could withhold vital information that might lead to the identification of the killer.

The warning to Hartlepool could have profound implications for her investigation.

Furthermore, Sylvester Netherby was not *not* a suspect. Mrs. Taylor adamantly refused to believe he was dangerous, but Bea was not certain the courtesan's opinion held much stock. Although her success indicated a profound under-standing of the male mind, she seemed incapable of seeing anything that was not firmly in her line of vision. The suspects she proposed were only those men who had issued threats to her directly—and within the past few months. Lady Audenshaw, whose pragmatic outlook and willingness to use trickery hinted at a potentially lethal indifference, was nowhere on her list.

Perhaps Mrs. Taylor had made the same mistake with Netherby.

Even more worrying, Bea allowed, was the possibility Mrs. Taylor had made the mistake with Hartlepool. Kesgrave had just admitted that his friend employed bribery and extortion to protect the greenhorn nephew's reputation as a means of insulating himself from criticism. He might have decided that killing the object of his nephew's fascination was an accept-able way to solve an intractable problem. Judging by his dismissive treatment of Bea, he did not hold women in particularly high esteem. Possessing neither beauty nor youth, she had nothing that required his attention, and not even Kesgrave's imprimatur was enough to persuade him otherwise.

Naturally, yes, your grace, all people who dislike you are inevitably murderers, Bea thought wryly as she composed the outlandish theory. If that was the criterion she was going to use, then there was a librarian at the British Museum she should add to the list as well as half a dozen members of Parliament who had scowled at her with ardent dislike during Mrs. Palmer's political salon earlier in the week.

Determined not to let her own prejudices interfere with her investigation, Bea agreed to the duke's suggestion.

Chapter Eleven

❦

A lthough Bea did not require confirmation of the duke's story involving Miss Lark, she was curious to hear an account of the incident from Sidmouth's perspective. During his tenure as home secretary, his lordship had demonstrated little empathy or patience for the plight of the common man. Famously high in the instep, he preferred squashing all dissent to assessing the validity of each complaint, and if the army had been allowed to act on the informant's false information, he would have eagerly seized the opportunity to suspend the writ of habeas corpus.

She did not doubt it for a moment.

After all, it would have been such a waste to go through all that trouble to manufacture a crisis and then fail to exploit it.

As his scheme had been thwarted by an insignificant servant, whom he should not have been obliged to acknowledge, Bea expected him to still feel the sting of resentment three days later and was surprised to discover he harbored no bitterness against the presumptuous footman.

The reason for the home secretary's sanguinity, she

learned upon further examination, was the eradication of Miss Lark from his memory. In his version of events, Kesgrave visited the Home Office on his own to warn him of Mr. Fitch's duplicity. It was, he took pains to make clear, more like a social call during which the duke happened to mention his concern about the quality of spy the Home Office had lately begun to employ.

Chagrined on Miss Lark's behalf, Bea asked about the footman who had accompanied Kesgrave and provided the information.

Sidmouth laughed at the absurdity of the question and insisted she was confused. "I think you mean the duke's groom, who waited in the hallway during our discussion. I could not permit him to enter my office, not carrying the faint stench of horse as he did."

Of course he recalled *that* detail, she thought cynically. It was always easier to remember the particulars you invented at your convenience.

Unwilling to allow him this fiction, she noted that the duke took the gig on Friday, which he drove himself. Therefore, the stable smell could not have emanated from a groom. "Do you mean to say, my lord, that Kesgrave was the source?"

Although Sidmouth drew breath to refute the implication, he was not allowed to issue it, for Lady Abercrombie interrupted with an elegant wave of her hand. "So this is where you are, duchess! I have searched the entire ballroom only to find you hiding in the home secretary's shadow. If you thought a deep-seated abhorrence of politics would forestall my looking for you here, then you were very much mistaken. There is no unpleasantness I would not overcome to greet you properly. I do apologize, my lord, for intruding. Please do finish your conversation before I begin mine."

Sidmouth swore he had nothing pressing to add. "I was merely enjoying her grace's wit. She is so very clever," he said with a courteous bow before stepping hastily away. In a matter of seconds, he was gone, swallowed up by the crowd.

It was quite a crush, Lady Diana's come-out, and Bea was jostled roughly as the countess suggested they retire to a quiet corner for a tête-à-tête. "It is always worse near the refreshment table," her ladyship added.

Alas, they had not taken a dozen steps before their progress was impeded by Bea's aunt, who lamented how awful it was that the Rowland girl was so popular. "I cannot move an inch without knocking into someone. Your come-out was so much more civilized, Bea, for hardly anyone attended, just a few dozen relatives and an assortment of old family friends. I believe Mrs. Ralston and her daughters came, which was very flattering, for they could not know then that you would one day marry a duke. None of us did. It was beyond anything we could imagine. And yet somehow, here you are, swathed in jewels," she said, her eyes growing wide as she drew closer to the necklace her niece wore. "Good lord, Beatrice, are those the Matlock rubies? They're as fat as grapes. And those earrings! There are so many diamonds, I cannot begin to count them all. Does Kesgrave know you are wearing them? I should think he would want to keep them in a vault. And you have always been so careless of your possessions. Do you remember that doll I gave you when you came to us? You misplaced it almost immediately."

It was true, yes, in the most literal sense, for she had indeed lost Esther a mere month after getting her. But it was not an accident. Horrified by the toy's deformities—its missing eyes, its caked hair, its legs devoid of stuffing—she had left it in the dairy cart and hoped never to see it again.

Lady Abercrombie scoffed at this lengthy speech, which contained so many faux pas, it was impossible to identify which one in particular she found objectional. Vera stiffened at the implied censure, acknowledging the countess with a tight smile. The last time she had seen the other woman, she had been driving away from Kesgrave House in Vera's own conveyance, which she had taken without permission.

Vera had little patience for a carriage thief's judgments!

Despite her larcenous tendencies, her ladyship was still a member of the aristocracy, and Vera's inveterate awe of nobility would not allow her to harp on the deficiency. Instead, she continued as if the beautiful widow were not present, noting that the ballroom was so crowded, she had not been able to keep an eye on Flora. "But I know I should not worry because she is with Holcroft, who is so attentive to her. I would not expect such consideration from a man with so many disgraced connections. It does not make sense. Perhaps the stories about his godfather are merely malicious rumors made up by resentful barristers. Now *that* is something you should investigate, Bea. You could put your unabashed curiosity to good use for once," she said firmly, satisfied with the quality of her advice.

Oh, but it was fleeting.

Scarcely a second later, confusion darkened her features as she reviewed her words and realized she had made a generalization far more sweeping than she had intended. Obviously, identifying murderers so they could be punished for their crime *was* a good use of her appalling inquisitiveness. "Although I am not sure I comprehend the purpose in ruining a perfectly lovely country party by arranging for your hostess to be arrested for murder. It strikes me as an inconsiderate way to thank her for her hospitality, and the rooms were so very comfortable! Mine overlooked the lake and a sprawling green field. And of course I do not have to mention how wonderful the food was."

But of course she did, for she had never enjoyed eels so tender. They practically melted on her tongue.

And the tartare sauce!

Simply the ideal balance of tarragon and chervil.

It was exquisite.

Lady Abercrombie, whose disgust of Mrs. Hyde-Clare was a product of the incoherent woman's triviality and her treatment of Bea's mother, regarded her with contempt as she described the tableware at Lakeview Hall.

The piquancy of the forks!

She is going to say something snide, Bea thought, tensing in expectation of an acerbic remark designed to cut her aunt off at the knees. Almost certainly it would be about the pending Matlock heir, of which the Hyde-Clares had yet to be apprised. Nothing would wound her relative more than learning the information secondhand.

Aunt Vera, turning her fawning appreciation to the elegant chairs in the country home's dining room, paused to draw breath. It was a tactical mistake, for it provided her ladyship with the opening she needed to interrupt, which she promptly did by asking Bea if she may borrow the manuscript her mother had been writing when she died.

"I should like to read it myself with an eye toward securing a publisher for the work," she announced blithely, as though noting the expertise of the orchestra or how lovely Lady Diana looked in her white gown. "It is what Clara planned to do once she had finished it, and I think it would be a lovely tribute to her memory."

Aunt Vera's face lost all trace of color, and she opened her lips to issue a protest.

Alas, no sound emerged.

She was incapable of speech, even to voice a complaint, which was her default mode of communication.

It was precisely what Lady Abercrombie intended.

The manuscript in question was Clara Hyde-Clare's reply to that shocking polemic supporting the education of females: *A Vindication of the Rights of Women*. Whereas Mary

Wollstonecraft claimed that improving women's minds would benefit families, making them better helpmates to their husbands and better mothers to their children, Clara argued for education for education's sake. Girls should have the same opportunity to study as boys because they were human beings in search of knowledge and understanding.

It was horrifying, her position, scandalous and misguided and utterly ruinous to the pillars of society, and Vera could hardly breathe at the thought of such a tome entering the world with her surname on the cover.

"I have already mentioned it to John Thomason of Thomason and Zane, on the Strand," the countess continued with airy indifference, as though completely unaware of the effect her words were having on Aunt Vera, who appeared on the verge of swooning. "We spoke of it only in general terms, of course, for I am nothing if not discreet, but he expressed interest and looks forward to reading it when it is ready. I thought you could edit it, Bea, and perhaps write a foreword introducing the ideas and explaining what they mean to you —as an historical artifact, that is."

It was astonishing that Aunt Vera was still standing.

Using a youthful folly to tarnish the reputation of a long-dead woman whose tragic passing had recently revealed to be a grotesque murder was horrible enough. But to bring her daughter into it—*that* was an abomination.

Only a madwoman would suggest the Duchess of Kesgrave associate herself with a book advocating for the elevation of female rights and co-education.

It was clear from the expression on her relative's face that she genuinely believed that the Countess of Abercrombie had lost her mind.

"She is teasing you, Aunt Vera," Bea said gently.

"Am I?" the widow murmured thoughtfully.

Darting an irritated look at the vexing widow, Bea reiterated that the countess was merely making a joke at her expense. "She knows how easy it is to rile you up. Do not give her the satisfaction."

The countess laughed, then pretended to pout as she owned herself grievously hurt by her grace's observation. "As if I spend *any* time thinking about how my words affect your aunt. My interest in the manuscript is in earnest, and I do hope you will allow me to read it even if you won't consent to publication."

Color returned to Vera's face at the notion of being mocked, and a bright red flush swathed her cheeks. She did not immediately reply, for she required several deep breaths to regain her composure, but when she did speak, it was with a quiet dignity. "I shall leave the matter to you, Bea, as I trust you to know what is best for your mother's legacy. If you decide publication is appropriate, then your uncle and I will support you."

It was staggering.

To hear Vera Hyde-Clare profess faith in her niece, to watch her react with calm equanimity to a proposal that horrified her to her toes, was an utterly confounding experience for Bea. She knew her aunt was trying to make amends. In the months since she had discovered the truth about her parents' death, Aunt Vera and Uncle Horace had both sought to repair the damage they had done in their ignorance and small-mindedness. Nothing could compensate for the misery of her childhood, but knowing that their regret was sincere enough to spur them to action was a balm to her soul.

She was genuinely grateful to resent them a little less.

And now Aunt Vera was willing to court ruination as an act of contrition.

Bea, who often struggled with a recent pledge to give her relative the benefit of the doubt, suspected it would not be as difficult going forward.

Equally flummoxed by the response, Lady Abercrombie frowned peevishly at Vera for spoiling her fun. She could not ridicule the woman if she refused to recognize the taunt.

It was, Bea noted with amusement, a brilliant stroke on Aunt Vera's part, and although her relative had not intended to outmaneuver the countess, she recognized a successful tactic when she stumbled across it. Consequently, she leaned forward slightly and mentioned that her second cousin on her mother's side also oversaw a publishing company. She could not recall its name, but she was certain it was based in Brighton, somewhere near the Royal Pavilion. It started with an R, she thought. "Reinhold? Reginald? No matter, I will find out if necessary. I am eager to lend my assistance, my lady, should Bea give the project her blessing. It is entirely up to her. I trust her implicitly."

Her ladyship, curtly refusing the offer, promised Bea she would seek her out later in the evening for their tête-à-tête. "We have much to discuss," she added pointedly before excusing herself to say hello to Lord Larkwell. As she walked away, she passed Waltham, and her nod of greeting signaled a familiarity with the new peer.

Catching sight of Bea only a few feet away Waltham approached and bid her good evening. After securing an introduction to Aunt Vera, he begged for a private word with her grace, which Mrs. Hyde-Clare graciously permitted. She was always delighted to perform a service to the nobility, and arranging her absence was among her favorite to provide. "I will go in search of my daughter, whom I have not seen since we arrived. I am not worried because she is here with Mr. Holcroft. Perhaps you know him? He is an upstanding young man of fine moral character despite the immorality of his relations. I am determined not to let the degeneracy of his family tease my nerves."

Uncertain how to receive this declaration, Waltham smiled politely.

It was a common reaction to her aunt, Bea thought.

His lordship began with an apology for interrupting her conversation. "I hope it was not about something pressing. I already feel awful asking you about the infernal situation in this lovely setting, and yet I could not resist the opportunity to find out what you know. I had a note from Piddlehinton this morning asking if I knew where Penelope was because he lost her. Is that not a damnable thing?" he asked with a bitter laugh. "A magistrate who cannot keep track of his prisoners! He says she ran away but how do we know she was not taken by the killer? When I spoke to her yesterday, she was resigned if not excited about going to Newgate to keep herself safe, which sounded like daft nonsense to me. Even so, I smothered my own horror and did what I could to bolster her courage. And now I am meant to believe she changed her mind without reason? I find that highly suspicious. I am consumed by anxiety for her. Please tell me, your grace, if you think I am making myself sick with anxiety for no reason."

"You are making yourself sick with anxiety for no reason," Bea said, duly following his command.

Receiving no comfort from her reply, Waltham chastised her for telling him what he wanted to hear. "You must be honest with me. Could she have been taken by the killer? Might she already be dead? Or is she wandering the streets of London alone and scared? Or is she the killer? I cannot believe Penelope would harm a hair on Millicent's head. They were such dear friends. Please tell me what you think. I am as tortured by the idea of her at the mercy of a hardened killer as I am by the thought of her hanging on the end of a gibbet. I got very little sleep last night worrying about it."

In his evening finery, he appeared well rested, the deep puce of his waistcoat adding a liveliness to his features, which

Bea knew from her own maid's skill could be more artifice than fact. But his rambling manner pointed to a deep apprehension, and she sought to assuage it by explaining why she believed the murderer had most likely made a mistake. Listing the factors that supported the conclusion, she ended by saying Mrs. Taylor could not be both things at once. "If she was meant to be the victim, then she cannot be the culprit. And it is to the killer's advantage that she stand trial for the crime, so he does not have an incentive to eliminate her. That is why I think she is hiding and safe."

Waltham nodded vigorously, but an eruption of laughter from a group of people near them made it difficult to hear his reply. She took a step closer. He was commenting on Mrs. Taylor's resourcefulness. "I have never met a woman more capable of ensuring her own welfare. And what of your investigation? Did you follow my advice and speak to Barlow? You will not find anyone in London who hates her more."

Bea nodded. "Kesgrave and I called on Barlow yesterday afternoon, and he has an alibi for the time of the murder. He could not have done it."

Waltham's face darkened with disappointment as he admitted he had hoped Barlow was the villain. "He is a sanctimonious prig, and I dislike him heartily. The thought of his going to prison for killing a woman of easy virtue has an appealing irony. I had even allowed myself the petty pleasure of imagining the headline announcing his arrest in the *Times*," he said with a hint of frivolity before letting out a discouraged sigh. "I suppose it is useless, then."

She assured him it was not. Although the list of suspects had grown thin, she was confident they could find new names to add and then there was the encouraging prospect of Hartlepool's nephew. "Through our interviews we have learned that one of Mrs. Taylor's suitors had made a habit of lingering in the square across from her townhouse at all hours, including early in the morning. There is a good chance Mr. Netherby saw the killer. Even if he did not witness the event itself, I am confident he will have useful information."

Bea spoke with more optimism than she felt in an attempt to increase her own confidence as much as Waltham's. Usually by this point in the investigation she had several intriguing possibilities, and she found the lack of them demoralizing. Despite her remarks to Mrs. Taylor earlier, two days was not in fact early in the investigation. It was a good deal into it, for most of her cases resolved within two or three days, and she was beginning to feel a little desperate. It was why she had put Hartlepool on the list for not wanting word of his nephew's attachment to Mrs. Taylor to reach his sister.

Obviously, she did not genuinely suspect him for so paltry a reason.

The problem was, she had so few suspects, she thought now, casting about for more promising contenders. With Lady Audenshaw's antipathy in mind, she wondered if Debenham's wife also bore a grudge against the courtesan. There was Mrs. Marshall as well, whose dislike of her neighbor had been mentioned several times. She lived right next door, which gave her the advantage of proximity and familiarity with the household's routines. Then there was the fishmonger with whom Mrs. Taylor was entangled in a dispute. She had made the comment only in passing but perhaps it was a source of genuine contention.

And, of course, there was always Piddlehinton, whose determination to see his dear friend hanged for murder was discouraging if not outright suspicious. Attempting to remove Miss Lloyd's body before Bea could examine it was either a bid to thwart her investigation or an outrageous resolve to hold to established procedure at the expense of decency or kindness.

Waltham, owning himself heartened by her conviction, swore he would not abandon hope and begged her to call on him if there was anything he could do to aid in the investigation. She promised she would just as the quartet near them erupted in laughter again and she had to lean in closer to hear his reply, which was still muffled by the chatter next to her. All she heard was *fable,* which could not be correct, and with an awkward apology, she asked him please to repeat it.

He smiled warmly and lowered his head, drawing nearer to her ear. "May I get you something from the refreshment table? The ballroom is quite warm, and I find that I am parched," he said, so close now she could feel the brush of his breath on her cheek and detect a faint hint of aniseed in the air.

Bea was struck by it at once, the warm scent of anise, and thought nothing of it for several seconds as she gently refused his offer. It was a common enough flavor, for it was in absinthe and fennel, and he could have come by it in a variety of ways.

But then it hit her, the strangeness of the coincidence, his breath smelling of licorice and the licorice candy on the landing. Mrs. Taylor said her exhausted friend had dropped it while climbing the stairs, but what if it had fallen out of a tear in a pocket created by a very sharp gate?

Waltham, no, it did not make sense, she thought, as he nodded at her and took a step away, her hand darting out as if to grab his wrist and tug him back to her side.

And then she would do what?

Order him to exhale so she could smell his breath again?

Obviously not, no, for that would be patently insane, and there was little to be gained from her confirming her own conclusion. It had to be someone without a preconceived notion, and she looked around for the duke.

Kesgrave would do it.

He was always game for a challenge, and this assignment was not as awkward as slipping his hand into another man's trouser pocket, a service he had performed without complaint or protest.

But as her eyes swept the room, he was nowhere to be found.

Oh, wait, there he was, performing the cotillion with Lady Diana herself.

Devil it!

Growing increasingly frantic, she searched for a substitute.

Russell, who liked an adventure.

Mrs. Palmer, with her matter-of-fact attitude.

Flora, who delighted at placing herself at the center of any exploit.

All she saw was Nuneaton.

He would never agree, she thought, imagining the satirical remark he would make about a man's breath belonging to himself, then urging her to save her own for more likely requests. Nevertheless, she grabbed his sleeve to halt his progress and stoically met his gaze when he glared at her stonily.

Realizing it was she, Nuneaton softened his expression and chided her manners. "I appreciate the enthusiasm, your grace, but I do not think—"

"You must smell Waltham's breath," she announced without preamble.

"No, I must not," he said firmly. "As I am neither a physician nor a veterinarian, the breath of man and beast is not my milieu."

Ignoring his refusal, she gently pushed him forward. "He is fetching himself a drink, so there is no time to lose. Please! It is a matter of life and death, I swear. I would not ask otherwise."

Amiably, he said, "I hate you," and walked away.

But in the direction of the refreshment table!

Relieved, Bea watched him stride with his usual grace across the floor until he was only a step behind Waltham. The most reliable ruse from that position was to bump him awkwardly on the shoulder or step on his heel and then smell his breath when he turned to issue a protest. But the elegant viscount could not dip into clumsiness, not even in service of a greater goal, and he somehow managed to place his leg at such an angle that it caused Waltham to knock into him.

Waltham turned in surprise and uttered a few words to Nuneaton, presumably an apology, for the latter nodded absently and continued to the refreshment table. Once there, he picked up a glass of lemonade before returning to Bea and handing her the beverage.

"I hope it is warm and bitter," he said.

Grateful for his assistance, she dutifully took a sip and reported that it was awful. "But I will finish the entire drink in penance," she said, then looked at him expectantly.

He stared back for several long seconds, then asked, "Whose?"

Confused, Bea tilted her head. "Excuse me?"

"To compel me to perform your absurd task, you said a life hangs in the balance," he reminded her. "I am now asking whose."

As it was a reasonable question, she did not hesitate to answer. Even so, she lowered her voice to make sure they were not overheard. "Penelope Taylor."

Although he could not have possibly anticipated her reply, he nodded as though the name was precisely the one he had expected to hear. "I have been anticipating this very development from the moment Twaddle began publishing sensational accounts of your escapades. Penny will do anything for attention, and she has always regretted the loss of a duke. All these years later and he was still the grandest feather in her cap. Did she tell you someone is trying to kill her?"

As this was remarkably close to what had actually happened, Bea stared at him aghast for a moment and then winced in embarrassment when she said, "Yes. But it seems to be true."

"Oh, you dear, sweet, foolish child," Nuneaton, oozing condescension. "I suppose Kesgrave has been gulled as well. Did she show you a broken planter and swear it had come within an inch of crushing her?"

"No, she showed us her friend's bloody corpse with five puncture wounds in the carotid artery," Bea replied, annoyed that she could not quite smother the hint of defensiveness in her tone.

"I see, yes," he said, although his expression remained doubtful. "In regards to my mission, which I discharged masterfully, as I am sure you will observe momentarily, the scent I detected on Waltham's breath was licorice. The burned note to it was unmistakable. And judging by the expression on your face, I can see that was the right answer. I wonder in what way."

"I am not entirely sure of that myself," she admitted softly before complying with his request to lavish him with praise for his deft handling of the assignment. "I was most impressed with the way you maneuvered Waltham into apologizing to you."

"I had to use the Barrington Feint—that is its official title —frequently during my tenure at Eton or I would never have gotten dessert," he explained with a deprecating smile as the duke joined them. "Kesgrave did not have to employ such measures because he was always tall for his age. Only runts had to resort to entrapment."

"Ah, but the Barrington Feint was a wonder to behold," Kesgrave said admiringly. "I can still recall the look of confu-

sion on Berthold's face as you nabbed the last plate of rasp-
berry fool from under his nose."

"I have not used the ploy in more than a decade, but I
brought it out of retirement as a favor to your wife, who
begged me to smell Waltham's breath," Nuneaton explained.
"The duchess is frequently outrageous, but I do think she
topped herself tonight."

Although the duke's look indicated he understood the
significance of the request even if its meaning escaped him,
he did not draw attention to it. Instead, he warned his friend
that there was worse to come.

Nuneaton refused to believe it. "Impossible!"

"Just wait until you are banished from Hoby's," he replied
with amusement.

As this horror was too terrible to contemplate, his lordship simply shook his head and walked away, causing Bea to
ask the duke why he was tormenting the viscount. "Now he is
going to be worrying about his standing with the bootmaker
for weeks."

"Why am *I* tormenting him?" Kesgrave asked as if
affronted by the query. "*You* are the one making him smell the
breath of our fellow party guests. I assume it is related in
some way to Miss Lloyd's murder. How so?"

It was not a question Bea could answer, not to her satisfaction, not in a way that explained Waltham's actions. She
knew only that he enjoyed Pomfret cakes and might be the
source of the one found on the staircase.

No, not might.

He was.

Bea would bet the library at Kesgrave House on it.

The candy had fallen out of the hole in the pocket of his
bottle green tailcoat. Mrs. Taylor said her friend scattered
them around her home, in charming little dishes on various
tables in assorted rooms, frequently offering them to friends

and visitors. It was not surprising that Waltham had developed a taste for them during their months together.

And yet none of it made sense.

Waltham had no reason to resort to murder. The young lord owed Millicent Lloyd nothing and was free to end their association in whatever fashion he deemed sufficient. That he had indulged in one last night of pleasure before informing her of his decision was in keeping with the bargain they had struck, and Bea could not fathom why a man who was already free of a commitment would kill to get out of it.

She could draw only one logical conclusion: He was not free of it.

If Waltham had been unable to extricate himself from the liaison, it was because Miss Lloyd retained some measure of control. She had a way to influence his behavior, and Bea assumed the courtesan was in possession of damaging information.

Blackmail was a tried-and-true form of manipulation.

Convinced it was likely, Bea imagined their final confrontation was more heated than the accounts provided by Mrs. Taylor and Waltham indicated—although not so contentious that it woke the servants, according to the information the former had provided that morning. The marquess had blithely dismissed Miss Lloyd's threat to start a rumor about the French pox as fleeting nonsense instantly regretted, but they had only his report. An hour later, however, Miss Lloyd was at her friend's house still prattling on about the pox, which meant she had not let the matter go. If that was the case, then Waltham might have had good reason to fear word of his condition circulating among the *ton*, especially if it was in fact accurate.

It was not implausible, was it, given Miss Lloyd's history in a brothel.

Maybe she knew he had it because she was the one who passed it to him.

If that was the case, then he would have two excellent motives: silence and revenge.

Bea examined the events from the assumption of Waltham's guilt.

First of all, he did not leave her home and return to his own as he and his tiger reported. The fact that the groom's description so closely matched his employer's, down to the use of the word *famished* for "hunger," intimated that the servant had been told what to say. Rather, Waltham remained outside Miss Lloyd's home. Bea could not believe he had anticipated that his mistress would don her pelisse and call on her friend at that hour. He had stayed for another reason, perhaps waiting an appropriate interval to pass before reentering the home. If he killed Miss Lloyd too soon, then he would be the obvious suspect.

Maybe he used the time honing his plan. He could not stride through the front door as was his custom. He would have to creep stealthily past the servants.

And how would he do it?

He also needed to figure out a means and a method.

Considering the complex factors that made murder an arduous undertaking, she wondered if she was overestimating Waltham's eagerness to strike. Accepting the inevitable, he might have lingered thoughtfully outside the residence as he contemplated the best way to kill Miss Lloyd. Then, while he was devising his plan, his victim obligingly stepped out of her house, presenting him with the ideal opportunity. Anything could happen to a lone woman walking through deserted streets a little after sunrise.

He must have hesitated.

Repulsed by the task before him, Waltham must have faltered in his determination, only regaining it when he saw her destination. Something about the prospect of the two women conferring compelled him to act.

His panic must have been overwhelming indeed if it moved him to kill his old lover in the bed of his new one.

It was a particularly vicious act, not only implicating Mrs. Taylor in the deed itself but also leaving her to find her friend with her throat pierced and her bedclothes drenched in blood.

Bea could not imagine anything more cruel.

But indeed she could, for Waltham had returned to Mrs. Taylor's home only a few hours later, bearing a bouquet of flowers and an eager affect.

The cold-blooded monster, taunting her with carnations.

And then she heard it again, the crash of the vase on the marble floor in the entry, the biting clap of shattering glass, and realized she had overlooked something vital.

The flowers.

Chapter Twelve

✿❀❀

As the orchestra began to play again, Bea gestured to the line of chairs along the perimeter occupied by companions and dowagers and suggested they talk over there, away from the press of the crowd. "Unless you have promised the set to someone."

Kesgrave's lips twitched as he replied, "Only my wife."

As he said the words, she recognized the familiar strains of the waltz, which he always saved for her. It was gauche, of course, to spend so much time dancing with one's wife, but he derived an inordinate amount of pleasure from twirling her around a ballroom. "I am sure there will be another, but if you would rather join..."

She trailed off invitingly.

"And wait to find out why you made poor Nuneaton smell Waltham's breath?" he asked, offering his arm to escort her to the far wall. "No, I would not. I am also keenly interested in how you bullied him into doing something so beneath his dignity."

Bea swore there was no coercion involved. "I merely appealed to his sense of decency."

The duke denied that his friend had one.

She smiled and conceded she might have begged a little as well. "But mostly he responded to my allegation that it was a matter of life and death. He is a better man than you give him credit for."

Kesgrave allowed this assertion to pass without comment and safely avoided a trio of matrons who tried to gain his attention by flapping their fans in his general direction. He feigned obliviousness beautifully, his eyes trained on a pair of seats toward the corner.

As they sat down, she explained that an agitated Waltham had sought her out to ask about Mrs. Taylor and the investigation. "As the laughter around us was too loud, he had to lean close to my ear to be heard, and I caught a hint of licorice on his breath."

Although his brow furrowed at this information, his confusion was fleeting and he readily connected it to the Pomfret cake on the landing. "Penny said it slipped out of Millie's hand while she was leading her up the stairs. But you think it was Waltham's. You think it fell out of his pocket—a pocket that was torn when he climbed over the gate."

"Precisely," she said, delighted as always by his ability to follow her line of thought. It would be so tedious to be married to someone who could only partially understand an implication. "Nuneaton confirmed it. He, too, detected licorice. I believe Waltham killed Miss Lloyd, although I cannot explain why. All I can think is she must have possessed sensitive information he did not want revealed. Recall, there was that rumor about his having the pox she said she would start. What if that was more than pure fancy? Could it be true?"

Although the duke did not dismiss the theory out of hand, he was far from persuaded. He did not think Miss Lloyd would be so cavalier with the information, for the rumor would cause her more damage than him. "She would not be able to continue to draw from the same grade of protector and most likely would have to return to the brothel where Piddlehinton found her. It was clearly an empty threat and Waltham recognized it as such."

Bea conceded the logic. A courtesan publicly identifying herself as pox-ridden was ruinous folly. "Something else, then. There has to be something she knew that he feared being exposed. Because he's the killer, Damien. I am certain of it. Recall yesterday, when he brought the bouquet. They were carnations."

"All right," he said in a measured tone.

"But he courted her with roses—a seemingly endless stream of roses in towering bouquets, according to Debenham," she pointed out.

"Pink carnations are a strangely uninspired gift from a man eager to consummate a new relationship," he replied with a glimmer of understanding. "And they are priced accordingly."

"Exactly, your grace," Bea replied with an approving nod. "Why waste money on a bouquet of beautiful roses when you are just going to drop them on the floor in stupefaction?"

Kesgrave, shaking his head in astonishment, murmured, "Diabolical."

"Perhaps, but the frugality will be his downfall," she observed with amusement. "Having decided to play the part of the eager suitor, then he should have played the part of eager suitor and brought a sufficiently impressive bouquet instead of saving a few farthings. It is not as though he cannot stand the expense if he hired Bedford's valet for twice his annual salary."

"No, I meant your deductive skills, Bea," he clarified, taking her hand in his and making gentle circles on the white silk of her palm. "They're diabolical."

A gentle flush colored her cheeks at the compliment, which astounded her, for she should be accustomed to his admiration by now, and issued a demurral. "It took me far too long to draw the connection. The juxtaposition of the plain bouquet and towering roses should have struck me as significant sooner. Regardless, Piddlehinton will not care."

The duke agreed that the magistrate would not find the evidence persuasive. Nor would he be swayed by a ripped tailcoat, assuming Waltham still had the incriminating garment in his possession. A man of Piddlehinton's ilk would much rather persecute a lightskirt whom he suspected was innocent than a lord whom he knew was guilty. "We will have to present him with incontrovertible proof."

"You mean such as a confession," Bea said pensively.

"I do, yes," he replied.

"It would require some manipulation," she observed, her mind beginning to buzz with possibilities as she contemplated the problem. "Presenting Waltham with the evidence we have compiled would elicit a shrug if anything. He would know we could not prove it. What if we discovered the information he killed Miss Lloyd to hide? We could use that to compel him to tell the truth."

Kesgrave was skeptical. He not only doubted the existence of a terrible secret but also could not conceive how its revelation would be more damaging than admitting to homicide. "The only thing worse than one murder is two murders, and I do not think Miss Lloyd would be foolish enough to threaten a man who had killed twice before. Be that as it may, I do not think there is harm in asking Penny specifically about a secret."

He added something about the intensity of Miss Lloyd's rage being overwhelming enough to cause an indiscretion, but Bea was no longer listening. She was stuck on what he had said prior to that remark: *The only thing worse than one murder is two murders.*

The title had come to Waltham unexpectedly through a circuitous route. He had inherited the earldom only after a distant relative succumbed to illness and the child's father fell from a cliff.

That was two deaths.

Something of her thoughts must have conveyed themselves to Kesgrave because he shook his head before she even uttered a word. "No, Bea, no."

But Bea pleaded with him to at least allow her to make the case. "Please, just give me a minute to put it together in my head," she said, closing her eyes so that she could think more clearly.

She began with the deaths themselves, locating their dates on the calendar. The boy died first, on Christmas, according to Waltham, with his father following four months later. She did not know the exact day, but based on what Mrs. Taylor had said, she could reasonably place it in the middle of April.

Waltham was in London on Christmas. Having encountered Mrs. Taylor in Hyde Park on Boxing Day for the first time, he could not have been in Bournemouth the day before. It was simply too great a distance to travel.

That meant he did not kill the boy.

Unless he was responsible for the infection itself.

It was, she supposed, a viable theory but also complicated to arrange and extremely difficult to prove.

Better to focus her attention on the second death, which would have been quite simple to execute. It did not require any particular skill or elaborate planning to push a man off a cliff. In that respect, Waltham could have easily done it.

In other respects, however, she was not so sure.

He was, she knew, absent from London in the middle of April. Debenham reported his leaving the city on April tenth, presumably in the company of the stunning Mrs. Taylor. In fact, the courtesan had been with Knutsford in Worcester, where she remained for two weeks. Waltham returned eight days later. By the time Mrs. Taylor herself was back in the capital, Waltham was gone again, summoned to Dorset after his cousin's tragic death.

Judging by those dates, Bea calculated that the previous marquess fell to his death within days of Waltham leaving London for an unknown destination.

Might it merely be a coincidence?

Without question yes, anything was possible.

But one fact was not speculative: With the death of the young heir, Waltham was suddenly and unexpectedly one heartbeat away from a marquessate. Having not been in the line of succession for the vast majority of his life, he was now at the front of the queue and all it would take to ascend to the prime position was one hard shove off a high cliff.

How easy it must have seemed!

And, she thought cynically, how easy it turned out to be.

No one suspected a thing.

Except Millicent Lloyd.

Ah, but she did not, not really, Bea realized, recalling again her threat to start a rumor about the pox. If it was a lie as Kesgrave insisted, then it was a lie created from whole cloth by a jilted lover in a fit of rage. If Miss Lloyd made one outrageous threat, then perhaps she made a dozen, all fictional, all hastily drawn from nothing, all hurled at Waltham in a vicious frenzy.

He said she recalled herself.

In his lordship's account, Miss Lloyd made a few mildly upsetting remarks and apologized sweetly, allowing him to take his leave on the best possible terms.

But what if that was not actually the case?

Miss Lloyd's subsequent behavior did not support the

claim that she coolly collected herself and bid her lover a pleasant adieu. She was still so furious she drank half a bottle of brandy and stormed out onto the deserted London street a little after daybreak to rail at her friend.

It was much more likely, then, that the parting was as acrimonious as the pox rumor intimated, and Bea wondered if Miss Lloyd had stumbled backward into the truth. Her rant in Mrs. Taylor's drawing room was nonsensical and sweeping, Bea thought, as she recalled the description: *She went on some strange tear about Hampstead Heath and the swimming ponds. She might have said something about gardening in diamonds. She laughed hysterically for several minutes, just giggling like a thief, and raged about fishing in a skiff. Oh, and then she told me I have an average house, which was the most baffling of all because my home is quite distinctive. Anyone who enters notes my audacious use of color and pattern.*

A great jumble, yes, but not all of it was incomprehensible blather. "Gardening in diamonds" was almost certainly a reference to the diamonds Kesgrave gave Mrs. Taylor in farewell, which she had recently worn to the Vauxhall pleasure gardens. Perhaps the jewels were another source of bitterness for Miss Lloyd, whose trinkets from suitors were never as beautiful or valuable. "Average house" was likewise not entirely inscrutable. Piddlehinton, citing the endless bickering between the two women, noted that Miss Lloyd had called her friend an "avaricious louse."

It all makes sense, she thought, repeating *Hampstead* and *Heath* over and over again in her head in an effort to hear the rhyme or adjacent word that might be germane.

Nothing.

She gave *swimming* and *ponds* the same treatment, ticking off fond, frond, bonds and blonds with increasing frustration before moving on to the next pair: fishing and skiff.

She heard it immediately—skiff and cliff—and wondered

if Miss Lloyd actually leveled the correct accusation at Waltham in her tumult of fury.

He must have known it was nonsense!

A scorned woman raining angry drivel on him like torrents of rain, she did not have knowledge of his evil deed or privileged access to his thoughts. She was merely spewing wildly, madly, vengefully, and even if she was determined to start an insidious rumor about the Marquess of Waltham, she would have very little chance of it taking hold. Her position among society was nonexistent, and she did not have the standing of someone like Mrs. Taylor. If her friend could be convinced to help spread the word, then perhaps the whispers might have started, but Mrs. Taylor had too much invested in his lordship's consequence to undermine it.

Waltham had nothing to fear and yet he stabbed his old mistress to death in his new mistress's bed and then returned a few hours later to ... what? she wondered.

Witness Mrs. Taylor's unraveling?

Confirm his scheme had proceeded as planned?

Offer himself as savior?

Bea could not fathom why he would return to the scene of the crime, a bouquet in hand, and it seemed like a particularly cruel stroke, the lovely carnations trodden underfoot in a simulation of shock.

Oh, but wait, she thought, as something about the trampled flowers played at the edge of her mind. The crushed blossoms. ...

The geraniums!

In the flower box in the front of the house—they were flattened. It was notable because Mrs. Booth had mentioned how well they were kept. Bright and perky, she had said, while Mrs. Marshall's petunias were straggly.

But when Bea had seen the flowers, they had looked

decidedly sad, as if someone had stepped on them with a boot.

Was it even possible?

No, the flowers were too high off the ground for them to be trampled underfoot, and the boxes themselves were too delicate to withstand the weight of a full-grown adult.

But flattened by elbows?

That was plausible, she thought, recalling the bucket, the one next to the door that the maid had put outside to get rid of the slop smell. Sarah had specifically said it needed to be aired out, yet when Bea saw it a short while later, it was facing down. Waltham had turned it over to use as a stool to increase his height, allowing him to listen at the window. Afraid of what his former lover would reveal, he had sought additional information.

And yet it still defied sense, for there was no danger in Mrs. Taylor having the information, false or otherwise. It was not as though she would pass it on to Mrs. Ralston or Twaddle.

Bea froze with a sudden start as the words Mrs. Booth overheard echoed in her head: *Here. I have paper. Let us write to him at once. What do you want to say?*

The *him* was Mr. Twaddle-Thum.

In her efforts to soothe her hysterical friend, Mrs. Taylor volunteered to write to the notorious gossip at once, and although it sounded like empty mollification to Bea, Waltham failed to detect the lilt of placation. Perched at the window, his forearms pressed into the soil as he struggled to hold his position, he heard only the threat.

And then he saw Mrs. Taylor sit down at her escritoire.

Could that really have been all it took to convince him his reputation and possibly his life were in peril? A few soothing sweet nothings and a dash-off missive, a missive that was— with no small amount of irony—written to him?

It was appalling and yet it made a horrifyingly simple sort of sense.

Bea opened her eyes and stared at Kesgrave. It was flimsy, she knew, her theory of why Waltham struck, and yet she was certain it was correct.

Having given the matter some thought himself, Kesgrave announced that he was willing to concede one murder. "Although you are prone to see foul play in every unlikely succession—"

"Not only Mowbray's father but his two elder brothers— all killed in a carriage accident," she said with meaningful emphasis. "The entire line wiped out in a single stroke. If that does not raise your suspicions, your grace, then I do not know what to say other than you're alarmingly trusting for a man whose own uncle tried repeatedly to kill him."

"It was a worn axle and a poorly shod horse," Kesgrave replied in a slightly bored tone, recognizing the reference immediately.

"Yes, yes, and the farmer with whom they collided was drunk," she said impatiently. "You are not saying anything I have not heard a dozen times before."

"Well, if you would stop implying the Earl of Mowbray murdered his entire family—"

"His mother still lives," she interjected. "And I believe there is an older sister."

"—then I would stop saying it," he continued as if she had not spoken. "Regardless, I agree there is reason to wonder about the previous marquess's death. It is not implausible for a father to either jump or stumble over the edge in a stupor of grief and brandy, but in light of subsequent events, murder does seem increasingly likely. But just the one murder, Bea. I cannot believe he killed the son as well. The boy died of a common childhood illness. There is nothing mysterious about it."

She agreed, citing Debenham's statements, which placed the suspect in London on the day the child died. "But after he died, Waltham saw an opportunity and did not hesitate to exploit it."

Kesgrave, who had also noted the neat alignment of Waltham's travel dates with his cousin's tragic accident, remained baffled by Miss Lloyd's part in the affair. He could not believe that Waltham was such a dunderhead as to embroil his mistress in his murder plot, and yet it was the only way she could have known the truth. "Regardless, it is the height of recklessness to threaten a known killer with exposure. Did she truly think he would simply capitulate to her demands?"

"Ah, but that is the thing: I do not believe Miss Lloyd knew she was threatening a murderer," Bea said, launching into the finer points of her theory. Kesgrave listened quietly, interrupting only once to reveal his surprise over her familiarity with the diamond necklace, which he assumed Mrs. Taylor would have sold years ago. Then he agreed with her explanation, not even quibbling over the paper-thin motive she ascribed to Waltham.

In fact, it made sense to him, for it explained why he decided to implicate Mrs. Taylor in such gory fashion. "He needed the scene to be cut-and-dried—something at which any reasonable person would look and draw an instant conclusion. After his cousin's fall from the cliff, which was shrouded in uncertainty, for nobody knows if he slipped or jumped, Waltham could not allow himself to be associated with a second mysterious death. And Penny was perfect because he needed to discredit her anyway because he thought she knew his secret. By making her the killer, he eliminated the threat because anything she said would sound like a desperate attempt at self-exoneration."

Bea, highly impressed with his reasoning, murmured, "One stone, two Birds of Paradise."

"Indeed," he replied, flashing a smile.

"He must not have known about her relationship with Piddlehinton," she said.

Kesgrave was not as certain. "I suspect he did know and rightly calculated it would not make a difference. Piddlehinton was convinced of her guilt from the start and would not listen to any argument Penny made in her own defense. Despite her pleas, he readily referred the matter to the coroner. No, what Waltham did not count on was you. It must have given him quite a bad start to arrive at her house to gloat over the success of his scheme and find London's premier Lady Runner on the case. Even if it had occurred to him to worry about your involvement, he would naturally assume you would not deign to talk to your husband's former mistress, let alone agree to prove her innocence."

As the duke himself had been seconds away from ejecting Mrs. Taylor from Kesgrave House, she hailed this assumption as reasonable. "It is little wonder, then, that Waltham sought me out this evening to ask about the investigation. He played the part of the anxious lover beautifully, displaying more concern for Mrs. Taylor's welfare than the progress of the investigation. Seeking to put his mind at ease, I told him about Netherby and was overly optimistic about his potential usefulness."

Kesgrave looked at her sharply. "You told him about Netherby?"

Aware of his sensitivity regarding the matter as it related to Hartlepool, she feared that she had made a grave misstep.

Should she apologize?

She did not want to, of course, and resented the very idea, but treading lightly around his lordship's nephew was one of the few constraints the duke had ever placed on an investigation. In light of that, it seemed like a small thing.

And yet the apology stuck in her throat.

Instead, she said cautiously, "I did, yes."

"I wonder ..." Kesgrave began thoughtfully, then paused as he appeared to consider an idea more deeply. "The only way to convince Piddlehinton or the coroner that Penny is innocent is by proving Waltham's guilt. The best way to do that is to apprehend him in the act of committing another crime—in this case, murdering a victim whom he considers a threat to his safety."

Bea looked at him in astonishment, scarcely able to believe what he was proposing. "You mean convince him Netherby saw him yesterday morning and can identify him?"

"We have the tailcoat threads we found in the gate," he pointed out meaningfully.

"So we know the color of the killer's coat and how he got into the house," she replied with growing excitement, rising to her feet as the urge to pace overcame her. If Waltham was caught trying to murder Hartlepool's nephew, then he would be irredeemably sunk. He would be charged for attempting to murder a member of his own class, and she and Kesgrave could convincingly argue it was done in pursuit of covering up his earlier crime. It would be more than enough to sway Piddlehinton and the coroner. "We could offer that as proof Netherby saw something. Waltham would panic at once. Kesgrave, it is a brilliant stroke."

He acknowledged the praise with a dip of his head. "But if Netherby saw Waltham, then why are we blithely sharing that information with him? There has to be a reason Netherby was unable to conclusively identify him."

"Does Netherby know Waltham?" Bea asked, chafing at the lack of space to roam freely. She had just narrowly missed thumping Lady Jersey in the shoulder. No doubt it was for the best, as the conversation should be conducted as quietly as possible.

"Well, they are at the same party," Kesgrave said mildly.

That was true yes, except it was a party so thick with guests, she could not swing her arms without swatting a hostess from Almack's. The likelihood of Netherby and Waltham meeting face-to-face was low. "Furthermore, Netherby is in his first season, so he cannot know everybody and most certainly cannot recognize every peer whom he spots mounting a gate from twenty paces. Let us say that he saw *some* of Waltham. Would that be enough to cause him to act? We need him to be genuinely concerned that Netherby will be able to recognize him with enough time. But we also need for him to feel some urgency, so we can control the circumstance. We cannot leave Netherby open to Waltham's reprisal for days on end. We have to provoke him into responding at once, now, preferably tonight. What could Netherby tell us tomorrow that he cannot tell us right now?"

"Given the requirements of the situation, there is only one answer: He is foxed," Kesgrave replied with amusement. "He came from his club already ape-drunk and you were able to get only the vaguest details from him—hence, the coat and gate. But you are confident he will provide useful information in the morning, when he is sober."

Bea, lauding the endless usefulness of alcohol, commended the inventiveness of the solution. "Let us also throw an artist into our fiction who can draw the face of the climbing figure to Netherby's description. Then it will not matter if Netherby recognizes him or not. You or I or Mrs. Taylor will."

Kesgrave, in turn, complimented Bea on this modification and suggested they present it to the necessary participants at once.

"Do you think we will have trouble persuading Netherby to leave the party early? It is a lovely affair," she asked.

"I think it will be difficult to stop him from calling out Waltham in the middle of the allemande," Kesgrave replied. "He will want to avenge the great injustice visited upon the object of his affection immediately. Hartlepool will have to restrain him, as it is beneath my dignity to sit on a flailing puppy."

In devising their scheme, Bea had not considered the uncle and wondered now what kind of obstacle he would present. Naturally, he would find it a violation of his avuncular duty to allow Netherby to make himself the target of a murderer.

The duke swore it would not be an issue, insisting his friend was too much of a gentleman to allow a woman to hang for a crime he knew she did not commit.

It was a matter of honor!

Bea rather suspected the chivalric code contained an exception for situations that involved one's nephew making a cake of himself over a bit of muslin, but she withheld commenting to that effect, merely suggesting they gather the relevant parties as quickly as possible. There was no telling when Waltham would leave.

Kesgrave agreed and proposed they find a private room to host the discussion. They would have to speak loudly to be heard over the orchestra, and it would be fatal if an inveterate gossip—why, yes, he *was* looking at Mrs. Ralston as he said it —managed to eavesdrop on the conversation. Familiar enough with the home, he recommended the small sitting room next to the study, which was more of a closet than a parlor, with trunks piled to one corner. Then he raised the complication of Waltham, observing that it would be beneficial to their scheme if he did not notice the quartet disappearing into a room together. It might appear disconcertingly conspiratorial.

It was a legitimate concern, and just as Bea pressed her lips together to contemplate a solution, her eyes landed on the familiar figure of Lady Abercrombie. She was perfect. The autocratic countess routinely prevailed over the wishes of her victims.

"I know," Bea said, then strode across the floor to grasp her ladyship by the arm. She apologized to the Harringtons for interrupting their conversation. It was horribly rude of her, yes, but she required the countess's assistance at once. The couple nodded, too stunned to object, but Lady Abercrombie, whose ability to protest had never been hampered by anything, least of all surprise, took her to task for the rough treatment.

Tartly, she said, "As much as I appreciate an assertive female, my dear, this is not how it is done. Did I drag you away from your aunt earlier? No, I did not, even though every instinct I have urges me to run like a fox from a hound any time she comes within ten feet. I squash my impulse and stand in place like a brave little soldier."

It was a fair critique, to be sure, and Bea apologized again for the peremptory behavior. "But I do not have time for niceties. It is, I swear, absolutely vital that I secure your assistance at once, for only you can provide the service Kesgrave and I require," she said as they came to a stop next to the duke. "We need Lord Waltham to be distracted for fifteen minutes or so. It is of the utmost importance, although I cannot explain why now and hope you will accept that we would not ask if it were not an emergency."

Lady Abercrombie did not argue.

Responding with appropriate gravity, her ladyship observed that the quadrille was about to begin. "Mr. Neery's youngest daughter has a disfiguring spot in the center of her nose and will be without a partner. Waltham is still establishing himself in his new position and will not want to slight a member of the Four-Horse Club. He will agree to lead her out," she said, before dashing off to settle the matter to her satisfaction, her stride elegant even as she hurried across the room. Unerringly, she found Miss Neery in her mother's shadow and graciously induced her to follow her. Then she sought out Waltham, who greeted her with a bow.

It was all very neatly done.

Kesgrave announced that he would find Hartlepool, leaving Netherby to her, and even though she had never spoken to the young man, she ably used her consequence to bring him to heel. He pouted, grumbling that his evening had already been ruined by the revelations the duke had made to his uncle. He stopped just short of calling Kesgrave a talebearer, but his meaning was clear, and he blushed when they entered the room to find his grace waiting for them. He mumbled a greeting and looked down at his feet.

He was indeed a puppy, Bea thought, as she closed the door.

Chapter Thirteen

H aving gathered the necessary participants to carry
out her scheme, Bea was surprised when the door
swung open not a full second later to admit the
Countess of Abercrombie.

"Really, Bea, you cannot enlist my help by crying emergency and not expect me to find out the details," she explained as she stepped into the room, taking stock of its occupants.

Hartlepool stood stiffly to the side, his pose emanating irritation, with Netherby to his left bearing an expression of pugnacious abashment, as if aware his behavior had been appalling and annoyed to be forced to acknowledge it. The men were similar in build, both of medium height with broad shoulders and narrow waists, but where Netherby's cheeks were gentle and soft, Hartlepool's were hollowed out. He had a wolfish look about him, augmented by his dark coloring, which made his nephew seem more like a literal pup.

"Not exactly what I was expecting but intriguing nonetheless," her ladyship added with an air of appreciation. "*Emergency* is one of those terms people use frivolously—

Winnie described the lack of ratafia at the refreshment table as a crisis requiring immediate action—so I was understandably skeptical. But now my interest is aroused. Please go on, my dear. Do not let me interrupt you."

As protesting would accomplish nothing and only waste time, Bea gestured toward the settee and invited her ladyship to sit down. "Thank you for joining us," she said satirically, closing the door again.

And again, it pushed open.

Nuneaton stood on the threshold, peeved that he had been compelled to foist his presence on Bea when she knew how much he loathed any exertion. "And after everything I have done for you! At the very least I deserved an invitation to"—he broke off as he examined Hartlepool and his nephew with a faint sneer—"whatever *this* is."

Keenly aware of precious minutes passing, Bea impatiently waved him inside and apologized for not realizing his curiosity was as vulgar as the countess's.

"Nobody's curiosity is as vulgar as the countess's," he murmured as he entered.

Lady Abercrombie accepted the tribute with a gracious nod as Kesgrave advised Bea to barricade the door before Flora appeared. As if summoned by this very statement, the youngest member of the Hyde-Clare family strode into the room.

"Ah, the little cousin," her ladyship said drolly. "How lovely for us."

Genuinely terrified that her aunt was not far behind, Bea shut the door with a firm snap and pressed her shoulders against it to hold it in place.

Laughing, Flora said she did not have to worry. "Mama is interrogating Holcroft about the size of his household staff. She says we cannot entertain an offer from someone who has fewer than three footmen, but obviously that is a plumper.

She would happily unload me onto a blacksmith who has an apprentice. Regardless, I am here now and stand ready to help. Who is our victim and who is our villain?"

"This is absurd!" Hartlepool exclaimed. "I am sure it is not what you intended, Kesgrave, but this summit has descended into a circus and I will not be part of it."

Bea stepped to the side to permit him to leave and intervened only when he ordered his nephew to follow. "I cannot allow him to consign an innocent woman to the gallows in a fit of pique. You may have all the fits of pique you like, my lord, as you are not integral to the plan. Mr. Netherby is. The only way to prove Waltham is the murderer is to catch him in the act of killing again. You, in fact, Mr. Netherby. We want to convince Waltham that you are such a great threat you must be eliminated at once. I do hope that is agreeable to you."

"I will do anything I can to save a falsely accused woman from a wretched death," Netherby averred fervently. "I would throw myself into the mouth of Mount Vesuvius if it meant sparing her one moment of discomfort."

"Good God, you are a clunkhead," his uncle muttered.

Bea, lauding the nobility of his sentiment, assured him the situation did not call for anything nearly so sacrificial. "All you have to do is leave the ball in the next ten minutes and seek shelter somewhere other than your rooms. Your uncle will let it be known that he sent you home to sleep off your overindulgence, after which I will inform Waltham that you had observed someone climbing over the railing on the morning of the murder. Naturally, you are too drunk to be helpful, but I am confident I will discover useful information when I interview you in the morning, along with a skilled artist who will make a drawing of a killer from your description."

Flora clapped, calling the plan brilliant and offering her

services as artist. "You will recall I made that sketch of Mr. Davies. And I really captured his personality. It was all in the scar. The scar was his essence."

Bea refused the overture on the grounds that no picture was actually to be made just as Hartlepool insisted he was not such a prattler that he would tell anyone his family's business.

Scoffing derisively, Netherby said, "You will not demean yourself in an insignificant way to save a woman's life, but *I* am the clunkhead! Even Nuneaton has been moved to help, and he cannot be bothered to lift a finger for anyone."

The viscount darted a meaningful glance at Bea before congratulating the young man on his astute assessment of his character.

"I am not refusing to debase myself," Hartlepool snapped. "I am pointing out that I am not known as a gossip, and if I suddenly start blathering to anyone who will listen about my jug-bitten nephew like an old biddy, then it might raise eyebrows. The best chance we have of lulling Waltham into a particular response is by behaving as expected."

"He is right," Lady Abercrombie said. "It would be strange if the typically reserved Lord Hartlepool blathered to Mrs. Ralston about the boy's condition. He will have to make a scene. I should think tripping over the refreshment table would do nicely. His mortified uncle will race to his side, grab him by the scruff of his collar and escort him out. Everyone will see it and not a word will have to be said."

Netherby, stepping forward with shoulders rigid and proud as if volunteering for battle, said, "I shall do it. I shall trip over the refreshment table!"

"Your heroism is a humbling thing to behold," Hartlepool said.

Either ignoring the sarcasm or failing to perceive it, Netherby vowed to stumble drunkenly over an entirely dining room full of tables if that was required to save Penny's life.

"That is, Mrs. Taylor," he amended with a sly glance at his uncle.

Her ladyship burst into gales of laughter so robust and sincere, she had to press a hand against her stomach to suppress them. "Penny Taylor?" she asked, giggles slipping out as she tried to speak. "All this fuss is about Penny Taylor? For shame, Bea, letting that scheming hussy lead you around like a dog on a lead! I would not expect Kesgrave to recognize the ploy because he is a man and they are decidedly obtuse about such things, but you are clever and suspicious. Whatever she has told you is a lie. She is trying to lure Kesgrave back into her clutches and availing herself of your assistance to do it. I knew something like this would happen! It is why I compiled those dossiers for you on Penny Taylor and all the others."

Netherby glared at the countess with vehement dislike, and although he seemed on the verge of ordering her to name her second, he offered only a mild rebuke. "You do not understand her character, which is unsurprising. Beautiful women are often resented and maligned by other women. They are jealous and cannot help being harsh in their judgments."

The notion that she would be envious of an aging Cyprian amused her ladyship, who laughed again, while Flora ran over to her cousin to offer comfort. Pressing Bea's head against her shoulder, she said, "You must not think it, my dear, no, not for a moment. It does matter that she is a ravishing creature and you are so very plain. Mrs. Taylor could sparkle with the light of a thousand stars and still not hold a candle to you. I am certain Kesgrave knows it as well. Besides, she must be quite old by now. It has been at least a decade since they were lovers."

It was impossible to say who was more insulted by the comment—Lady Abercrombie or Netherby—and they both inhaled sharply, the former seeming ready to offer her own challenge. Seeking to avoid a needless squabble, Bea twisted her shoulders to free herself from her cousin's grasp, for she could not make a reasonable comment constrained like a rooster. Flora, however, mistook her struggle as an attempt to draw closer and tightened her grip with a soothing murmur.

Fortunately, Kesgrave was of the same frame of mind and told the company to stop wasting time. "Tilly, you are right to be suspicious, but in this instance you are wrong. The threat against Penny is real. Bea and I examined the corpse ourselves, and Miss Lloyd was very much dead. Flora, your concern for your cousin is touching. Now do release Bea or she will get a crick in her neck. The quadrille will be over soon and we have to disperse before then. Are there any issues left unresolved?"

Netherby, manfully overcoming his anger, said there was one detail that had yet to be addressed. "Her grace said I should seek shelter somewhere other than my home. But if I am not in my home, then how will Waltham try to kill me?"

"He will not," Bea replied, taking several steps to the left as a precaution against another burst of affection from Flora. "He will try to kill me."

Amiably, Kesgrave said he would take Netherby's place, not the duchess.

"It will never do, your grace," Bea said with a firm shake of her head. "Your hair is too light and you have at least five inches on him. Waltham would know at a glance you are not Netherby."

"It will be dark," the duke countered. "He will know nothing."

But Nuneaton could not agree, pointing out that Waltham would have a candle. "He will see your golden curls from across the room and realize something is amiss. Of course, the duchess cannot do it either. That is madness."

"It is practical," Bea asserted.

"I suppose you think it should be you?" Kesgrave asked with amused cynicism.

Nuneaton shuddered dramatically as he regarded his friend with injured disbelief. "Good God, Kesgrave, what have I ever done to make you think I would agree to lie on another man's sheets? What an utterly appalling opinion you have of me! No, I was going to suggest Hartlepool do it, as he bears a close resemblance to his nephew."

"You see, *that* is a practical solution," said Hartlepool, whose churlish look in Bea's general direction conveyed a disgust for women who volunteered to put themselves in danger while there were able-bodied men in the room. "I was going to propose the very thing myself."

"This is idiotic!" Netherby exclaimed. "To talk about who looks more like me when I look the most like myself! I should be the one who risks his life to save Penny, not my uncle, who does not even like her. He has never said one kind word about her. Just two days ago you called her a mercenary little hen, which is decidedly unfair because her nose is small and dainty, nothing like a beak at all. That is why I should be the one who saves her. *I* should be the hero of the piece!"

"And that is why you will have nothing more to do with it after you stumble into the refreshment table," his uncle said with a severe frown. "You do not understand the gravity of the situation and think it is all a great lark. It is not a lark. It is serious business, and although I do not like or respect Penny Taylor, I will do everything in my power to make sure she does not hang for a murder she did not commit. But make no mistake: This is a shameful episode with no heroes."

"Bea is heroic," Flora asserted. "Saving the life of the beautiful woman with whom her husband was enamored for almost a year when she must wish her to perdition. I would not have the generosity of spirit if Holcroft introduced me to one of his convenients."

Although Bea swore she bore no resentment against the courtesan for events more than twelve years in the past, her cousin refused to believe her, and for the sake of expedience Bea agreed to wish Mrs. Taylor to a place slightly less unpleasant than hell, such as St. Giles.

"Then it is decided," Kesgrave said firmly. "Hartlepool will bring Netherby somewhere safe and then proceed to Lexington Street to wait for Waltham's attack."

"I shall deposit him at my townhouse and my butler will look after him," Hartlepool said, earning a spiteful glare from his nephew, who did not appreciate the description, which made him sound like a toddler in leading strings. "You will have a Runner on hand to apprehend the villain?"

"Yes, as well as the magistrate," Kesgrave said. "If Piddle-hinton catches Waltham in the act of trying to kill the man he believes is a witness to his crime, then there can be no wiggling off the line."

Everyone was satisfied with this plan, except Netherby, whose objections were already known, and Flora, who still felt her drawing skills qualified her to be present at the time of capture.

Neither protest received a response.

In the dwindling minutes before the quadrille ended, the duke reviewed the order of events—Bea would inform Waltham of the encouraging lead before Netherby made his drunken scene—and Nuneaton consented to arrange for Piddlehinton to meet them at the house in Lexington Street, which required him to leave the ball at once.

"Lady Diana will be devastated by my early departure," he warned soberly, "and if Mr. Twaddle-Thum takes note of it and makes a fuss, I expect the duchess to do something outrageous to take the focus away from me."

"Do not fret, my lord," Bea said with a light chuckle. "I have spent two days making social calls to various Mayfair addresses in the company of my husband's former mistress. Whatever outrageous thing you wish me to do I have already done."

To avoid undue attention, they left the room one at a time, waiting a full thirty seconds in between. The precaution further irritated Netherby, who grumbled to the duke, "You are all prudence and no action! I cannot fathom why Mrs. Taylor finds you so attractive."

Lady Abercrombie laughed throatily and said, "No, I imagine you cannot. And that is precisely the problem, you cawker."

Netherby turned red but did not reply.

Returning to the dance floor, Bea spotted Waltham right away. He was with Lady Patricia and her mother. As urgency denoted importance, she swept across the room and interrupted their exchange with a heartfelt apology. Neither woman took exception to the treatment, owning themselves delighted to meet the duchess and hopeful they would have an opportunity to talk with her again later in the evening.

"Perhaps we may sit together for supper," Mrs. Akhurst added. "Or we can call at Kesgrave House for tea. I do enjoy taking a stroll around Berkeley Square."

"Perhaps supper," Bea replied vaguely, not wishing to imply she would be gone by the time the meal was served. Then weaving her arms through Waltham's, she drew him away, toward the fringe of the room but also within sight of the refreshment table so that they could watch the performance. "You will never believe it, my lord, but my supposition was correct. Netherby did see something! He was across the road on the morning of the murder, pining for Mrs. Taylor like the veriest moonling."

Waltham smiled, as if vastly relieved by the news, but it was overly bright. Bea thought she could feel his anxiety as he replied, "Why, that is remarkable! He was across the road the whole time."

"It is very remarkable," she replied. "I have conducted several investigations, and this is the first time I have found an eyewitness. I am thrilled."

"As am I," he insisted, his smile widening as he struggled to maintain his enthusiastic affect. "And what did he see?"

Bea held her answer for a moment to increase his suspense and then leaned forward to reply with relish, "A man in a bottle green topcoat! He saw him climbing over the locked gate at the top of the stairs leading to the servants' entrance. Can you believe it? That is two new significant pieces of information: Now we know how the murderer got into the house and what he was wearing. It is an astounding stroke of luck and it is just the beginning."

Waltham blinked his eyes furiously as he pressed one arm against his stomach, trying, Bea supposed, to squelch a sudden squeamishness. "The beginning, you say? You think he knows more? What more can he tell you? A bottle green tail-coat seems very specific to me."

As if responding to her prompt, Netherby stumbled forward, his elbow jabbing Mrs. Ralston as he slipped between the confirmed gossip and her daughter. Alas, the space was too narrow and he also stepped on the former's toes. Mrs. Ralston squealed and called him a graceless nincompoop.

Gesturing to the scene, Bea explained that the witness's utility was limited at the moment by his condition. "It is unfortunate. But he will be more clear-headed in the morning, and that is when I intend to approach him again. I have already found an artist to accompany me so that she may draw a picture of the murderer based on Mr. Netherby's description of his physical appearance."

Netherby apologized to Mrs. Ralston by leaning in close, and she pulled back as if revolted by the familiarity.

Watching the display, Waltham seemed to grow more and less anxious at the same time. "He is a graceless nincompoop, as she said. You really think he knows more? He cannot know more. I do not believe he knows more. Maybe he does?"

"I am certain he does," Bea replied firmly. "When asked for a description, he rattled incoherently for several minutes. I was able to figure out only a small fraction of it, such as the green tailcoat. I am convinced tomorrow, when he is sober, Mr. Netherby will provide us with a cogent description of the killer. If neither Kesgrave nor I are able to identify the image produced in the drawing, someone else will. Mrs. Taylor, for example, or maybe you, Lord Waltham?"

Startled, he squeaked, "Me? You think *I* know the killer?"

"You are quite popular, are you not?" she asked fawningly. "Since assuming the title, you are invited everywhere and may soon receive an invitation to join the Four-Horse Club from what Lady Abercrombie tells me. I think it is likely you will recognize him."

"You think the murderer could be a member of the Four-Horse Club?" he asked, seemingly appalled by the notion.

"Well, bottle green is the fashion this season, which indicates to me the killer is a gentleman," she replied. "My experience is not vast, but I have not seen any fishmongers or bank clerks sporting a bottle green tailcoat. For that reason, I think we can reasonably assume either you or Kesgrave or Mrs. Taylor will recognize the face in the drawing, presuming we can find her. It is a huge relief to me, Lord Waltham, and I am not ashamed to admit it. Miss Lloyd's murder has confounded me more than any other I have investigated in my brief career as a so-called Lady Runner, and I had begun to believe the villain was too clever to be found. If not for this remarkable bit of luck, he would have likely succeeded in sending an innocent woman to the gallows in his stead."

"So it all comes down to that graceless nincompoop," Waltham murmured with a hint of wonder in his voice as he watched the object of his contempt stagger forward and knock into the refreshment table. Several glasses toppled to the floor, shattering as a bottle of claret tipped over. The dark red wine spread across the tablecloth, which Netherby grasped in a bid to steady himself. The slick fabric slipped through his fingers and he tumbled to the side, somehow throwing himself clear of the broken glass. He landed on his shoulder with a groan of pain and then guffawed as he drew his knees to his chest. "'Graceless nincompoop' is too kind a description. He is a buffoon."

Bea conceded the accuracy of the assessment, for Netherby had made a convincing fool of himself in a brilliant performance that exceeded all her expectations. There he was still, on the floor, cackling and moaning, as concerned mamas warned their daughters to watch for slivers of glass.

Hartlepool arrived at the same time as the footmen with brooms and held out a hand to help his nephew to his feet. Netherby clutched it gratefully, then slid backward as he failed to regain his balance. He dropped back down to the floor as the crowd tittered with embarrassment, and Hartlepool's face darkened with exasperation.

And it was not pretend, Bea noted. His lordship was genuinely annoyed at his nephew for the extravagant display. He had anticipated a more modest fall.

"His uncle is taking him in hand," she said approvingly as Hartlepool tugged on Netherby's arm, ostensibly to support him but really to tell him to stop the nonsense. His nephew ceased tottering and slurred an apology. "That is good. He will make sure the boy gets home safely and is put to bed. In his condition, he is liable to stumble into the road and get run over by a carriage."

If the idea of a drunken accident appealed to Waltham, he gave no indication. "You should delay your visit until the afternoon, as he will have a pounding headache in the morning and will not be fit for company."

"You are probably right," Bea said reluctantly. "But I am too impatient to get a proper description of the murderer to wait until two o'clock. Let us hope Mr. Netherby recovers quickly. He is young and should rebound with a little care and sleep. My uncle recommends a concoction of raw egg, barley water and cardamon to counter the effects of excess. I will send his housekeeper a note advising it. Or perhaps a package with the necessary ingredients. I do not expect the pantry in a bachelor's establishment to be well stocked."

Now Waltham made no attempt to hide his interest. "A bachelor's establishment? You mean he is not staying with his uncle?"

"He insisted on hiring his own house, in Lexington Street," she replied. "He wanted the freedom to come and go as he pleased without his family staying abreast of his activities. I suspect if he were lodging with Hartlepool, he would not have been lingering outside Mrs. Taylor's townhouse so early in the morning. So you and I must be grateful."

"As by your own report, he was pestering Penny with his lurking presence, I am not sure *grateful* is the right word," he said with a cynical twist of his lips. "But your point is well taken, your grace. The situation is what it is and cannot be altered. I must commend you on your excellent work on Penny's behalf and beg that you keep me apprised of developments. I look forward to seeing the drawing."

Bea promised to call on him the next day if necessary. "My hope is Kesgrave or Hartlepool will recognize the culprit and convince Piddlehinton to apprehend him on the strength of

Netherby's word. Then we can put this whole sordid episode behind us."

Waltham echoed this sentiment, noting that murder was indeed a dreary business and marveled at her grace's willingness to expose herself repeatedly to its palling effects. Although she had been asked this question several times, Bea still did not know how to explain her strange compulsion. Her lack of response did not pose a problem, however, because his lordship was not interested in an answer. His eyes followed Hartlepool as he led his nephew out of the ballroom, and she could see his mind already knitting away at the thorny problem of Netherby's murder. Not wishing to interrupt the process, she pledged one last time to see justice done for Mrs. Taylor and bid him good evening.

In return, he thanked her for her stubborn determination. "Without your persistence, Penny would have no hope at all."

The footmen finished sweeping the last of the shards into the dustbin as Waltham walked away, and Bea fetched a glass of warm lemonade before finding Kesgrave to report on the success of her undertaking. Although one could never predict the behavior of a murderer with one hundred percent accuracy, she felt confident Waltham would move against Netherby. He certainly had all the information he needed.

Had she been a little too obvious in providing it?

She did not think so, no, but worried about it for the hour they remained at the event. Although she was eager to leave, she knew it would never do for them to be seen making a hasty exit, especially so soon after Netherby's disgraceful departure. Consequently, they lingered until supper was served, then gently made their excuses to their hosts, who were sorry to see them leave but delighted by their attendance.

Waltham had left about fifteen minutes before.

Kesgrave gave Netherby's address to Jenkins, who eyed

them skeptically as they climbed into the carriage in their finery. Although they assured the groom that no, they did not want to return to Berkley Square to change their clothes first, Bea lamented the constraints of her attire. If her everyday booties were insufficient to the task of chasing and apprehending murderers, then her silk slippers were an actual impediment. In light of the circumstance, she had no expectation of having to run after Waltham, but the lack of options still bothered her. It was patently unfair that she had to choose between delicate silk and flimsy leather.

Twenty minutes later, they arrived at the address, which was on the edge of Mayfair, adjacent to the fashionable section, although not quite achieving that distinction itself. Not outright decrepit, the house was nevertheless shabby and Bea could easily imagine Waltham being emboldened by the sight. The rotted doorjambs would pose no bar to entry.

It was perfect, Bea decided.

Jenkins said nothing as she climbed down from the carriage, but it was apparent from his posture that he heartily disapproved. He had accompanied them on enough escapades to know when they were behaving recklessly.

In fact, there was no risk involved in that night's venture. They had set the scene and now all they had to do was wait for Waltham to saunter onto the stage like an obliging player. But she could not explain that to him, of course, for one did not seek to soothe the anxieties of the servants. It would mortify the groom to even imply he even had feelings.

As the Duke of Kesgrave's carriage was not part of the set decoration, she instructed Jenkins to return to Berkeley Square. "We will find our own way home."

The groom flinched at the notion of their graces making do with whatever slapdash contrivance they could arrange but acquiesced without protest.

As the servants had been dismissed for the night, Hartlepool answered their knock. Although he had had the opportunity to change out of his formal attire, he had contented himself with removing his cravat and waistcoat. Still sporting his silk breeches, he looked like a gentleman prepared to enjoy a restful glass of port in his study before retiring to bed.

It was, Bea thought as he led them down the hall, an improvement.

"Sylvester was much subdued by the time we arrived at my home," his lordship explained as he mounted the steps. "I think the gravity of the situation finally struck him, and he accepted that it was best to allow the grown-ups to handle the matter. Although I cannot like his fascination with Mrs. Taylor, his sincere concern for her welfare appears to be the only thing that influences his behavior. He understands that ambushing Waltham in this way is the best chance she has to be exonerated for the crime."

Arriving at the first-floor landing, they were greeted by Piddlehinton, who was mopping sweat from his forehead with a handkerchief, visibly distraught by how close he had come to sending his dear friend to the gibbet for a crime with which she had nothing to do. He could barely breathe for picturing her lifeless eyes at the end of a noose.

As he seemed inclined to rattle on for quite some time about his distress, Bea asked him to kindly fetch her a sherry from the parlor downstairs. "And please pour yourself one as well. It would never do to get a trifle disguised in this situation, but a single glass might help to ease the tension. While you are doing that, I shall introduce myself to the Runner."

The magistrate dashed off to fulfill her request, and Hartlepool paid her the first compliment of their acquaintance. "A clever solution, that, sending him to get drinks. I wonder why that did not occur to me. It is simple enough. I suppose his blather impeded my ability to think. It was so much noise."

"He does not seem to have the temperament for an ambush," she replied as he led them down the hallway, the floorboards creaking with every step. Although the home's dilapidated condition made it an unwelcoming place to live, its various groans and squeaks were well suited to the circumstance. They would easily hear Waltham's approach.

The bedchamber was small and square, with a brick hearth on one side and windows along an adjacent wall. The drapes, once a deep navy blue, were faded in splotches and hung two or three inches off the floor. Although the length was not ideal for hiding, she imagined the curtains would be adequate in a darkened room. There were few items in the room—a clothespress, a trunk, a writing table—which meant the curtains would have to do. Relatively narrow, they would provide concealment for only two people.

Ah, but which two, she wondered.

Well, Mr. Rusk naturally.

The whole point of the plan was for someone with authority to catch Waltham in the act of murdering a witness to his crime, and the Runner struck her as a reliably sturdy witness. A jury, if it still came to it after that night's work, would find his testimony convincing.

Piddlehinton was also a candidate for one of the curtains, but Bea did not believe the older gentleman was capable of standing still for a significant amount of time, not with his current level of apprehension. She recalled the beads of perspiration and imagined the drapes bulging with his elbows as he dabbed his forehead. Furthermore, he was not exactly in peak physical condition and would be at a disadvantage if the encounter turned violent.

It was this threat that Kesgrave was sure to cite as the reason he should hide behind the second curtain, and Bea could not bestir herself to counter it. She could see arguing if their skills were equal, but she was still at the beginning of her training and could admit without any tweak to her ego that he was more qualified to engage in a fight. She had yet to discharge a pistol, and he had been taking lessons at Gentleman Jackson's for a more than a decade.

As the options were limited, Bea had no choice but to hide in the dressing room with the magistrate. A cramped space to the right of the bed, it was lined with shelves on two sides and stuffed with trunks. It accommodated only one chair, and Piddlehinton, having dragged it over from the writing desk, insisted the duchess take it.

"I will sit here," he said, gesturing to a chest of drawers against the back wall. It was about three feet high with a wide top and sturdy legs. To make room for himself, he stacked three books on top of each other and rested a trio of lamps on top of them. Then he cautiously lowered his bulk onto the surface and noted it was quite comfortable. "I will be fine here for the duration. I do hope everything goes according to plan, your grace. I will be wretched if Waltham does not appear. I would much rather arrest him for murder than Penny. But neither I nor the coroner can do anything if his guilt is not uncontestably proven. I know you understand."

"I do, yes," Bea said, fully aware of the constraints of his position. If Mrs. Taylor were a woman of rank and means, the men would be able to use their discretion. Lady Skeffington, for example, had been permitted the dignity of exile to the Continent. But no lightskirt, not even one with whom he was friends, could be given the benefit of the doubt. It was a horribly unfair system in dozens of large and small ways.

Before closing the door to their little room, she peeked her head out one last time to confirm that everyone was in their proper place. Hartlepool was in bed, his head facing into the room, away from the entry, to make sure he did not reveal his wakeful state unintentionally. Kesgrave and the Runner were tucked behind curtains, the tips of their black shoes peeking out of the bottom. Barely able to make out the outlines of their feet in the thin light she carried, she had no concern Waltham would spot them in the darkness.

"I am shutting the door now. Let us hope Lord Waltham has the courtesy not to keep us waiting all night," she said with a hint of facetiousness, as a murderer could not be relied upon for punctuality. Then she settled into the chair, placing the lamp on the trunk beside her, its flickering glow too dim to seep into the bedchamber from the small crack under the door. It barely extended as far as Piddlehinton, who was three feet away, his unruly nerves still jangling, and he shifted in his seat, unable to find a comfortable position. He moaned, either with anxiety or frustration, and she sent him a quelling look as she pressed a finger to her lips to indicate absolute silence. If Waltham suspected their presence, the plan would fail.

"I am sorry," Piddlehinton said, then immediately slapped his own hand against his mouth as he realized he had made no effort to modulate his volume. Then he apologized again, this time in a whisper, and promised to do better.

And he did.

In the half hour that followed, the magistrate sat silently in the dressing room, his limbs barely moving as they waited for Waltham to appear. Bea, who had been on the edge of her seat, as though prepared to leap up at any moment, leaned back as she realized it was going to be a long night indeed.

Then suddenly she heard a creak.

Chapter Fourteen

B
ea tensed in expectation, her hand reaching for the lamp beside her as she rose to her feet to apprehend the villain as soon as Hartlepool called out, and she drew to a sudden halt as a loud clamor filled the dressing room

Shattering glass, she thought.

It was the sound of glass smashing against a hard surface, and incapable of making sense of the noise, she turned to Piddlehinton to see if he shared her astonishment.

But he was staring down at the lamp shards at his feet, seemingly baffled by how they had gotten there.

As if he himself had not knocked them over!

Disgusted by his clumsiness, she inhaled sharply to rebuke him for foiling their plan and pivoted to the door as she remembered Waltham.

Goddamn it!

Still clutching the lamp, she wrapped her other hand around the handle and then froze because she had no idea how to respond. They had to have heard it too—Hartlepool and Kesgrave and Rusk—but if they had held their positions, then her rushing out would ruin everything.

But surely it was already ruined, with Waltham recognizing the danger and retreating at once. Even if he did not suspect an ambush, he could not be so foolish as to attack a man who was fully awake and possibly in the company of his valet.

He would wait until later or try something else.

Or recognize how strange it all was: the silent, dark house exploding with sound.

It was patently wrong, and any villain with a modicum of sense would run.

Bea tightened her hand on the door as she heard a thump from the other room followed by a cry and a yelp.

Then: "I say, Uncle Tony, your elbow is on my windpipe and it is dashed hard to breathe."

Netherby!

She swung open the door, the lamp raised high, to see Hartlepool on the floor beside the bed, his left leg under his nephew's hip, his right arm pressed against the boy's throat. His lordship's face was hidden in his shadow, but it required no imagination to picture its thunderous expression as he regarded his scapegrace relative with fury.

"Of all the woolly-headed nonsense," Hartlepool sneered, pressing down harder in his anger. "What in the blazes are you doing here?"

Even in the gloomy light, Bea saw Netherby's face turn an unnatural shade of red, but before she could say something, the duke interceded. Stepping forward, he laid his hand on his friend's shoulder, and she realized both he and the Runner were there. They had darted from their positions to apprehend Waltham before he could disappear.

Only it was not Waltham.

Insolent puppy!

Bea shared Hartlepool's anger, and as she watched the gentleman tug his nephew roughly to his feet, she wanted to give the boy a severe set-down.

But that would take time—time they did not have.

Waltham could arrive at any moment.

Devil it!

"We must save the recriminations for later," she said firmly.

"No, I will offer them now!" Netherby said heatedly, his color returning to normal as he broke free of his uncle's grasp. "Your treatment of me is indefensible, patting me on the head and sending me off to bed like the veriest child. I am not a child! I am a grown man who is the only witness to a murder and I deserve to be in on the fun."

"The fact that you consider this fun proves that you *are* a child," Hartlepool said with mild scorn, which somehow made the condemnation harsher. "And you did not witness anything. That is a ruse, you idiot."

Seemingly taken aback by the reminder that he had not actually observed anything significant, Netherby faltered for a response before saying, "Well, this bedchamber is not a ruse. It is real and it is mine and I deserve to be here. You cannot kick me out."

He crossed his arms pugnaciously, as if daring his uncle to eject him forcibly, and Hartlepool turned to Bea. "You deal with him. As you were the one who came up with a plan that hinged on this numbskull, I leave the problem in your ingenious hands," he said, trying for scorn but landing closer to sullen. Then he capped off his tantrum by straightening his clothes and climbing back into the bed.

It was impossible not to be amused by the arrogant earl's descent into sulkiness, but she revealed none of it as she tugged on Netherby's sleeve. "Come, you will hide in the dressing room with me and Sir John."

Aghast, he pulled his arm free and said, "Impossible! That room is too small for two people, let alone three. I would never fit. I almost did not take the house because the dressing room is so tiny. I do not mind faded walls and pockmarked floors because those are merely aesthetic concerns, but a dressing room that is too compact to fit all my clothes is a practical problem with no solution. But I suppressed my misgivings because it was only for one season, and now you expect me to squeeze myself into it? No!"

"Yes," Kesgrave said.

The duke's tone was mild, possessing none of the surly exasperation of a relative who had been exposed to the boy's antics for several months, and Netherby acquiesced petulantly to his authority. His shoulders rounded with resentment, he slunk slowly across the floor like a toddler being sent off to bed.

As Netherby disappeared into the dressing room, the duke asked, "What was that crash? It sounded like breaking glass."

Bea rolled her eyes. "Piddlehinton's nerves got the better of him. Fortunately, the lamps were the only fragile items in the dressing room, so nothing else will break the next time he is startled by the creak of a floorboard. In that respect, I suppose we should be grateful for Netherby's unexpected arrival. It allowed us a rehearsal."

"Bite your tongue," Hartlepool said sourly from the depths of the bed.

But Kesgrave agreed that it had been useful and noted that the room had actually been too dark for him or Mr. Rusk to see anything. "I think a gentle glow from the hearth would improve our vantage and provide Waltham with a little assistance."

Rusk proceeded to start the fire with the duke's help. Then they tamped down the flames until they were flickering embers. In the glimmer it was possible to discern figures but not features.

Satisfied, Kesgrave slipped behind the curtain as Bea returned to the dressing room to find Piddlehinton where she had left him: perched on the chest of drawers, his legs drawn to the side to avoid contact with the shards of glass that surrounded the piece of furniture. She decided his reluctance to change his position was probably a good thing, for it indicated that he understood the gravity of the situation and did not want to make another wrong move. Netherby, either gallantly leaving the chair for her or warned off it by the magistrate, sat on a trunk against the left wall, his head bent forward to accommodate the shelf directly above.

Neither man was in the ideal pose for an extended wait, and she imagined them both growing unbearably stiff after the first hour.

Alas, it took only thirty minutes for Piddlehinton to eject the first groan.

Bea glared at him meaningfully, and he bowed his head with contrition.

Netherby, in contrast, did not make a single peep, though she knew his neck must ache. All he did was shift his weight from one side of his body to the other every so often.

In that way, he was the ideal ambush companion.

As the second hour dragged on, Bea felt herself go restless and began to worry again that she had overestimated her ability to convey pointed information in a subtle fashion. She thought she had been sly in her conversation with Waltham, extolling the opportunity Netherby presented in an enthusiastic but restrained fashion that appeared natural.

But she would think that, would she not?

Unable to observe herself, she had no idea what her manner had truly been like and perhaps what she thought was wily could have appeared to the killer as blatant.

He might have known what she was doing from the very beginning.

It was a discouraging thought, for it meant not only that their plan to apprehend him that evening would not prospect but also that he knew she did not have a promising—

A floorboard!

Tensing suddenly in her seat, she turned first to Piddlehinton to see if he had heard it as well, but he was staring at the ceiling. Netherby, likewise, showed no response, his expression blank as he contemplated his own fingers.

Now she was imagining things, Bea realized, her muscles loosening as she forced herself to recline in the chair. After two hours in the airless space, she was so desperate for something to happen, her mind was inventing noises. It was not altogether surprising given—

Creak.

Oh, but that time it was unmistakable, the sound so very close, practically in the room with them, and everyone around her reacted, Netherby jerking forward, deftly avoiding the shelf with his head as he rose to his full height, Piddlehinton jumping to his feet, then shrieking. Even Netherby knew this was asinine behavior and lunged forward to cover the other man's mouth with his hand. Muffled, the magistrate continued to scream, his pain seemingly too intense to be silenced, and Bea realized crouching in the dressing room was pointless.

The jig was up.

Thrusting open the door, she was met with a confounding scene: Rusk supine on the floor, Hartlepool wrangling with the blankets and Kesgrave falling to his side at the entrance to the room.

And a scent.

A horrifyingly pungent smell, like sour milk, Parmesan cheese, and feces, assaulted her nose the second she stepped out of the drawing room. Running to the doorway to assist Kesgrave, she gagged twice and almost slid herself on a wet substance that covered the floor by the threshold.

It was stinky and thick.

Vomit, she thought, finding it incomprehensible yet undeniable.

She heaved again as the realization hit her, and clutching the doorjamb to steady herself, she caught movement out of the corner of her eye.

A shadow racing to the staircase.

Waltham!

Leaving Kesgrave to fend for himself, as he did not seem at passing glance to be gravely harmed, she chased after the killer, first along the hallway, then onto the staircase, where she pivoted sharply as she grabbed the balustrade, her wet silk slippers gliding with worrying ease on the smooth floorboards. Grasping the handrail tightly she ran as fast as she could, keenly aware of the darkness, mindful of tripping and vaguely terrified of misjudging the bottom and pounding into the floor.

But there was light below, from the window over the front door, and she could see the last step as Waltham reached it. She was so close and yet too far, and gauging the distance while calculating her angle, Bea propelled herself off the third-to-last tread. It was a horrible sensation, being lodged in midair, feeling herself horizontal to the floor, but before she could perceive its terribleness, it was already over. She thwacked Waltham on the back, driving him to the rug with a walloping thud and landing on his rear end, which broke the worst of her fall. He howled in fury, the sound ferocious and inhuman, as he lurched upward in an attempt to dislodge her and then wrenched to the side when that effort failed. Stunned from the drop and struggling to regain her breath, she felt the fabric from his coat slip from her fingers as he yanked his body and drove something hard into her eye.

His fist.

He was punching her.

Once.

Twice.

Her head exploded with pain as her neck snapped back a third time, his weight heavy as his torso pressed her into the floor, and all she could think was, *I know this one, I know this one,* as if struggling to recall the answer to a simple question, such as the capital of Spain or the square root of eighty-one.

I know this one.

I know this one.

Zimmer had drummed it into her head, the most vulnerable part of the human male. Over and over, he pointed to his groin, ignoring her blushes, and insisted, "This is your secret weapon, your grace. This gives you the advantage every time. Do not hesitate to use it."

But Bea had known she would hesitate, for she could not imagine striking a man in his crotch. Something would stop her—an entrenched decency, a crippling mortification—and yet the moment she remembered Zimmer's words, she bent her knee, raised it sharply, and bashed him as hard as she could.

The effect was immediate.

Waltham yelped, his body recoiling in pain and surprise, and Bea shoved him to the side as his tightened fist first dropped to the floor, then joined the other hand in cradling his injury. He curled into a ball and whimpered. Bea scrambled to her feet, tripping over her skirts several times and finally rising to her full height just as Kesgrave arrived to enfold her into his arms.

She stood there for a moment, her head throbbing, her

left eye feeling as though it had receded into her brain, and relaxed into the comfort of his reassuring embrace.

Then she thrust him violently away as the stench assaulted her.

"You reek!" she said, bile rising in her throat as the smell oozed deeper into her nostrils. "What in sweet unholy hell is that intolerable odor? Is it vomit? It smells like vomit. Is that even possible?"

But in stepping away, she had moved into the weak light, allowing Kesgrave to glimpse her face. He swore hotly himself and closed the distance between them in three indignant strides.

"For God's sake, I told you to wait!" he said, gently taking her chin in his hand to inspect the damage. "You are bleeding, damn it, and your eye has already begun to swell."

He pressed a handkerchief to her nose, but it also stank of regurgitated stomach contents and she shoved it away. She darted back again, apologizing profusely for being unable to bear his presence. "It is just that you are so very disgusting and I am unduly sensitive to disgusting odors due to my interesting condition."

But he ignored her, drawing close enough to seize her by her shoulders and cursed again. "You do not have to remind me of your condition, for I was keenly aware of it every step I took in the pitch-blackness. I will not have it, Bea! You could have tripped and broken your neck! And if you say one word about how a proper pair of boots would have made the endeavor safer—one single, solitary word, Bea!—I swear I will lock you in the cellar for a week and allow you nothing but gruel—to hell with your interesting condition!"

Although she could hardly take her next breath for the stench, she realized she had to bear it for the sake of her marriage and forced herself to stay still.

But it was difficult.

Very, very difficult.

She also recognized the strategic value of acknowledging the recklessness of her actions, not in the least because she had felt the danger herself as she careened down the steps. If she had given the matter thought rather than just responding on instinct, she would have been too terrified to attempt the stairs. In that case, it was all well that ended well, she thought, for if Waltham had been allowed to leave the house, then they would never have gotten a second chance to prove his guilt.

Even so, she knew better than to tell him about the lurching jump that had literally brought down the killer because Kesgrave would be incandescent with rage at the thought of her hurtling through the air—and with good cause.

The truth was, she had failed to consider the cherub.

Instead of trying to defend herself, she adopted an expression of contrition that lasted a whole three seconds until she recalled how she had bested the killer.

Drawing back as she inhaled with excitement (and promptly gagged), she said, "It worked! Mr. Zimmer's secret maneuver! I struck Waltham in the groin with my knee and he squealed and loosened his grip, allowing me to get out from underneath him, and then he curled up into the ball he is in now. It is remarkable, for it was exactly as Mr. Zimmer said. We really must send him a note thanking him for his excellent service."

Kesgrave's expression did not soften.

If anything, it grew harder at hearing she had been trapped beneath Waltham.

But he must have found something mollifying in her explanation because he resorted to pedantry, pointing out that the generous compensation Zimmer received for the sessions *was* his thank you.

"And it's all thanks to you that I was able to defend myself so deftly, your grace," she gushed. "It was so clever of you to arrange my training."

Now a smile quivered on his lips. "Is that how you think to wrangle out of this one, brat, by flattering me?"

"It is my intention, yes," she stated candidly.

He shook his head, clearly unimpressed with her plan, but rendered no verdict on its chance of succeeding. Instead, he turned to look at the staircase, where Netherby was bounding down the final step followed by his uncle, who held a candle, which he used to light the sconces in the hallway. Netherby took one look at Waltham wailing on the floor and said, "I cannot pretend that I did not want to be the one who leveled him, but I can appreciate a job well done. Nice work, your grace. You are a prime goer!"

Kesgrave demurred. "That is the duchess's handiwork. By the time I arrived she had already subdued him. Unfortunately, it came at some expense to her."

Although Hartlepool appeared horrified by the bruise blossoming on her cheek—and by the prospect of his friend being leg-shackled to the sort of woman whose cheek blossomed with bruises—Netherby took one look at her face and said he had seen worse. "When my horse got spooked by a mouse and kicked the stable boy and when Paddington Jones knocked out Jem Simpson. He had two black eyes and a broken nose. I say, your grace, you have blood dripping from your nostril. Here, I have a handkerchief. Would you like it?"

"Only if it does not reek of vomit," she said hesitantly.

"Nothing about me reeks!" he said with confidence as he withdrew the linen square from his pocket and handed it to her. "But your caution is well justified, as my uncle smells like the vicar's home after his wife served spoiled goose for Martinmas, and he did not get the worst of it."

It was still utterly dumbfounding, the advent of vomit,

and Bea turned to the duke and begged him to explain. In reply, he said he could only hazard a theory, for they would not know the correct answer until they interviewed Waltham.

Dabbing her nose gently with the handkerchief, Bea accepted his terms. "Please speculate wildly, your grace, as to what you think happened."

But of course the duke would never indulge in wild speculation, only restrained supposition based on the facts available to him. "Waltham brought the vomit with him in a bucket, which leads me to conclude he planned to make it appear as though his victim choked to death on his own vomit, which is not an entirely implausible turn given his state of excessive inebriation at Lady Diana's ball this evening. Had he succeeded, I do not think any of the several dozen people who watched Netherby fall over the refreshment table would have questioned it."

Netherby stiffened in outrage. "I have never heard of anything so despicable! It is one thing to murder a man in his sleep but to defile his corpse, to saddle him with a grotesque death, to make him the subject of mockery and scorn when he cannot defend himself, is beyond the limit!" he cried, marching to where Waltham lay still clutching his privates and ordered him to name his second. "I *will* have satisfaction!"

His lordship did not respond to the challenge other than to moan incoherently, and while Hartlepool called his nephew an absurd puppy, Bea continued to address the duke. "Then he heard Piddlehinton and panicked?"

"He was beside the bed when Piddlehinton shouted," Hartlepool said, preemptively drawing his nephew away from Waltham. Although the boy should know better than to kick a man when he was down, the fury in his eyes indicated he might not remember. "I had heard him on the stairs. He was near silent but old steps will creak. I turned over to watch his progress, so I saw him enter the room with the bucket. I had just closed my eyes to affect sleep when the magistrate yelled, and I opened them again and Waltham appeared frozen by surprise."

"He was," confirmed Kesgrave, who had also observed Waltham's progress into the room. "I could not make out the detail of the bucket from my vantage, but I could see his legs, and as soon as Piddlehinton screamed, he halted and just stood there, over the bed. I felt certain he would turn tail and run, so I darted out from the curtain, and Rusk followed me. I was halfway across the floor when Waltham threw the vomit at me. I had no idea what it was. I smelled it before it even hit me, and when it did hit me, the revoltingness almost stopped me cold."

"And Rusk?" she asked, recalling the figure lying on the floor.

"Waltham threw the bucket at him and hit him square in the forehead," Kesgrave explained. "The man fell like a stone."

"And I got entwined in the bedclothes," Hartlepool added in disgust. "As the night wore on, I grew increasingly restless and wound myself in the sheet as I shifted positions. And then I was sprayed with some putrid liquid, which I instinctively began wiping away, and as I was trying to climb out of bed at the same time, it became a hopeless tangle. I am sorry I was not more helpful. Had I been able to free myself sooner, perhaps the duchess would not be sporting two black eyes."

"Two?" Bea asked, wincing at the information. "I thought it was only the left."

Hartlepool assured her it was both.

"The good news, then, is the right one does not hurt," she said cheerfully, although the truth was, now that she knew about the second bruise, it began to throb as well.

Frowning, the duke replied, "That is not the heartening report you seem to think it is."

"Ah, but Mr. Zimmer's secret maneuver!" she reminded him. "The injuries are a small price to pay for the peace of mind that comes from knowing I have the means to fend off even the burliest villain."

"If you think the idea of your being attacked by a burly villain gives me peace of mind, then your understanding of our relationship is sorely deficient," Kesgrave said blandly.

"A duchess with a false sense of confidence," Hartlepool murmured. "Terrifying *and* fascinating. Your situation is more dire than I ever suspected, Kesgrave."

Ignoring the slight, Bea asked the duke how he ended up on the floor.

"He slipped," Hartlepool said with an amused chuckle. "All those years of fencing lessons, of mastering the riposte and parry, of attaining a dexterity of which the rest of us could only dream, and he slips on vomit like an ungainly turnip. You are to be congratulated, Damien. Grimaldi himself could not have done better."

Kesgrave received this praise with a dip of his head, taking no affront in being compared to the famous clown, and noted that the substance was unexpectedly slimy, which he attributed to a high concentration of mucus in the mixture. "Either Waltham drank rancid milk to make himself throw up or he has too much dairy generally in his diet."

Delighted, Bea looked pointedly at Hartlepool and said, "Trying to discern the source of the vomit's texture—*that* is terrifying and fascinating."

"There, we are in agreement, your grace," Hartlepool said, regarding her with good-natured understanding for the first time since they had been introduced. "He was always a dead bore in class, toadying up to the lecturers by giving more detail than the question required."

"Accuracy is not sycophancy," Kesgrave replied smoothly. "And we are straying from the topic. What happened in the dressing room? Why did Piddlehinton cry out?"

"Because he is an overgrown baby," Netherby said scathingly. "All that racket over a sliver of glass in his foot. It barely broke the skin."

"He was sitting on a chest of drawers that was surrounded by broken glass from the lamps he had shattered when Mr. Netherby arrived," Bea explained. "And then when the floorboard creaked with Waltham's arrival, he startled again and jumped to his feet, forgetting about the glass."

"Several shards went through the bottom of his shoe," Netherby confirmed. "But only one cut him, and it was little more than a scratch—less blood than from her grace's nose. And yet he caterwauled as though one of his toes had been severed. I am amazed that a man of his years and experience could be so infantile. If I am that ridiculous at his age, Uncle Tony, then you may call me a cawker with my blessing."

"You are a cawker now if you believe I want or need your blessing," his relative muttered.

Having attained a reasonable grasp on the events, Bea asked Netherby to fetch Piddlehinton so they could interview Waltham. "And do check on Mr. Rusk. He should hear what his lordship has to say as well."

Although Netherby tightened his lips at the request, he assented without protest. "But if Piddlehinton cannot manage the stairs with his wound, I am not carrying him down! He will just have to stay there in the dressing room with my clothes."

"Yes, thank you," Bea said, agreeing to his terms before turning her attention to Waltham still whimpering on the floor. "Should the pain not have begun to lessen by now? It has been several minutes since I delivered the blow, and it cannot be *that* debilitating."

Kesgrave assured her it was but agreed that Waltham should have some ability to collect himself, as the shock of the first wave should have subsided. "But I do not see what incentive he has to talk to us, as there is no way he can defend his actions this evening. There is simply nothing he can say that would make breaking into a man's room at three in the morning with a bucket of his own vomit seem innocuous. He will hang for Millie's murder whether he admits to it or not."

Taking this speech as an invitation to devise an enticement, she asked if exile to New South Wales could be arranged for Waltham in exchange for his confession. It was what the duke had done for his uncle's killer. "Discovering the truth about the previous Lord Waltham's demise is the least we could do for his poor widow."

Realizing he was on the hook for two murders, however, was all the inducement Waltham needed to speak and he swore he had nothing to do with his cousin's demise. "He fell or leaped to his death in grief and despair," he insisted between agonizing groans. "You will not blame me for that!"

Curiously, Bea looked at the duke and asked if his lordship's selective denial could be considered a tactic admission of guilt in Miss Lloyd's murder. Kesgrave agreed as Hartlepool announced that he could make sense of none of it. What reason could a man of Waltham's wealth and standing have to kill an insignificant lightskirt?

"She could not have been such a henwit that she took offense at being discarded, for she and her ilk are *meant* to be discarded," he added with perplexed astonishment. "If one wanted the inconvenience of constancy, one would take a wife."

Bea conceded the validity of the statement, which revealed more about Hartlepool's prejudices than society's, and replied that Miss Lloyd, in her irrational resentment over

LYNN MESSINA

being chucked over for her dearest friend—and, yes, the emphasis she used on the word *irrational* was meant to be satirical—she had stumbled across the truth. "Miss Lloyd, furious at being cast aside, made a series of unfounded and outrageous threats to Waltham, which she repeated to Mrs. Taylor, who could scarcely understand a word she was saying because she was so drunk and angry. To soothe her friend, Mrs. Taylor suggested they write a letter to Twaddle telling him all these unfounded and outrageous rumors. Waltham, who was listening by the window, heard the remark and was either too distraught or too daft to recognize the statement for the hollow mollification it was. He believed the threat was real and decided to eliminate both women in a single stroke: killing Miss Lloyd and ensuring Mrs. Taylor hanged for it," she explained before addressing herself to Waltham on the floor. "At least, that is my understanding of events. You must feel free to correct any mistakes."

Waltham glared at her balefully and, moaning again in pain, curved his body toward the wall. But only a second later he twisted around to look at her. "Penny knows Twaddle! She met him last month and had tea with him and knows his direction, and sometimes she sends him little gossipy notes in hopes that he will begin to pay her for information. The story about St. Ives swimming in the Serpentine—that came from her! It was no idle threat! And it was not *my* vomit! I am not a street urchin to drink rancid milk. I had it from a drunken lout in a tavern."

Although he turned back to the wall, Bea paused before replying to make sure he did not have other points he wanted to clarify. The concern regarding Mr. Twaddle-Thum was wholly without merit, and she was willing to wager that Mrs. Taylor had not enjoyed tea with the notorious gossip but rather with Mrs. Norton, a society matron determined to do everything possible to earn back her vouchers to Almack's.

Hoping to learn crucial information that would win Kesgrave's forgiveness, she had assumed Twaddle's identity to conduct interviews with many of the duke's former associates.

That was almost four weeks ago, and Bea still found her archnemesis's ingenuity as surprising as it was impressive.

Waltham, however, was not nearly as astute, and she pointed out that Mrs. Taylor had no reason to orchestrate his downfall when her own fortunes were tied to his. "She had already severed her connection with Audenshaw to give you her undivided attention, so in harming your reputation she would be only hurting herself. The incentive went in the other direction, with her wanting to do everything in her power to protect you from Miss Lloyd's spite—although, again, I must remind you that Miss Lloyd did not know anything. She was merely tossing out thoughts to nettle you. I cannot fathom why you ruined a perfectly good first murder with a sloppily done second one."

Having failed to account for his mistress's self-interest, Waltham slowly tilted his shoulders to stare at Bea with a dumbfounded expression, the pain in his groin momentarily forgotten in his bewilderment. As he seemed disinclined to provide an answer, Kesgrave offered his own opinion, proposing the corrosive effects of a guilty conscience. The murderer, knowing he was unworthy of trust, could not extend it to others. Hartlepool endorsed this explanation, proposing fear of discovery as an equally destructive force, and her interrogation of the suspect devolved into a high-minded discussion on the nature of guilt. By the time the duke cited Lady Macbeth, Waltham was doubled over again, mewling softly, and Bea could not decide if the source of his agony was the groin injury or the conversation.

A few minutes later, the Runner came gingerly down the stairs, a bloody cravat wrapped around his head like a bandage. Although the wounded man was clearly in danger of falling, Netherby lent his support to Piddlehinton, who flinched with every step. Patently absurd, the arrangement was nevertheless in keeping with the whole enterprise, for the magistrate had been little help from the beginning.

If anything, he had been a hindrance, ruining their ambush not once but twice.

It was almost impossible to believe any human being could be so clumsy, and then to come inching down the stairs as if grievously harmed when Rusk's gash was so deep blood had soaked through the fabric square—he was every bit as infantile as Netherby had observed.

And yet this childish creature had somehow managed to oversee a magistrate office with reasonable competence for more than a decade.

It was unbelievable.

Except what if it was not, she thought suddenly.

The man who wailed at a cut on his foot was irreconcilable with the one who sustained a knife wound while pursuing a thief and continued to give chase.

One was an act.

She had no doubt which.

The question then became why, and Bea could not fathom what Piddlehinton stood to gain from helping Waltham murder Miss Lloyd and blame Mrs. Taylor.

Well, no, she amended, Piddlehinton did not help with the murder because all evidence indicated that the killer had acted spontaneously. But the second part—ensuring Mrs. Taylor took the blame—was unquestionably true. Bea's faith in that conclusion was unshakable.

And yet she could not fathom why.

Ah, but she could, for Piddlehinton had mentioned his precarious financial situation on more than one occasion and Waltham's coffers were overflowing.

Perhaps it was merely that simple.

"Kesgrave, can we arrange exile for Waltham if he gives testimony against his accomplice, Sir John?" she asked, staring pensively at the coiled form on the floor.

The magistrate gasped as he tripped down the last few steps, Hartlepool goggled at her as though she had lost her mind, and Waltham slowly unfurled himself.

"I am certain something can be worked out, yes," the duke replied.

Needing no further inducement, Waltham sat up and cried, "He helped me! I could not have done it alone. I will tell you everything!"

"He is lying," Piddlehinton said frantically, marching across the floor to stand over the killer. "Her grace has given him the words, and now he is parroting them back to her. You cannot believe him. He is desperate and grasping at straws."

"His foot is fine!" exclaimed Netherby. "A second ago he could barely hobble down the stairs and now he is walking without difficulty. *He* is the liar! I wager he did not even knock over my lamps by accident. He did it on purpose. How dare you destroy my property? Expect my solicitor to deliver a bill for the damages by the end of the day."

Piddlehinton colored at the accusation and even switched his weight to his left leg as though to claim the cut still stung, but then he shrugged and admitted the injury was trivial. "But that does not mean I am in league with a murderer. I have no deal with Waltham."

Waltham disagreed. "I bribed him. I knew a magistrate would be a valuable ally, so I offered him money and he accepted and we have been working together ever since. And that is just a fraction of what I know, your grace," he said eagerly. "I can tell you so much more. If you arrange for my exile to the Continent, I can tell you how the entire magistrate's office is corrupt. It will be a bigger scandal than the master of the rolls resigning in disgrace."

Although Piddlehinton jeered at this accusation, sweat began to trickle down the side of his face in a clear indication of his nerves. Laughing with a hint of hysteria, he conceded that he had made some small, minor, insignificant, really very tiny effort to keep Penny as the main suspect in Millie's murder. "But only because I owe her money! I swear I never entered into an agreement with Waltham. Press him for details. Ask him how much money he offered and when the offer was made and where we were when he made it. Ask him how the money was delivered to me and in what denominations. Go on, please. Ask him!"

But even as he urged the course of action, he insisted it was not necessary. "You already know it! I am certain Penny mentioned our arrangement when discussing the state side in Newgate. She has been giving me money for years to invest for her, and I used the funds to pay my own debts, then printed lovely stock certificates for her. She has dozens of them, all from companies I made up, all worthless. In recent months she has pressed me to sell some of her investments so she can buy her townhouse, and arresting her for Millie's murder seemed like the ideal solution to my problem. But only because I thought she was guilty! I felt so much relief at my good fortune I could barely breathe with the shame of it, for she really is such a dear friend. That is why I agreed to call on Berkeley Square. It was a gesture of penitence! I did not think anything would come of it. I did not even realize she would ask the duchess for help. I assumed she was going to beg the duke to intervene on her behalf because of their prior relationship. It reeked of desperation to me and I knew it would come to naught, but I would not deny a condemned woman her last desperate act."

"He is lying!" Netherby said.

"I do not think he is," his uncle countered.

Bea was inclined to agree with Hartlepool's assessment. The magistrate's insistence on asking Waltham for details was persuasive, and it would be easy enough to confirm his story. If he had truly given Mrs. Taylor dozens of fake stock certificates, then she would have a drawer full of useless sheets of paper.

Poor Penny.

So proud of her financial security, hard won and nonexistent.

"But my lamps!" Netherby protested. "He broke my lamps to warn his confederate of our trap when he thought I was he and then screamed holy hell when Waltham arrived. You cannot deny it."

"I cannot, no," the magistrate said, lowering his head in disgrace. "But I did not do it on purpose. I acted without thinking, in the heat of the moment. I panicked, you see?"

Netherby rolled his eyes. "Twice? Really? What sort of chuckleheads do you think we are, Piddlehinton?"

"I thought it was nonsense!" he replied ardently, his eyes pleading for understanding as he looked first at the duke, then at Beatrice. "When Lord Nuneaton told me that Waltham was the culprit who had arranged everything to make me think Penny had done it, I thought it was folderol. It was complicated and messy, and I had seen Millie and Penny bicker so many times. They hated each other. They loved each other, too, but they also hated each other, so I believed Penny had finally lost her temper. But then Lord Nuneaton told me an even more fantastic story about Waltham and his cousin and a cliff and a sick little boy, and it all sounded daft. Even when I was sitting in the dressing room with the duchess, I thought she had the wrong end of the stick, and then I heard the creak of the floorboard and I panicked because I did not want it to be Waltham. Everything would just be better if the murderer was Penny. It was Netherby and I believed more strongly than ever it was all nonsense. Then it happened again and I had the same panicked response to warn him. But that is all it was: panic. I was never in league with Waltham and he certainly never gave me any money. My situation would be quite different if he had. Now I must keep lying to Penny."

"No," Kesgrave said sharply. "You will tell her the truth."

Piddlehinton blanched. "But she will set Hawes on me. You know it!"

Indeed, he did, yes, and the duke did not care. "You will tell her the truth tomorrow or I will the day after."

Netherby seethed with frustration. "You're letting him hoodwink you! He is guilty, I tell you. The lamps do not lie!"

Hartlepool rapped his nephew on the ear and told him to stop being an ass. Then he turned to Kesgrave and said he should take the duchess home. "The Runner and I can handle matters from here."

"And I!" Netherby asserted.

A faint smile appeared on Hartlepool's lips. "And my rattlepate of a nephew."

Although Bea wanted to object, she could think of no reason why. Waltham was defeated. He would stand trial for the murder of Miss Lloyd, and even if the prosecution could not prove that he killed his cousin as well, the suspicion of it would be enough to finish him off. The very thing that he had stabbed his mistress to prevent—gossip besmirching his good name—would happen as a result of it.

Hartlepool was competent. He would make sure the villain was brought to prison and Rusk taken to a doctor to have his wound treated. Piddlehinton would scurry home with his tail between his legs.

That was everything settled, she thought, accepting the offer.

"As you do not have your carriage, please take mine," Netherby said with unprecedented graciousness.

Now Bea grinned and flatly refused. "I am not climbing into an enclosed space with the duke in his current condition."

Kesgrave, drawing his brows together, seemed prepared to argue, but he merely reminded Piddlehinton he had only the one day to tell Mrs. Taylor the truth. He would find her at Miss Lloyd's home pretending to be her slain friend. Then he apologized to Rusk for the abuse he had suffered in the pursuit of justice and thanked their host for his hospitality.

Netherby beamed with pleasure and said, "It is a good house. A little wrung out and very drafty but well suited for chicanery. Uncle Tony will not give me credit for it, but I chose the best home for entrapping a murderer. I will not mention that to the landlord, of course, for then he might increase the rent and it is already more than I can afford."

Horrified, his uncle asked how much he was paying for the drafty eyesore as Kesgrave led Bea to the door. Once outside, she took her first deep breath in almost a half hour and reveled in the fresh scent of spring on the cool evening air. She could still detect hints of the odious stench and complimented Kesgrave on courageously walking the streets of London swathed in vomit and smelling like something that had died four weeks ago, especially at that hour, when so many of his peers would be traveling home from the Kempton affair. They were sure to be spotted. "Although, as you like to say, once the Duke of Kesgrave starts wearing eau de puke, everyone will start wearing eau de puke."

"I think this time we have reached the limits of my influence," he replied, smiling with cheerful self-deprecation. "At least, I hope."

Bea laughed, imagining Floris in Jermyn Street mixing elixirs of bile and sour milk, and took his hand as they turned onto Brewer. It was a lovely night for a walk, brisk but not cold, and she felt curiously at peace. Here, she had brought him to yet another new low—this time, literally bathed with some unknown lout's putrid bodily fluid—and she did not care one whit. Every time she thought they had finally hit rock bottom the ground somehow opened up to reveal another inconceivable nadir.

Would it ever stop?

Apparently, no, never.

The realization thrilled her.

BEA AND THE DUKE RETURN WITH ANOTHER MYSTERY SOON!

In the meantime, look for Verity Lark's latest adventure:

A Lark's Conceit.

Available for preorder now.

My Gracious Thanks

Pen a letter to the editor!

Dearest Reader,

A writer's fortune has ever been wracked with peril — and wholly dependent on the benevolence of the reading public.

Reward an intrepid author's valiant toil!

Please let me know what you think of A Murderous Tryst on Amazon or Goodreads!

Notes

CHAPTER 8

1. To learn the facts of the situation from Kesgrave's perspective, see the prologue of A Lark's Flight.
2. To read this exchange from Verity Lark's point of view, see A Lark's Flight.

About the Author

Lynn Messina is the author of almost two dozen novels, including the Beatrice Hyde-Clare mysteries, a cozy series set in Regency-era England. Her first novel, *Fashionistas,* has been translated into sixteen languages and was briefly slated to be a movie starring Lindsay Lohan. Her essays have appeared in *Self, American Baby* and the *New York Times* Modern Love column, and she has been a regular contributor to the *Times* parenting blog. She lives in New York City with her sons.

Also by Lynn Messina

Verity Lark Mysteries Series

A Lark's Tale

A Lark's Flight

Beatrice Hyde-Clare Mysteries Series

A Brazen Curiosity

A Scandalous Deception

An Infamous Betrayal

A Nefarious Engagement

A Treacherous Performance

A Sinister Establishment

A Ghastly Spectacle

A Malevolent Connection

An Ominous Explosion

An Extravagant Duplicity

A Murderous Tryst

And Now a Spin-off from the BHC Mysteries Series:

A ~~Beatrice~~ Flora Hyde-Clare Novel

A Boldly Daring Scheme

Love Takes Root Series

Miss Fellingham's Rebellion (Prequel)

The Harlow Hoyden

The Other Harlow Girl

The Fellingham Minx

The Bolingbroke Chit

The Impertinent Miss Templeton

Stand Alones

Prejudice and Pride

The Girls' Guide to Dating Zombies

Savvy Girl

Winner Takes All

Little Vampire Women

Never on a Sundae

Troublemaker

Fashionista (Spanish Edition)

Violet Venom's Rules for Life

Henry and the Incredibly Incorrigible, Inconveniently Smart
Human

Welcome to the Bea Hive

The Bea Tee

Beatrice's favorite three warships not only in the wrong order but also from the wrong time period. (Take that, maritime tradition *and* historical accuracy!)

The Kesgrave Shirt

A tee bearing the Duke of Kesgrave's favorite warships in the order in which they appeared in the Battle of the Nile

Available in mugs too!

See all the options in Lynn's Store.

Printed in Great Britain
by Amazon

38400406R00162